ICE, WIND AND FIRE

MEL KEEGAN

ICE, WIND AND FIRE

THE GAY MEN'S PRESS

First published 1990 by GMP Publishers Ltd
Reissued 1999 in association with Prowler Press Ltd
3 Broadbent Close, London N6 5GG

World copyright © 1999 Mel Keegan
Mel Keegan has asserted his right to be identified as the
author of this work in accordance with the
Copyright, Designs and Patents Act 1988

A CIP catalogue record for this book is available from the British Library

ISBN 0 85449 291 7

Distributed in Europe by Central Books,
99 Wallis Rd, London E9 5LN

Distributed in North America by LPC/InBook,
1436 West Randolph Street, Chicago, IL 60607

Distributed in Australia by Bulldog Books,
P O Box 300, Beaconsfield, NSW 2014

Printed and bound in the EU by WSOY, Juva, Finland

ICE, WIND AND FIRE

1

*T*HE torch beam probed into the dark interior of the warehouse, illuminating crates and boxes. My wary eyes saw a hundred shoot-holes, my nerves were crawling and the palm of my hand itched on the door's peeling paintwork. If this was a set-up it was classic. If it was not, it would be tomorrow's headlines. Byline or obituary, a risk Matt Lansing's journalists seem to run too often.

The bitter north wind must have come straight off the Arctic. It numbed me as it stirred litter in the shaft of the torchbeam. The English cold still cuts me to the bone, eight years after I left Australia for pastures greener. A young journalist with his eyes on the future wants the spotlight, the big cities where tomorrow's news is made, or the world's war zones. There is an old saying about being careful what you wish for.

I stood in the partial cover of the warehouse's open door, listening for any sound from inside, but the place was like a crypt. It was abandoned, already vandalized. I saw telltale signs of squatters, refuse and the black brands of fires on the concrete, but no sound betrayed people. A ginger cat mewled at me from the gloom. It scooted out past my legs, as nervous as I was. Then I was alone.

It was four in the afternoon on a dim, cold March day, and I had gone out to pick up a package. A phonecall, anonymous, offered Lansing the kind of information that has made *Perspective* the magazine it is. Outspoken, radical, dedicated to the truth, irrespective of the toes it crushes. We have been into court three times in the last two years, and staff journalists have been known to be worked over. We tread a lot of toes, make a lot of enemies. I knew as well as my boss, the anonymous call could as easily be an engraved invitation to an ambush as a genuine drop of information.

I edged into the warehouse, playing the torch about. The scuttle of rats behind the boxes had my heart in my mouth. I did not begin to breathe properly until I saw the manilla envelope waiting for me on an upturned crate. The word 'Perspective' was scrawled on it in felt pen. If I was still in one piece ten metres through the door, it was not likely to be a set-up. A man outlined against the daylight, blinded by sudden darkness, makes an easy target – so does a torch. I got a grip on my paranoia. The envelope could have been wired, but sense argued that a knife between the ribs is equally effective and less risky.

No, the envelope was just an envelope. I could feel a sheaf of papers inside, and what had to be a video cassette. It went into the inside pocket of my top coat as I left the warehouse. Daylight was like an affirmation of survival. My heart began to slow as I hurried back out to my battered old Escort.

Traffic was congested, London drab and grey under its overcast. With Lansing's information on the seat beside me I was at liberty to pass the time in fantasy. England in a cold, rainy March is a place for escaping from. I felt a million miles away from Sydney. It was two years since I had been back, and that visit was on assignment for Lansing. The family greeted me with mixed emotions, nothing ever changes. How can it?

I thought of Sydney's sprawled city-scape, remembered the way the heat you can still get in March, which is early autumn, seems to shimmer over the buildings while the streets are like canyons, filled with city dust and hot wind. London is another world, but a world I call home now. Though I dreamed of escaping for a while as I drove back to the office, my plans did not include Australia.

The plane tickets were in the drawer at home, under lock and key, and our bags were packed with two days' grace. Greg and I were out of there, tourist class on British Airways, on Friday morning – nothing short of the outbreak of nuclear war would stop us.

A lot of people regard working for a news magazine like *Perspective* to be a glamorous occupation, but the first year on the job cures you of that. We draw a lot of desk work, a lot of routine surveillance, and there can be danger when you make enemies, as we do, telling the stories we tell. It may thrill some to be a glorified clerk one half of the time, and up to the eyeballs in mud and leeches, or dodging Khmer Rouge snipers, the other half, but the novelty quickly wears off.

I've seen a lot of action since I put Sydney behind me. I was a green kid, needing to grow up, learn. The Falklands, Grenada, Chad, Lebanon, Kampuchea. There is not much I haven't seen, and some I wish I'd missed, if only because I like sleeping at night. My friends say I'm addicted to adrenalin. They are partly right.

But I'm even more addicted to the truth, and the myth of human rights. Eloquent speeches can not disguise the fact that human rights are still little more than a nice idea in this world. Black, Jewish, gay – every city is full of victims who will tell you the truth.

Perhaps I'm more motivated than the White, Anglo Saxon Protestant male, over twenty-one and married with 2.4 children. He has nothing to fight for since he was given everything as his birthright. I'm gay. Lansing knows it, knows about Greg and me and approves. He isn't homosexual but he stands on the principles of the magazine, that prejudice is the only real, mortal sin. *Perspective* "arrived" in 1985, with that story lifting the lid off persecution in the suburbs, the cross gays have to bear with AIDS rearing its ugly head. The byline was mine.

The office was starting to gear down for the night. The day staff were on their way out and the skeleton crew beginning to drift in for the late shift. I threw the envelope onto Lansing's desk and hung my coat over a chair. The heating was on, making the air stale. Matt Lansing is not a young man, and won't make old bones. He was blue about the eyes, chain smoking, surrounded by spent coffee cups and dogends. He looked like a walking coronary, but he's looked the same for the eight years since I met him. I arrived in London with a letter of introduction from a *Bulletin* editor, and high hopes. Green and painfully young? Still, Lansing liked what he saw. I was on probation and would have been out on my arse at the first cockup, but the cards fell my way.

Lansing shoved the swivel chair back against the venetian blind and jammed one foot against the edge of the desk as he took a knife to the envelope. The cigarette bled ash onto his shirt, unnoticed.

"Anybody at the place when you got there?" He has never lost those flat, north-country vowels, as he's proud of them. Working Class Hero.

"Not a soul." I perched on a corner of the desk among the detritus. He started on the sheaf of papers, eyes narrowed against the smoke. "Has Greg been in yet?"

He shook his head, engrossed in the scribbled sheets. "Your better half's still in Putney talking to some bird with an axe to grind. RAF wife wanting compo after her husband

9

flew his Jaguar into the ground. Nice juicy tidbit – big government grinds little people underfoot."

"Same old story," I said acidly.

"And a public favourite." He peered at his watch. "You keen to punch the clock, Connor? You're not going to get on that plane one second faster by shoving off early today. Sweat it out, enjoy the anticipation."

I shrugged philosophically. I like Lansing. He's a forthright kind of a man who demands a lot but gives a lot in return, one reason I've turned down offers and stayed with *Perspective* since 1980, running risks when I could have been photographing orchid shows and horse races. "I'll hang about till Greg gets in, if it's all the same to you."

He scanned the bottom of the last sheet and knocked the stack back into shape. "Good stuff. Headline stuff," he muttered, smug and loving it. "Let's see the French wiggle out of this one."

I craned my neck to see the top sheet. The writing was big and bold, not an educated hand. The strokes suggested anger. The group protesting had the cause of the century! French nuclear testing in the islands around Tahiti, a nest of cancer, deformity and sickness. No way will the French admit their testing is responsible for the misery and human suffering. No amount of evidence matters a damn – the kind of situation that draws Matts Lansing like a magnet.

And makes his best journalists put their necks on the block again. I hoped there was enough in Lansing's hand to spark a storm and idly speculated as to the chances of Greg and me getting an assignment out of it. Australians are mildly concerned over French nuclear testing, but normal Pacific weather patterns take the fallout and polluted water away, and the situation seems too far from home to be worth protesting. That is their mistake, but it's going to take freak weather dumping French fallout in Queensland to drag them out of the complacency that seems to come naturally, living in Australia.

If the information proved out, Greg and I could be heading south soon. I soberly contemplated the wisdom of a side trip, home to Sydney as I heard my lover's voice in the outer office. He was joking with the sports editor, making various ribald cracks about body builders. Greg has no time for "narcissism" while half the world is trying to kill the other half. Herb Sadler, meanwhile, has a morbid fascination for overinflated bodies, and a low flashpoint.

10

Lansing gave me a push off the desk with his elbow. "Get out of here, Connor, and take bloody Farris with you before he starts a shindig."

I laughed at the idea. Greg would mop the office floor with Sadler. My lover may be slightly built, and a hand's breadth under my height, but they do not come tougher than Greg Farris. Greg is a fighter, has always had to fight. He was a battered child, institutionalised, tortured at school because of his emerging homosexuality, and finally, a teenage runaway. A lot of boys would have committed suicide. Greg says he came close before he took himself by the scruff of the neck and dragged himself out of the gutter.

I stood at Lansing's door to watch him. Greg is only two year my junior, but you'd take him for a kid. He's built like a dancer, all legs and shoulders. His face, if you can tear your eyes away from his bum, is almost feline, with cat-like grey eyes and high cheekbones, and a mouth that pouts and says "kiss me". He's beautiful. "Handsome" is a word that sits badly on Greg, his features are too unusual. But beauty surrounds him no matter where he is or what he's doing. He wears his hair long, thank God, thick chestnut waves on his brow and collar, seducing your fingers.

He looked up over Sadler's unhealthily tidy desk, winked as he saw me, and I watched him slide in behind his typewriter for the last job of the day. I brought a couple of polystyrene beakers of dishwater coffee from the machine, looked over his shoulder as he typed up a rough copy from the notes he had taken in Putney. Sadler had his coat on. He left as the typewriter began to chatter, and we had the office momentarily to ourselves. I took the opportunity to be close. I felt the tension in Greg's shoulders, and rubbed his neck as much for my own pleasure as his.

"You're strung up," I said quietly. Lansing was still working next door and the kids who mind the shop and answer the phone on the graveyard shift were just outside.

"You've noticed." He looked up and back at me, grateful for my massaging fingers. "One of those bloody days, Alex. Been one of those weeks. Two days, and we're out of here."

Greg is a Londoner, born and bred – and quite well bred, which makes it all the more troubling that he should have been battered as a child. You can never tell what goes on behind the polished oak front doors of the middle class. It's a mistake to assume that domestic violence springs out of poverty, and the better oiled are above it. That in itself is a kind of prejudice, against the poor. Greg's father was in banking. He smiled at me, a lover's smile, and went back to the rough copy.

We had been counting the days till our escape and could taste freedom. Sunshine, blue skies, green sea. There is enough of the Aus in me, still, to chafe at England's grey skies and cold winds. I took my hands away from him as the boss appeared at his door, shouting for a typist and Greg finished up the rough in record time. The typescript slid into Lansing's copy tray for approval, and we left at once.

"Chinese, Italian or Indian?" I asked as the lift took us down. The freezing March wind hit us in the face and I turned up my collar. We had the choice of several decent restaurants on the road home.

"Indian," he decided, and we ate scalding curry at the Taj Mahal, talking shop. I watched his eyes brighten as I told him about Lansing's feed of information from the Tahitian activists, out to light a fire under the French government.

Greg is an idealist as well as a damned fine journalist. Anger is an emotion that looks good on him, makes his eyes glitter and his face all the more feline. "Tahiti," he mused as we ate ice cream to douse the curry's fire. "You fancy the assignment, do you?"

I had mixed feelings about it, and said so. "Dangerous. Not just the French contingent – the place is ticking like a clock. Headline today, cancer in ten years." I picked at my own dessert. I remembered the other incident, years in the past now, when the French took prisoner the crew of a Greenpeace protest ship. What followed was brutal. "Not the kind of risk I like to run," I said, alluding to the radioactivity. "Armed French sailors are one thing, cancer is something else."

"And if nobody runs it?" He arched one brow at me. Pushing.

"You're game," I observed, refusing to be needled.

He sat back with an eloquent shrug. "Maybe. If we could get results."

"You're up against the French government," I argued. "The original immovable object. Anyway, Lansing's got hold of enough to make trouble. See what happens when the shit hits the fan next month. It's worth the cover." I enjoyed just looking at him in the restaurant's soft, amber lighting. There were ivory elephants and lanterns behind him, and a potted palm, an exotic background that suited him, fanned my sensual mood. They say curry's an aphro. They could be right. He looked up at me over the dessert, caught the look on my face and laughed quietly. "So I've got a one track mind," I said indifferently. "It hasn't bothered you till now."

"Doesn't bother me yet." He stood up, jingling the keys to his Triumph. We had left my geriatric Escort at the office. "Home, James?"

"And don't spare the horses," I finished.

Home was a flat in Islington, a quiet, private building where people looked sideways at us, suspecting, but still smiled and nodded as they passed by. A locked door, the sanctuary of our own space . . . I had wanted him since he returned to the office, and he knew it. He was teasing, flirting, at the restaurant, and knew I would jump him a foot through the door. I pinned him to the hearthrug while the gas heater warmed up. He did not even try to wrestle me off, but relaxed into a boneless sprawl under me. "Wanton," I accused. "Randy animal."

"And not the only one!" He wound both arms about my neck and pulled me down. I gave him my mouth to ravage and he bucked his slim hips against me to rub us together. If there was ever a time I could resist Greg, or wanted to, it's long in the past. He was undressing us while our mouths were still sealed tight. I had his shirt off, delighting in his chest, which has a pelt of fine hair as chestnut as his head.

He arched his back, waited for me to attend to his nipples. I know what he likes. It's the beauty of being lovers, the knowing. I suckled, bit down on them as they hardened to little brown pebbles in my mouth, and he moaned. I know every sound he'll make. He wears his Levis so tight I've seen people stop, in the street, to watch him walk away. I zipped them down, tugged them off him with difficulty, and paused only to toss away my slacks before I was on him again.

His cock slid in snugly beside mine as we humped together, slick with pre-cum and loving it, eating each other alive. I was feverish when he sank his fingers into my forearms, stopping me so that he could hook his legs over my shoulders and have what he really wanted. I held myself on knees and palms, looked down into big, grey eyes that were luminous in the lamplight. He had collected our pre-cum from his belly. His hand brushed my cock as he reached down to make himself ready, and I was alight, heart trying to skip out of my chest. He knew, kissed me as he waited for me to get a rein on my runaway glands. Then I was in him, deep

13

in him, cocooned in the hot, moist velvet insides of him.

Did I tell him I love him? I know I moaned something, but it could been curses or abstract blasphemies. His hands were talons on my back, pulling me closer, as if he could not get enough of me, until I lost rhythm and control and erupted into him. I felt him pumping his cock, the few quick, hard strokes he needed as I began to come. He plunged headlong into orgasm with me.

Sticky, stiff and tangled on the hearthrug, we rolled over and laughed at each other. My knees were two big bruises and he was rubbing his back. I looked down at myself and made a face. "Bath," I decided, less than impulsively.

We shared it, yawning over double brandies as we lounged in the water, and arousal began again. He has the hands of an artist. I sat back against the side of the tub and let him make free with my charms, watched lazily as he held me in one fist and himself in the other. He paced us perfectly until our cream fanned in the water, almost at the same moment. For that, I leaned over and smacked his mouth with a kiss.

"I thought we were going out tonight," I said, allowed to breathe again after some minutes of silence.

"You're kidding?" He yawned deeply. "For a start, I've got to be in Manchester at nine for that rally. Women Against Nukes, remember?"

In fact, I had forgotten. I should have been on assignment with him, laden with my cameras, but I was due in court in the early afternoon. Lansing had told me to be there on time or get my behind kicked. There was a chance Greg could be delayed in Manchester till late, so Bobby Craven was going up as his photographer, on Lansing's orders. He reached for his glass, which was balanced precariously on the side of the tub, a little brandy left. He drained it and rinsed it in the bathwater before delving under my sensitive arse for the plug. I gave a yelp as he pulled it, making him snicker as I stood up quickly.

"You're wicked," I growled at him as I reached for towels.

"Evil," he agreed. "Also knackered. Go out if you want, mate, but I'm hitting the hay." He yawned, emphasizing the sentiment as he headed for our bedroom.

I stood in the doorway, weighing the allure of the disco against warm sheets and Greg's weight, sleeping on my chest. The disco lost. It was early. I made dry jokes at my own expense as we slid into bed – old age catching up with me, bed at ten, a nice mug of cocoa if I was a good lad. Greg snorted in disgust, wriggled that tight little bum at me, perhaps to remind me of what I had done to it an hour ago. Then he was all over me, limp, sound asleep in minutes while my mind continued to race itself in circles with the day's business.

I was vaguely aware of him slipping away at some ungodly hour of the morning, but when I woke properly he was gone. An early rendezvous with Craven at the office, a dash up the motorway to the delights of Manchester, and a date with a crowd of mothers, school teachers and no few Lesbian sisters, to whom the future was a matter of survival – whether we make it, or don't.

Grey would enjoy himself tilting at windmills in Manchester. Demonstrations, lost causes and idealistic crusades are basic to his nature.

For myself, I was due before a magistrate at one, choked in a collar and tie and minding my manners. I was a reluctant witness, counting the hours until my last day on the job was done, and Greg and I would take those plane tickets and use them. I sat in the waiting room outside one of the Old Bailey courts, indulging my fantasies of Montego Bay, Jamaica, and what I was going to do to Greg there. Lansing arrived five minutes before my name was called. I went into the box, under oath with my hand on the Bible, for what that was worth. I'm a sinner and an unrepentant one at that. Is the Bible the right book for me to swear on?

The case involved a frame I had shot months before. It was a view across Trafalgar Square with Greg's interview subject, a retired general, in the foreground. In the background, to the surprise of everyone, a petty crime was taking place. The action showed up clearly on four of my frames. I was in the waiting room for an hour and a half, and in the witness box for about a minute. Lansing was not amused. It was a day's idleness on wages, even if it did give us a tasty little piece to print. *Perspective* acting in the public interest yet again. Altruism is our middle name.

I waded through a backlog of desk work in the afternoon, caught Herb Sadler leering at me at four, and tolerated his jibes about Greg and me, and our holiday. He was green to the gills with envy. We had promised ourselves a real "fly away" holiday for years, and for almost the first time in our lives we could afford to do it. We had both toured the world repeatedly on business, but Montego Bay is a dimension away from Beirut and Kampuchea. To begin with, nobody is taking pot-shots at your unwanted white face.

Greg was back at five, hustling me out of the building before we could be detained on any pretext. We stood on the pavement, looked up at the red and black lettering spelling the magazine's infamous name, and I wished it good riddance for the next glorious fortnight. Greg was in an exuberant mood, boisterous as a kid. He bought me ravioli and chianti, took me home, tumbled me on the bed and fucked me senseless before we showered, changed and hit the disco for the evening.

The crush and noise of threshing bodies and hard rock are not Greg's usual taste. He inclines toward classics and film soundtracks, but that night he wanted to dance. If only the mood would overcome him more often. He is a natural dancer who does not seem to have bones and joints like ordinary mortals. He danced me into the floor, and I let him. You are only young once.

And you fly away to Jamaica once in a year, if you're lucky.

The first time I ever saw Greg Farris, he was leaning on the wall of a hotel called The Upland Goose, in a place that was unknown but would soon be one of the best known names in the world. Port Stanley.

It was bitterly cold. Only two years out of Australia, I felt the cold right through to the bone marrow, but the Falklands islanders did not seem to notice it. Greg was standing in a patch of wintery sun, wearing the customary Levis and a brown sheepskin jacket, a grey fisherman's jersey, boots, sunglasses. He had his shoulders against the brickwork, weight on one leg, hips thrust out, thumbs hooked in his back pockets. I remember the way my heart picked up, just at the sight of him. A walking wet dream, with the wind in his hair and his face turned to the sun.

I had been living and working in London's unhappy places, doing a story about the gay related diseases that were becoming recognised as AIDS. I felt depressed, tainted by the drugs, the booze, the privation and illness I had seen, and before me was what seemed to be a boy, beautiful and disgustingly healthy.

Lansing sent me to the Falklands because, without arrogance, I am bloody good at what I do. I was good as a sprog working on Sydney's *Bulletin*, and I had matured with experience. It was the March of 1982, and history was about to be made. *Perspective* was then four years old. I had been a staffer since I came out from Australia in '80. Lansing had sent me to Vietnam, Laos, Chile, places where a news photographer's life can be dangerous. Lethally so.

I learned on the job, survived by the skin of my teeth while I kept my mouth shut and watched professionals at work. The breed of veteran battlefield journalists who will tell you horror stories about Tet, and Khe Sanh. My heroes were Neil Davies and Tim Page, and still are. Even now there is a little boy inside me, looking for heroes to worship. Lansing sent me into situations that were suicidal, and paid me well when I came back alive, with the goods. Pictures that helped make *Perspective* the magazine it became.

The saying goes that a picture is worth a thousand words. In fact, it's closer to five thousand. And some are bought at the price of a man's life.

When our sources in Argentina phoned home with the first sibilant rumblings of what would soon be a full Atlantic storm, Lansing put me on a plane, southbound for Port Stanley. We had a man there, so I was told, a good freelance who had worked with us several times already, sending stories from East Germany and Libya. I knew the name and respected the man from his writings, and agreed to work with him at once, when Lansing offered me the assignment.

My head was still ringing after the flight. My bones vibrated with the phantom sensations of aeroplane engines. I had no idea the walking wet dream leaning against the wall of the hotel was my writer, and had half decided to send him signals, see what bounced back. I fell in lust the moment I set eyes on him. The rest came later.

He must have been waiting for me, and recognized me by the weight of camera gear I was carrying. When he asked if I was Alex Connor from *Perspective*, and gave me his hand, I felt that sinking feeling.

There was the delightful anticipation of working with him. There was also the disappointment of realising I now had to mind my manners. Making the wrong advances to the wrong person can screw a job up royally, which is professional suicide. I pinned on a smile, shook his hand, bought him a beer in The Upland Goose and feasted my eyes instead. Indulged my private fantasies. There is no law against window shopping.

Did I broadcast the signals without realising it? Perhaps. That was March 31st, and we were in adjoining rooms at the hotel where we met. Two days later, it started.

The shooting began at four in the morning, waking us and everyone else in Stanley. Greg was suddenly in my room without bothering to knock. We could see nothing from the window. What we would not learn for days yet was that a hundred and fifty Argentine *Buzo Tactico*, or Special Forces troops, had choppered in, landing just three miles south-west of us. I dragged on what clothes were closest to hand, grabbed my gear and ran. Writers can compose copy at their own convenience, but a photographer fights like hell for the frame that will put him on the cover of *Time* or *Life*. Or *Perspective*.

Greg often works with a pocket cassette recorder. I had grabbed the Canon, with a Nikon for backup, extra batteries and all the film I could stuff into my pockets. I did not know how long it would have to last, so I chose my frames with care. The fire fight went on for hours. We felt an absurd sense of unreality.

Islanders called in to Stanley's radio station, describing what they could see and hear. If not for the gunfire punching sporadically through the freezing night, you would have been forgiven for thinking it was a Mercury Theatre production – young Orson Welles scaring the pants off America with a Martian invasion.

But just before nine in the morning, I got several shots of Argentine tanks on Ross Road, pictures of infantrymen in blackface. The Police Chief had called a state of emergency at half past seven, and at quarter past nine I lay flat on my belly in the mud with a long lens on the Canon, watching the Royal Marines surrender. For the lads of "Naval Party 8901", as the garrison was coded, and for the islanders, it was over.

For Greg and me it had just begun.

We could have masqueraded as tourists, but we expected the curfews, the preoccupation with pieces of paper that would begin soon enough. We sat in a ditch not far from Mullet Creek, where the *Buzo Tactico* had landed in the middle of the night, and made plans. We would stay on the outside, keep out of their way, wait and watch, and do the damned job Matt Lansing was paying us for.

It was cold, it was muddy, and if Greg felt anything like me, he was scared witless. Fear is healthy. It reminds you you're alive, and keeps you alive. We hid in a barn to get out of the weather that night, not even daring to let the farmer know we were there. We burrowed into a pile of straw and

18

cuddled up to share body heat.

And I turned on. By then I was beyond caring if he took umbrage. I did not attempt to hide what was happening. If he wanted to be a son of a bitch about it, that was his prerogative.

In fact, he practically raped me. And I helped him do it. Afterwards we laughed at each other, buried in a heap of smelly straw, insides growling with hunger, feeling on top of the world. He had wanted me since he watched me walk up the road to The Upland Goose, and had practised the same laudable restraint as myself, not eager to risk alienating the photographer he must work with, come hell or high water, for the duration. I think I wore his finger bruises for a week.

We were on the outside, living from day to day, cold and wet, literally under the gun. In those brutal conditions you come to trust another human being quickly, or to despise him just as quickly. Greg earned my trust a dozen times over. It was a joy to watch him work. He was just twenty-six then, two years younger than me, and as tough as they come, mentally and physically.

I got his story out of him in the cold dead of night, as he got mine, anything to talk about while we held each other for warmth, for pleasure. Stories of a skinny little kid whose father called him a "nancy", and who thrashed him regularly to beat some "starch" into him. A kid pushed beyond endurance until he got out and ran, and survived by a fluke in a world that should have eaten him alive.

We could not hope to keep ourselves secret for long. The farmer was a dairyman, a veteran of World War II. He took us for looters at first, and showed us the wrong end of a twelve gauge. My stubborn Australian accent, and Greg's London, seduced the old man into a kind of French Resistance fantasy. He told us we could stay, and fed us occasionally.

We were still shacked up in his barn when a thunderstorm seemed to erupt in the middle of the night, almost a month later. It was the Vulcans hitting Stanley's airfield, but we did not discover this till later. The batteries in my transistor held out. We would listen to garbled reports of disaster. *Belgrano* went down the day after the Vulcans came, *Sheffield* two days later.

There was a lot of bombing, but that was not the worst of it. The Argentines had imposed a curfew and after dark would shoot at anything that moved, any chink of light, or just at buildings. Rounds would punch straight through walls, and God help anyone inside.

And yet those were weeks when I felt more alive than I had in years. The danger, the adrenalin, were addictive. So was Greg. Lansing had given the pair of us up for dead. A fortnight later, when the Argentines surrendered at last and I picked up the phone to call home, he pulled strings somewhere. We went back on an RAF "trash hauler". Lansing must have something on someone high up.

My pictures and Greg's copy were picked up by several of the national dailies, and Greg was hired onto the staff. It was strange, falling into a proper bed together after six weeks of straw and thistles. Lansing gave us a tasty bonus and three weeks' holiday. Scotland was paradise by comparison to Stanley.

I wanted Greg to live with me, be my lover, embrace monogamy and live happily ever after, but the little sod turned me down flat. He had a fierce independence. I knew it was a leftover from his nightmare childhood, when, if he had not learned self-dependence he would have gone under. So I let him take his time, wined, dined and bedded him every chance I could. Those months, I had no one else, wanted no one else. Greg was more than enough.

In the end, it was a new nightmare that buried the old one and brought us together properly, after a year and a half of my wanting and his evasiveness. AIDS put the fear of God into us. Invited to a wild party, Greg attended. Boozy, druggy, it spiralled into orgy, and when he woke up he could not remember a single face, it was a blur. His arse was sore as hell, he knew damned well he had been fucking, but with whom, and how?

He came to me one day, fretting and shamefaced. We both took the tests, sweated it out till we were given the all-clear, and we've stuck together like glue since. Monogamy can be boring if your partner is boring. Greg is anything but.

It is over three years since we set up shop together. It seems more like three weeks. Our old lovers threw confetti at us. Lansing made the customary jokes about Greg "keeping me off the streets". Mockery aside, we were running scared. You can't help wondering about the humble condom when there are kids born daily who wouldn't be if the damned things worked a hundred percent. We were scared enough, and deeply in love, to break Greg's addiction to independence. Lansing teamed us, reckoning that to split us for weeks or months would be the quickest way to finish us. Temptation is everywhere – monogamy is a decision, not an accident of fate. I won't say I haven't been tempted. I will say I've been faithful, and I trust him when he tells me the same. It's staying alive.

We were together in Chad, Libya, Beirut, Laos, the last in the world you would be in by choice. We shared a dream of escape and aimed all year at that morning in mid-March. Plane tickets in our pockets, bags packed, sights on Montego Bay. Two weeks of sheer idleness and delicious indulgence . . . We should have known better.

2

JAMAICA.
 Lush, tropical, balmy, full of tourists who spend a couple of hundred million quid a year there. Poverty-stricken, depressed, troubled, if you care to look further than the white beaches and highrise hotels. The land of rum and pirates, Maroons, freed slaves, sugar plantations, moonlit beaches and jungle-clad mountains. Scuba and cricket. The thought of being turned loose for a fortnight in a place like this with the person you love, and whose delectable little body still drives you wild with lust six years after you first lay down with him, are enought to make you salivate.

London had been cold and wet, and the aircraft had been so cold we both drank too much to keep warm. They keep it cold to offset the effects of so many passengers who have that prediliction to throwing up. We were squiffy when we left the plane and whistled for an absurd little Jeep taxi at the Sir Donald Sangster International Airport.

It was, by local standards, a little cool, but Greg was stunned by the sudden heat. To me it was like stepping out into the soupy air of a warm, moist March afternoon in the old country. If I closed my eyes, it could have been Sydney, and I could be on my way out to Ashbury for a guardedly polite and indecently brief visit with a family that has not quite disowned the black ram. Yet.

Greg had shed his pullover and jacket just before we

landed, and he was still sticky before we dumped our baggage and did an exaggerated double-take at the size of the bed. The management of the big hotels look the other way when tourists book in. Two guys can go to Jamaica to watch the cricket, dive and ball their brains out with whomever they choose, but West Indians take a dim view of homosexuality in their own people. Fortunately, they leave the tourists alone, perhaps despising them but at the same time wanting to separate them from their money.

Two men can share a room in reasonable innocence. We had booked as G. Farris and A. Connor, and asked for a double. After discreet "fishing holidays" in Wales and Scotland I naïvely expected two narrow little single beds. The hotel must have expected a regular couple and it was too late to change now. The hotel was fully booked.

There were apologies as we were given the key and the management realised the mistake. I called it serendipity. Would they guess? If they did, they'd turn a blind eye. They want your shekels, they take no further interest in you, trying to ensure that you "come back to Jamaica", as the slogan goes.

"You could get lost in that," I said glibly, referring to the bed. "Pack your hiking boots, did you? If you fancy a bit in the middle of the night you'll need bloodhounds to find me."

"We'll rope ourselves together," he said, just as glibly. "Like climbing the Eiger only not so exhausting." And then he caught my eye and we both laughed, grabbed each other. "Well, maybe more exhausting, I admit." He nipped my ear, kissed me and gave the bed an amused look. "They ought to hand out a map." He yelped as I dumped him into the middle of it. The mattress was horizontal heaven.

Being larger and stronger has its wicked benefits. Usually, Greg resents being picked up physically, manhandled right where I want him. He normally bellows in outrage. Perhaps it was the booze we had both put away on the plane, but he was laughing that day as I sat on him, pinned his wrists over his tousled head. "We've got all day to try the bed," I said, attempting a disapproving tone as he writhed around under me. The kind of gyrations he knows turn me on faster than it takes to tell.

"All day," he agreed with mock gravity. "And I want to swim, so get your bloody carcass off me and let me unpack!" He struggled up, kissed me before I could even blink in surprise, and with his tongue in my mouth there was no way to even pretend annoyance. Instead, I subsided, let my whole weight sink him into that mattress, trying to get a curse out of him. He preferred to ravage my mouth and hug like a boa-constrictor until I was the one begging to breathe.

My lips were bruised as I sat up. "Swim?"

"You seen the beach?" He bounced up off the bed, a dynamo of energy and enthusiasm that made me feel like his father. He stripped as I watched, tipped out the contents of his suitcase in search of the shocking-red bathers I had bought him. French. Sheer. Almost indecently so. "Wonder if there's a place around here that hires tanks? There's a reef just off the point. I haven't dived warm water for years."

There is a myth about the big, sunbronzed Aussie. A six-foot-four-inch hunk of glorious masculinity, blond, blue eyed, wearing a tiny scrap of lycra that conceals nothing, and a ridiculous little lifesaver's cap tied atop sunbleached curls, while the salt water courses off the perfect curves of his muscular body, leaving behind waxen droplets riding the soft, slick sheen of suntan oil . . . They do exist. Once, long ago, I would spend my adolescent afternoons at Dee Why, gazing lustfully at these demigods. The myth is that all, or even most, Aussie males match the image.

And then there is the truth. Some of us cannot bare our skin to the sun, and I was cursed as one of them. My family came out from Dublin at the turn of the century, not long before Australia became a nation. My Irish genes will not tolerate the sun, and Greg knows it. People have the idea I'm modest, even prudish, and just refuse to strip in the Great Outdoors. I hate to puncture their illusions, but the truth is simpler. This skin, which Greg likens to marble or alabaster, was never designed for the sun. I don't tan, I burn. And burn. Then I'm a mass of peeling blisters until I'm right back to alabaster. By lamplight in bed, alabaster has its charm, but in the cruel blue light of day I would be more inclined to describe my tender skin as fish-belly white, and shudder at the sight of it.

By March Greg's tan had faded too, but he still had a residue of the gypsy-brown colour left, making him the colour of honey, or apricot jam. Saturdays on the river, I remembered. Afternoons spent fucking on a rug at a friend's farm in East Anglia. I groaned, knew it was all my own fault as I searched my own bag for my bathers, sunblock and the blue beach robe I'd bought with the thought in mind of covering the alabaster, saving myself some pain. "Slip, slop, slap", as they say in Australia – "slip on a tee shirt, slop on some sunscreen and slap on a hat." My battered old Akubra came out of the bottom of the bag.

Greg laughed rudely. I shot a glare at him, intending to be furious. But he was hopping on one foot, bathers half on, naked and supple, enormous grey eyes filled with mischief. Instead I just smiled, mock-sweetly, like a bad impression of Boy George, and turned my back on him.

Arms slid about me a moment later and he pressed against my back. We stuck sweatily together despite the room's airconditioning. "Hey, I'll rub the oil in for you," he promised sultrily. "I don't want to watch you burn. And altruism's got damn all to do with it, mate." A kiss devoured my ear. He bit my lobe quite painfully. "I'm getting randier by the minute and I don't fancy getting laid by a lobster."

"Such kindness and considerations overcome me," I lisped. I pulled out my bathers and a plastic bottle. "Bugger off and see if you can get some beach towels and stuff. Buy 'em if you have to. And Greg." He was at the door, turning back as I called his name. I threw his robe after him. "Put that on, or you'll be gang banged and sold to white slavers before you get to the service desk."

He laughed, caught the green terrycloth robe, and I made noises of resignation. I changed into the skimpy nylon bathers like a martyr on his way to the scaffold. The big walk-in wardrobe sported a long mirror, and I studied myself critically in it.

I'm just on six feet tall, and I build muscle easily. I look after my body, partly because, so looked after, it returns the favour; partly because in my job unfitness is dangerous; and because I work, constantly and hard, to keep Greg mine. My looks are Irish, the pale skin, blue eyes and hair that is almost black. I favour my father in features. Connor men were always handsome creatures, and we know we are. But that white skin was going to cost me. My fault for bringing us to Jamaica instead of Sweden or somewhere intelligent.

There were compensations. Watching Greg frolic like a seal in the surf, duck-diving with him, pulling him under and then watching him splutter for air while I swam to a safe distance. Running for my life as he chased me out of the water and up the beach.

By lunch time we were both exhausted. The hotel had a five star restaurant but we spent a few dollars on bananas, sweet rice and corn at a little stall a mile or so away from the tourist trap. Two white faces amongst a crowd of beautiful black children. Some of the most beautiful people in the world are Jamaicans. The adolescent boys are enough to awaken the chicken-hawk in a man.

I was sticky with sun oil and sea salt and dragged Greg back to the hotel for a shower when he wanted to explore. "We've got a fortnight, for Christ's sake," I argued. "Why run yourself ragged the first day?"

He was itching, more than ready to share the shower, and surrendered on a whim. Piped reggae music played quietly in the room, someone called Jimmy Cliff, a local folk hero, and the rhythms were infectious. Greg lounged under the shower while I picked up the phone to send down for drinks.

The scotch and ice arrived fast, as if the management were still trying to make amends for the "mistake" of putting the two of us in one vast, king-sized bed. I longed to share the water but waited for the drinks, deliberately discreet. Sharing a room with a man is not the same thing as being caught under the shower with him. West Indians have an old fashioned moral code. It paid to be careful.

"I'm like a prune, waiting," Greg told me as I stepped under the water. "Where the hell were you?"

"Sending for drinks." I ladled shampoo onto my hair and shook soap out of my eyes. "And you don't look like a prune to me." I kissed him, got a mouth full of suds. "Look more like a plum. Fancing being plucked?"

"Nice word for it." He leaned against me, warm and wet. I soaped his buttocks for the sake of it. "Before I fall asleep and it's too late," he added with a theatrical yawn. "Going to hire a car tomorrow. There's a roadmap by the service desk – dirt roads up into Cockpit country. Old haunts of Cudjoe the Maroon."

"Cudjoe the what?" I turned the water off.

"Jamaica's answer to Robin Hood." Greg inspected his fingers. "And I am like a prune!"

"Wrinkled as old Aunt Florrie," I agreed dolefully. "Wrinkles on your bum, even." I had him. For half a second he screwed his spine around to peer down his own back, and I laughed rudely. He glared at me but good humour ruined the performance. "I lied," I confessed, chucking a towel at him. "Come here."

Warm and wet, he is irresistible. No one else I know smells like him, tastes like him. I ate him alive from mouth to knees and back. Soon he was swaying, dizzy with arousal, his cock

25

hot and hard against my cheek. I sucked it, to feel him come on my tongue, but he had other ideas.

A lush groan, and he shoved me away, stepped out of my reach. "You've had lunch already. Come on and do me properly. I'm squeaky clean." He took my wrists and hauled me to my feet. "And I feel like the de luxe treatment." With that he turned away, tilted his hips, gave me a glance over his shoulder, heavy-lidded. "Or have you got other plans?"

Six years since I first tasted his mouth, touched his body, and although there is not one square inch of him I don't know by sight, feel, taste, he can still drive me into what writers understate as that frenzy of lust, with a gesture or a look. Perhaps because I know his body so well, and it's like going home. Or because I've always known he'll do anything to make it great for me, and frustrated disappointment has yet to happen between us. Just Alex going soft in his declining years? If that is the case, so be it. I shall go on being soft -- I like it.

Greg heaved and panted, wild under me. I was out of my head, just as wild, and almost did not hear his muttered curse, but I never liked to hurt him. Half believing I some-how had him in pain, I stopped with an effort, shook my head clear of its scarlet cotton stuffing. "What?"

"You know what we forgot to pack?" His face was taut, fingers clutching at my forearms, and I already had his left knee hooked over my shoulder. "We left the stuff in the bedroom!" He said indignantly. He came down a little, eyes clearing. "The new tube."

"Oh brill, utterly brill," I said lucidly. Our pre-cum was scattered far and wide and I offered him my palm. "Care to spit on that?"

He winked at me. "Got a better idea." My sunblock was within arm's reach. He shoved the bottle into my waiting palm.

"Better get a towel as well, or we'll have this fancy duvet in one hell of a mess." I dragged the beach bag closer. "How would you like to come all this way and be ejected from the premises for unnatural practices?"

"I could always prostrate myself on the floor," he offered, not quite solicitously. My fingers inside him silenced these expressions of wit.

Eons later I groped after the bottle of Grouse and glasses and slopped the rich, expensive amber fluid into gorgeous Waterford crystal. I balanced his drink precariously on his chest. He lay spreadeagled like a swastika, limp and almost asleep. It's in moments like that I love him most. I think I am the only person alive who ever saw Greg Farris let go to that extent, boneless and wrung out, so unselfconscious and at peace, he doesn't care what he looks like.

His old lovers have called him aloof, distant, standoffish, as if Greg always had the safety catch on, even in intimate scenes. With me, his defence mechanisms shut down all the way. Total trust. In these moments he is mine, utterly.

I dabbed a little whisky over one nipple, suckled it dry and looked his body up and down. His hair was damp, his semen spilled carelessly on his flat belly, his legs splayed as when I released him. Wanton. Like nothing human, I thought – Pan, was it? Faun or satyr. I wriggled around to lap at the silvery trails of his milk until he laughed at me and tousled my hair.

We slept for hours, dressed in slacks and colourful "surfie" shirts, and I loaded the Nikon for a stroll along the water-front. Afternoon grew hot, sultry. There was going to be a storm. The sky brooded, dark out over the hills in the east, but in the West Indies that is nothing to worry about. It can be thundering at noon and the sun blazing again at two. A tropical paradise, in every sense of the word.

The island has a long, lurid history, from the time Columbus discovered it in 1494 to the British capture of the Spanish colony in 1655, and the awful years of slavery. In those hell years only the Maroons, under their General Cudjoe, were at liberty. Jamaica is steeped in history, the whole place reeks of it, and the tourist industry is an unhappy graft of a new limb on an old body.

The Jamaicans are so poor many of them can't feed themselves adequately, and meanwhile tourists – people like Greg and myself – go there to lounge around in the sun, eating, drinking, screwing and swimming, without a care in the world. Justice? In my experience, it's a myth.

The poverty exists back-to-back with the tourist traps. We strolled a couple of miles away from the hotel and I watched Greg's face harden. Poor people's houses are the same no matter where you go, but you expect them in countries like England, which have no delusions of Paradise. Here?

We came to a halt in the deep shadows under the palm trees just above the beach. It was late, we would have to turn back soon or miss the last call for dinner at the hotel. We were alone. The beach stretched away before us, Montego Bay like something out of an Errol Flynn fantasia, no one to share it with, just the two of us.

I pulled him against me, felt him relax into my arms, and when he lifted his mouth I kissed him, long and hard. We came up for air, and he was smiling again.

"I was just thinking about the people who live here, Alex. They've got it hard."

"About as hard as growing up on the Sydney docks," I said, trying not to remember my own childhood, which was lacking until I was out of the nest and gone. "Or having your father beat shit out of you till the authorities confiscate you, and then growing up in a government home." His mouth compressed. "That's the way life is." I licked along his deep upper lip. "You're born, you die, and what you do between times is up to you. Got to get out and make things happen."

"You're becoming a philosopher," he teased. "Come on, Socrates, they'll be serving dinner soon."

"Jog back?" I asked. "How's your rump?" I glanced meaningfully at his slim little backside, in its white slacks.

"Okay." He winked at me. "You're too good to hurt me."

We had been working on the streets since Christmas, and it was tough work. We seemed to have been running for weeks and had acquitted ourselves very, very well against hardcases a lot of years younger. A week before, we ran the gauntlet of a truckers' picket and it turned nasty. And then a meeting with gay youth representatives became a brawl. I watched Greg gallop the legs off a kid ten years younger, catch him going over a wall and not even get out of breath. The lad had stolen one of my cameras.

We have ten years left at this kind of work, if we stay fit, but by Lansing's calculations we have been on borrowed time for the last couple already. We were in Thailand in '82, not long after the Falklands circus, doing a story on the drug trade and the plight of the beggar brats in Bangkok. I took a bullet in the shoulder. Greg was shot in '79, in Tehran, and again in 1981, that time just a graze when he got between a Klan youth and the black boy he was out to shoot, one balmy night in Florida.

The shootings are the worst of our mishaps, but both of us have been pasted for sticking our noses in where they were not wanted, taking pictures and making trouble. We both ache on cold days, the leftover pains of sundry fractures. Sometimes, in the middle of winter, I can ache in a dozen places and I know I'm slow.

Greg must be too. Lansing watches us like a hawk,

although he doesn't say much. No jock on his payroll will be much better than us. We have all been through the grinder in a dozen countries. It goes with the job. *Perspective* is a law unto itself. One day Lansing will put us out to pasture, no doubt about it. But not yet.

We aren't oblivious to the fact we push our luck, and more than once Greg has expressed his feeling that it's loyalty to Lansing and his ideals that keeps us at work. I ask myself sometimes what we will decide if the boss suffers the coronary he richly deserves on his steady diet of coffee, whisky and cigarettes. Buried or retired, Lansing will be sorely missed. But if we find ourselves working for a starched collar we don't know and don't want to know, I doubt we will be so keen to go on.

Holidays away, like our interlude in Jamaica, are balm on raw nerves, getting us out of the hot water, helping to even up the odds. That was the big theory, and as usual we were dead wrong.

Trouble follows us about like a stray dog.

We showered after jogging back, dressed in our gladrags and strolled down into the Grand Hotel's dining room in time for the last sitting. We could smell the lobster, caviar and champagne on the warm night air. After the poor people's houses along the waterfront we found the rampant wealth strangely disgusting.

It always makes me smile to see Greg turn up his nose at the upper crust, and those who put on the dog like them. If he had endured taking the beatings, straightened out his act for his father's benefit and let the old sod pay his passage through Oxford or some business college, Greg could have been the one with the silver spoon in his mouth. Instead he vilifies that whole caste, mimics the accent brutally. It is a point of honour that he refuses to hobnob with them.

There was champagne in a bucket of ice, prawn cocktails served in brandy balloons, fillet steak in French dressing, crepes, mint chocolates, coffee, cheese and crackers. I could feel my waistline thickening while I watched Greg nibble his way through what would have fed a regiment. The one item that could make me envy, even resent Greg, is that he can eat and never gain an ounce. He falls underweight under stress. Then I have the delight of watching him consume chocolate and eggnog, and brave the scales each morning only to groan in anguish as he discovers he has not gained.

Very mellow after good food, good wine, good company, we lounged at the bar, watched the couples dancing under nodding lanterns. We could hear the sea. The tide was on the turn. Lights glittered like jewels on the boats, riding at anchor out on the bay. The band was playing soft calypso rock, a big mamma crooned old love songs in one of those tenor, blues voices that come from decades of indulgence in moonshine. The night wind was warm, almost too warm, and when we looked up there were no stars. The whole sky was blanketed in with a dense overcast.

"Looks like that storm's going to hit." Greg was looking eastward, where the Caribbean islands trail out onto the Atlantic. "Lightning over the hills."

The bar, with its calypso band and lantern-hung dance floor, was on the hotel's patio. We were not the only ones to notice the worsening weather. Waiters were unobtrusively taking in the chairs and bolting down awnings. "Just our luck. We leave England for the tropics and the rain follows us," I grumbled, trailing Greg into the foyer.

In fact, it was a light show spectacular. We stood at the window, watching the lightning rip across Montego Bay. It was a sight we would not have missed. Like a laser show over a rock arena, but a thousand times more powerful, generated by nature, unpredictable, violent. The palm trees bent double before a gale we could not feel. West Indian hotels are built to withstand the battering of full blown hurricanes.

Long after midnight we called it a day. I had intended to capitulate in bed with a flourish, fling myself at his feet and tell him to do his worst. Or best. It would have been the perfect end to a perfect day, but I was sound asleep as soon as my head touched the pillow. The next I knew, the sun was waking me, streaming in under a blind we had thoughtlessly left up on an east window.

I gave a grunt of disgust at the interruption of my dreams and turned my back on the dawn. I bured my face somewhere in the regions of Greg's armpit, luxuriating in the smell of him, clean and warm and male. He was still asleep but once I wake there is no chance of me settling down again, and I amused myself for some time, watching him dream. Asleep, even blue about the jaw, he looks so young I can feel pangs of guilt, as if I'm shamelessly exploiting youth.

And then he woke, stirred, yawned, fluttered his eyelashes as he stretched. I heard a joint crack and leaned over to kiss him. No one should taste so good in the morning, or wake up so randy. Last night my capitulation would have been a grand affair with music and passionate words wooing abandon, and such drivel. This morning I had no time for the hooplah. I kissed him breathless, pushed the bottle of sun oil into his hand, snorted with laughter at his expression of surprise, and turned over on my side, arse presented demandingly.

He took it. Greg has never been a lad to turn down a priceless opportunity. When he is in me I can't remember my name or what day it is. There are more important things in life than these mundanities. I was running slick with oil, it was everywhere when we returned to our senses. We took a look at the bed, at each other, and were caught between ribald laughter and sheepish contrition.

"Better not do that again."Greg was always practical."We'll find a chemist, get a tube of something. We're going to start getting hate mail from the laundry."

I wriggled around. I could still feel him inside, phantom sensations I wished I could share. My buttocks were slippery, tender between, but the sheets were in a messy condition. "We could always tell them you got a sunburned bum." I yawned in his face.

"Me?" He demanded. "You're the one with the alabaster bod, for Chrissake, and you're the one one with sun oil up your –"

"Point," I said aridly. I slid carefully out of bed. "I'm going to take a shower, honey. Phone down for some breakfast and share the water?"

We had the radio on while we shaved and ate, learning, not to our surprise, that the storm over Montego Bay which we had watched until the lightning was spent, was the worst in years. The hotel had not suffered. It was built to survive even moderate earthquakes. But in the poor quarter there was a great deal of hardship, even loss of life. Cascades of water off the hillsides, murk in the sea, broken palm trees, flattened shacks.

An hour later we hired out a cabin cruiser and scuba gear. Tanks, buoyancy compensation device, octopus regulators – only the best of equipment here. The sign on the wall assured us that the dive shop attached to the hotel was an affiliate of the Professional Association of Diving Instructors. The boat was a nice little thing, sunshine yellow, with an acre of plate glass and twin Johnson outboards. Its name,

Light Fantastic, was stencilled over the transom.

Montego Bay is a great dive. For that matter, anywhere in the Caribbean is a fantasy come true for the hobby diver. And there is always the chance of picking up a few coins, a Spanish trinket worth the price of your plane fare.

We took the boat out about a mile. The tide was idle, slack water, and the sea like a pond, slapping gently at the boat. Barely a breeze stirred, although it was degrees cooler there than onshore. The depth was no more than thirty feet to the coral spires of the reef, so there would be plenty of light, and these waters are not so cold you have to suit up in rubber. Greg put on his BCD, weight belt and tank over bare skin. I followed his example. You cannot burn in thirty feet of water, even with skin like mine.

The storm had stirred up the whole sea. The visibility was poor even though the sky was clear now and the sun strong. The murk was disappointing, but the sea bottom settles again quickly. We had plenty of time to wait for it. Today was for fun.

We poked about, played tag with the reef fish, admired the coral and enjoyed reacquainting ourselves with our old skills. We were both well trained, with the Advanced Open Water certificate. I did my training as a pimply adolescent on holiday in Cairns, nursing a terrible crush on the instructor and blowing every cent I had on fees, gear, boat hire. The Great Barrier Reef is probably the best dive in the world, even today, when the ravages of tourism and pollution are taking a cruel toll. A decade ago the damage and commericalism had still to set in badly, and north of the Sunshine Coast one might have entered another world. Happy memories.

At the same time, but thousands of miles away, Greg was doing his own dive training in the Aegean, all of it financed by an admirer. A benefactor. Greg's first big break in life, and long overdue. I know he has his own happy memories of two years that must have been the best of his life, to that point.

The water was cold enough for us to be chilled in half an hour. We needed to think about surfacing by then in any case, or we would not have enough left in the tanks for a second dive when we had warmed up in the sun. I gave Greg a nudge and tapped my watch, and when he nodded we inflated the BCDs to rise back to the boat, which seemed to hover above us against the sun.

We had bought potato crisps, fresh fruit, beers, the flotsam on sale at the boat ramp. We lay in the well of the boat to soak up the sun, and made short work of the food. I was sinking into a pleasant torpor when I felt his fingers sliding into me. I pried open my eyes to watch. "Enjoying yourself?"

"Oh, yeah." He kissed my nipples. "You're too beautiful to let you fry. God, look at you." His expression became smug. "Look at what's mine."

"Possessive bugger," I observed lazily. In fact, I crave such expressions of possessiveness. What is there between us but promises, trust and love? No pieces of paper, no legal gibberish, nothing to tie us together if we wanted to drift apart. We are where we choose to be. I wondered how many married couples could say that as I opened my arms and invited him to lie on me. His body was warm now, hard and bony, just the way I like it.

"Yeah, I'm possessive," he said with curious indifference. "I keep what's mine. Thought you knew."

"I do." I hugged both knees firmly around him, fondled his rump through its wisp of damp, clinging lycra. I slipped my hands between fabric and dewy skin and kneaded him, which he loves. His eyes closed, as if he were a pampered cat. "Want to dive again? There's half an hour's worth left in the tanks."

He nodded dreamily and took his weight on his palms, on either side of my chest. "You know, I've always had evil fantasies about this. Being on holiday, far away from Lansing and bloody telephones. Get you in some beautiful place. Things to do. Privacy, so we can do what we like in the fresh air! You realise how long it is since we had the chance to do it outside?"

I racked my brains and shook my head. "When?"

"Last autumn." He gave me a dig in the ribs. "Groping around in the orchard at my cousin's place."

I licked my lips salaciously. I recalled that afternoon fondly. "Want to neck? Go on, live dangerously."

Where half an hour went I would not attest to, but it was almost lunch time when we went over the side for our second dive. A breeze was getting up, a little cross chop rocking the boat, but a few feet below the surface it was like being suspended in weightlessness. The water was cool, shockingly so on our sun-hot skin, and the murk was clearing as the tide began to run. We cast out seaward, ambled along the coral spurs where rainbow fish ducked and wove in startlement as we swam by.

It was easy to forget the time and wander too far. We had reached the outmost arm of the reef and were on the point of turning back when an object caught my eye. A mass of geometric angles where none should have been. The murk of the storm-churned water made it difficult to pick out what it was and I caught Greg's attention with a hand on his shoulder. He turned toward me, and I pointed him at the object.

As curious as I am, his journalist's instincts rule him. He kicked out, a couple of powerful, jetfin surges, and was ahead of me by yards. I followed, and as we drew closer the geometric object I had glimpsed became much clearer. It was a light plane, a Piper Navajo, high wing, single engine, the kind of plane that buzzes about the Australian bush the way a VW waddles through city traffic. Hundreds of kilometres can separate one station from the next. Flying is a matter of survival. This Piper carried an American registration.

And the pilot was still in it. Or, his skeleton was.

The fish had picked it clean, right down to white bone, as the windscreen had smashed away. He sat slumped over against the side of the cabin, but the plane had settled the right way up. Aerodynamics are as functional in a liquid environment as in the air. The plane would have glided slowly down, tugged nose-first by the weight of its engine.

For the life of me I could see no reason for it to be there, on the ocean floor in thirty feet of water. The whole aircraft looked to be in perfect condition, no sign of explosion or fire. It must have feathered down into the sea, since there was no sign of crash damage. The registration read N5612L.

The Navajo is not a new plane. This one could have been built twenty years before it crashed, in the days before American civil aviation was strangled to death by a legal system that provides any damned fool pilot with the power to sue the manufacturer for an arm and a leg, irrespective of the fact he piled up the plane himself. But pilots and the authorities regulating them have far stricter standards and practices than divers. Aircraft that are structurally unsound are automatically grounded. So this one, no matter its age, must have been airworthy.

Yet here it was, parked neatly, broadside-on to the outmost spur of the reef, with a skeleton in the pilot's seat. Greg's hand on my arm brought me back to reality with a start and I took a look at my watch. Time to go up, without delay. We were down to a few bars in the tanks, getting close to the safety limit of five atmospheres. I filled my BCD and kicked out toward the shape of the boat above us. Greg was a little behind and below me.

"Going to have to report that," he said as he dumped the empty tanks into the rack behind the boat's cabin. "Somebody will be having fits over that plane."

"I couldn't see a damned thing wrong with it." I cracked open a can of Budweiser, American beer that is like bitter brown fizz after one acclimatizes to European beer. "Might have been pilot failure – the man could have had a heart attack. These things happen."

"Could be." He took the beer from me, disposed of half of it before he handed it back. "N5612L. That should speak volumes to the insurers, also the registration authorities." He cracked a second beer, needing it. Tank air is dry air – there can't be so much as a molecule of moisture in it, or the inside of your tanks oxidise and become toxic. Which means your whole respiratory tract dries out as you breathe. Greg savoured the frothy Fosters as I started the Johnsons and headed the *Light Fantastic* for home.

I still wonder, if we had known the hornets' nest we were disturbing, would we have left nature to itself? We had flown thousands of miles to get away from police and hardcases, and almost the first thing we did was blunder into the midst of a local intrigue. It was, I admitted as I nudged the cabin cruiser back into its berth at the boat ramp, bloody typical of our luck.

I recognized one yacht turning gently at anchor, just off the beach. *Condor of Bermuda*, the beautiful, gracile maxi belonging to Marlon Brando, twenty years old and still one of the fastest hulls in the water. She brought back memories of bouncing around on a dinghy-sized spectator craft with half a dozen young hopefuls, looking for close-up shots as the maxis butted out toward the Sydney heads at the start of the Sydney To Hobart. Sand in your lenses, water in your camera – and a frame that appeared in the *Sunday Telegraph*.

The man in charge of the boat ramp was a bloated tub of lard with a high, squeaky voice. He was like a beached whale. His skin was like black leather in the sun, his head bald, teeth tobacco stained. His name was stencilled over the shed that housed the phone and paperwork. Thelston Conway. It was an odd name for a man so very *un*Irish, but meant only that, however long in the past, one of his forefathers had been owned by an Irishman. Slaves owned by a man took that man's name. And slave children born into a householding were as often as not fathered by the owner, so they were due it. Only humans would think of a system like that.

Greg passed the tanks over the side of the boat to me and hopped onto the blistering concrete of the ramp. He waved for Conway's attention, and when the beached whale looked over called, "Where's the nearest police station?"

"Police?" Conway's voice sharpened in surprise. "You got trouble, man?"

"Just something to report," Greg shuffled urgently on the sun-hot concrete slabs as he searched our bag for his sandals before the soles of his feet scorched off. "How long since they searched for the light plane that disappeared around here?"

Conway's eyes narrowed to slits. "How de 'ell you know 'bout dat?" He demanded, as if we had no damned right to know.

"We found it," I said indifferently. "Just now. Out that way." I waved in the general direction of the reef. Some weird, animal sixth sense warned me to say no more. "How long since it happened?"

"Nearly a year." Conway took the tanks from us, one in each enormous hand, as if they weighed nothing. He marched off to the shack to dump them in the back of his utility. They would go for refilling to the service station up the road. "Dey turn de place inside out, man, never find nothing. It vanish jus' before a storm, an' by de time dey lookin' for it, it was gone."

"Buried," Greg speculated. "The storm yesterday probably cleared it off again. The whole sea's churned up. Which way did you say the police station is?"

"I didn't." Conway turned back to us and for just a moment there was an odd look on his face – a look I did not like. It was quickly masked behind a fat, cheerful smile that bared his stained teeth. He pointed the way to the copshop, but I had seen it and felt a tingle, like spider feet, running down my spine. Paranoia?

As we walked up from the waterfront Greg cast a glance over his shoulder. "What d'you make of that?"

"You picked it up too?" I shrugged. "Maybe he had something to do with the search. Half the boats on the island must have been out looking. Maybe he knew the pilot – or maybe there was trouble. Not our trouble, mate. Sleeping dogs and all that."

"Too right," he agreed with that annoyingly accurate Australian accent he conjures to tease.

It was a short hike back to the hotel and along the road we were passed by an orange Jeep with a sun roof up. "Got to hire some wheels," Greg decided. He had turned up the collar of his shirt, aware of the weight of the sun on the back of his neck. "Today."

"After lunch." I shouldered my way through various "holiday wallies" queueing to buy icecream. "Talk to the police after lunch, too."

We had planned to eat at the hotel but our shortcut introduced us to a tiny, dim cavern where locals dined on seafood and rice. A quick shower in our room, fresh clothes, and we were back there, conspicuous among the Jamaicans. It was rough and ready, not the kind of establishment that would attract tourists, which is exactly why we were there.

If you can escape the tourist trap you will see the real face of Jamaica. It may not always be pretty but it is honest. Sometimes painfully so. There is poverty, unemployment, privation, need. Illiteracy, ill health and every other malady of modern civilization. Drugs, religion and radical politics make strange bedfellows.

The cricket was on the radio. I pricked up my ears as I heard some magic names. Richards, Dujon. In England we are accustomed to seeing these men play on the same team, captain and wicket keeper for the West Indies touring team. There, at home and playing for the Shell Shield, they were on opposing sides. Richards captained Antigua and the Windward Islands, and Dujon captained Jamaica, both brilliant players and as good to watch as dancers. The game was being played on the other side of the island, at the ground in Kingston.

"Want to go over, tomorrow?" Greg forked the hot rice and prawns into his mouth. "Sounds like they're going to make a match of it."

"You're on." I cocked an ear to the radio. "There's three days left, and there's a domestic shuttle." Then I leaned closer, teasing. "I wouldn't mind catching you in the gully at deep fine leg myself."

He has gone beyond the stage of choking on his food when I say such things at awkward moments. Now, he gives me the kind of smile you would pay money for, and demands I deliver on rashly made promises. That remark would cost me later, I knew. I looked forward to paying up as we finished lunch with fruit and chocolate, and left the locals to their cricket commentary. It would be good to hop over the mountains to Kingston on some banana airlines flight tomorrow. But business came before pleasure, and there was still a niggling, needling feeling in my insides as I remembered that look on Thelston Conway's face. He knew something, and no way could it be anything innocent.

3

*T*WO car rental agencies operated within a hundred yards of our hotel. One was Avis, hiring little American J-cars, the other was a local Jamaican enterprise, renting out the absurd little orange Jeeps we had seen running about. We looked at the staid, prosaic "grocery getters" from Detroit and headed for the rank of gaudy junkers.

"Going to regret this," Greg said ruefully as we paid over a few notes and collected the keys. "This contraption's older than we are. It'll probably break down every hundred yards and we'll be up to our elbows in grease fixing it."

"Live dangerously," I chided. I slid the key into the ignition. "First stop, the cops."

Live dangerously. I should buy a crystal ball and go into the business of prediction – I must have second sight. We had been on the road under ten minutes when I saw the big, black Dodge behind us. I thought it was trying to pass and pulled over to let it go. These American cars are too big to argue with, especially if all you have under you is a wheezing Jeep, circa 1944.

The Dodge did not go by, but rode our tail until we knew we were in trouble. We expected the solid shunt. It was no shock when our Jeep lurched and almost destroyed itself on the cobbled wall on our left. My neck gave a sharp protest at the whiplash. Beside me, Greg cursed fluently.

"What the fuck are these guys playing at?" He twisted around in his seat, squinted into the sunglare as he noted the licence plate like the schooled observer he is. "Can't see the driver. Black guy in shades, could be anyone. There's another guy in the car. Big. Hold on!"

Another shunt slammed into the Jeep, rattled it on its nonexistent suspension. I changed down and put my foot down, wondering if we could outrun the Dodge. It would wallow through corners where the Jeep would be faster.

"I think we've annoyed someone," Greg said tartly. He lifted two fingers at the driver of the black Detroit tank.

"Annoyed –?" I echoed. I slammed my foot to the floor. Ahead of us was a blind bend with kids playing cricket on the hot asphalt. This was getting damned dangerous. "Grab something, there's a lefter coming up."

The Jeep skidded around the bend, one wheel off the road, then I stamped on the brakes and prayed as I saw the marketplace coming up fast. Fruit stall, curios, anything and everything for sale. Island beauties, overweight matrons, kids and old men scrambled out of our way as I brought the Jeep to a bouncing halt.

Greg and I were out of it before the brakes had stopped squealing, expecting a fight, itching for it. The Dodge wallowed to a halt. The driver sat, like a fool, begging to be rear-ended by traffic coming up behind while he revved the big V8 motor. The passenger window cranked down as we watched, and suddenly my mouth was dry.

"Down," I hissed at Greg, but he was faster, ducking into the cover of the Jeep. Both of us expected to see a gun muzzle through that window.

The big, gas-guzzling motor revved again, like a gravel-voiced threat, a promise of retribution to come. Then rubber burned on the road and it was gone. We could hear it burbling along the main thoroughfare, away from the hotels and tourist country and deeper into blacktown, where few white faces are ever seen.

We straightened, dusted down, and Greg arched one brow at me. I knew that expression. Curious and angry, he can be a bulldog. "What in God's name was that about?"

I could only shrug. "Maybe they just don't like tourists."

The market was silent as we looked around. No one cursed or shook angry fists at us for dangerous driving. The locals wore shuttered expressions, as if they had not seen anything. I pasted on a smile and approached a middle aged woman. I offered to buy some mangoes. What I wanted was information, but her face was blank. "You saw the car?" Greg asked, a pace behind me. She shook her head, looked up at us with vacant eyes.

"You must have seen it!" I said sharply. Again, she shook her head. I took the mangoes and addressed the same question to the elderly man selling fishing tackle and bait at the next stall. He was just as blind. Or just as scared.

Greg's hand on my arm drew me back to the Jeep. "Leave it alone, Alex. Somebody's corked their mouths good and tight." He slid into the car, took one of the mangoes and sank his teeth into it. Juice dribbled down his chin. I watched his pink tongue flick out to collect it, unconsciously erotic. "Question is, who? And why? And why run us off the road? What the hell have we done to beg for trouble?"

I twisted the key in the ignition, listened to the tinny rattle of an old motor, which had stalled under brakes. "I've got the traditional bad feeling about this," I admitted, looking at his face in the shade of the sunroof. Pensive. "Police?"

"Police." He tossed the remains of his mango onto the road.

The station was a single storey building, no more ostentatious than a post office, with a pebble-dash facia and dusty trees. We parked by the side wall in a patch of shade and stepped into a sudden dimness and relative cool. The officer on duty was just a boy in short sleeves, listening to the cricket on a transistor on the desk.

Big, velvet eyes looked indifferently at us, and he passed us on to an older man with sergeant's stripes. He showed us into an office in the back, turned on a fan to stir the soupy air, and took a statement from us. I have lost count of the number of these I have made and signed. This one was no different, save for the passive reactions of the sergeant.

His name was Payne, and although he was polite he did not evince a twitch of excitement either about the light aircraft we had found, or the run-in with the Dodge. We gave him the licence numbers of both. He took down all the information, but the bottom line was that a couple of tourists had a legitimate complaint to lodge against a local, for irresponsible driving. They would "look into it".

Back out in the car, Greg slid in behind the wheel, and I watched his knuckles whiten on it, an expression of simmering anger. "You know, I'd have sworn there was a sniper in that car. Just a feeling you get after the first thousand times you've been shot at," he muttered.

I knew the feeling. Beirut, Tehran, Saigon. The places

where the news is made, and stories, pictures, are sometimes paid for in blood. "Right." I wiped the back of my hand across my face. Sweating is a way of life in Jamaica's humid afternoons. "It's that bloody plane. It must be."

"Payne didn't bat an eyelid about it," Greg mused. "Maybe he wasn't on this patch when it crashed. You know, somebody else's nine day wonder."

"Maybe." I remembered Payne's bored face. Or maybe the man was just tired of the job and longing to be out fishing. Paranoia is an occupational hazard in our business.

We loitered in the shade of the dusty trees outside the station and lock-up, annoyed and frustrated. Then Greg gave the key a vicious twist in the ignition, starting the motor and revving it hard. Four old cylinders rattled in protest as he dropped the aged, sloppy box into gear. "So much for the melodrama. Screw the whole show, Alex – where do you want to go? Drive up into the hills? Be cooler up there. Waterfalls off the slopes after the storm."

"You're on." I slid green glasses onto my nose and slid carefully into the passenger's seat. The upholstery was so sun-hot, my backside was like a slice of sirloin in half a minute. Broiling gently. "And we'll take that buzz over to Kingston, see the cricket, tomorrow. Fly over?"

"Sooner drive," Greg said shrewdly. He gave me the roadmap he had bought at the hotel's service desk. "Get the hotel to pack us lunch, hire a proper car, do the grand tour."

"We're on holiday, not charting the Congo," I remonstrated. "Why not ride over on Banana Airways, a DC3 over the mountains? Or take the train if you insist on doing everything the hard way."

"Simple." He backed the Jeep out of its space. "If we drive it we can stop half way there and screw each other's brains out." He shot me a heavy-lidded look. "Can't we?"

"Point," I admitted. I felt the familiar throb deep down inside as he spoke. Greg is a randy creature. Sex is like breathing to him. I imagine there was a time when he used to shave his palms.

The dirt roads led upward, sheer. The hillsides still streamed with runoff after the storm. The temperature quickly dropped to a comfortable level. When we found a place that was flat and offered a postcard view Greg pulled off the road under the trees and turned off the Jeep's roasting motor. We could smell it, and I wondered about refilling the old Jeep's radiator before we started back.

The quiet was startling. The wind sighed in the forest, which stretched in all directions. Only the sounds of birds broke the stillness. We could have stepped back centuries. The sea was a ribbon of blue-green low down on the horizon under a sky like a cobalt blue dome over us. I was reminded of home, startled into the sudden realisation that, at the bottom of me, there is still the inclination to regard Australia as "home".

This was the cockpit country. It was here, in the eighteenth century, where Britain was at war with General Cudjoe the Maroon, and his renegades. A band of Koromanteen tribesmen, brought over from Africa as slaves when the indigenous population had been worked to death and must be replaced. The Koromanteen were warriors, and refused to surrender, accept their slavery.

I could relate to that powerfully. Freedom has more value to gays. Born twenty years earlier, Greg and I could have been robbed of our liberty in our own country, for the "crime" of being what we are, something that is as much a part of us as a black man's skin is to him.

"Beautiful," said Greg quietly, as if he was reluctant to break the peace and silence. "Wild. Virgin." He swung out of the Jeep to stretch his back and legs after the bone-jarring ride. "Hard to think that brutality ever happened here."

But it did. Brutality that only presaged the atrocities to take place later in New South Wales. Irishmen have been as persecuted as the Koromanteen, and by the British, just as Cudjoe's people were. My father never let me forget my heritage, the bloody past on which modern Australia is built.

"Listen," Greg murmured a moment later. "What is that? Stream?"

"Sounds like it," I agreed. "Could do with some water for this heap. I wouldn't trust it not to boil on the way home." A coke bottle was loose in the footwell. I leaned in to fetch it, and the Nikon. I never go anywhere without a camera – force of habit. Greg set off through the trees without waiting for me, and I followed the sounds of water on pebbles.

He had found a brimming washaway. Kneeling beside it to drink, he presented me with a target that made my heartbeat double in a moment. I framed him in the Nikon's lens and popped a couple of shots. The sound of the shutter made him look up. His face was dripping.

"Know what you look like?" I teased.

His eyes were enormous, dark. I thought for a moment he

would make a joke of it. We enjoy a razor-edged banter that has not flagged since one night in a barn outside of Port Stanley. He has a sharp tongue, often savagely astute. I had spoken half in humour; I do have a one-track mind. Not being ashamed of it, I readily confess it. In fact he looked like something out of Greek myth. Some sculptor must have seen a creature like this in a wood, who knows how many thousands of years ago, and tried to capture it in marble. And yet the reality was mine, real, warm and alive.

We have been in love for a long time. Is love supposed to cool with time, fade into an affectionate friendship, so that you live with your "lover" but all your lovemaking is a series of tricks and brief affairs? Perhaps for some. And in a way love does cool with time. Our frenzied rounds of nearly violent lust did become more rare as familiarity grew between us, but in its place is a kind of knowing. A comfort that is without price. Living without it would be like having my legs lopped off. Perhaps you have to have found someone like Greg to understand.

He did not say a word, but got to his feet, took off his clothes and stood waiting for me to take whatever I wanted. Afterwards we dozed. The shadows were long when we stirred, yawned awake, the batteries recharged, the afternoon's frustrations soothed. I realised I was hungry as I sat up. And I was itching. We had curled up in the shade without bothering to dress, and there is a price to be paid for such foolishness.

Greg examined his own legs and swore. "Shit, insects! We want our brains examined. I'm eaten alive." He thumped my shoulder. "You ought to know better!"

He was right. We had a dustbowl for a backyard when I was a boy. The ants nested by the millions and were up to an inch long. When bulldog ants bit, you knew about it. "They'll have something at the hotel to put on them," I said hopefully, studying his bites and my own. "First aid – stings and bites must be the most popular mishap around here."

"Oh, right, and I'm going to drop my pants and ask the nurse in charge to plaster my arse in ointment!" He made a face as he pulled on his slacks and raked his nails over the cotton, still scratching.

"So we'll find a chemist on the way back, and I'll plaster it for you," I offered, scratching my own thighs. "Then you can daub the stuff on me. In case it's escaped your notice, I'm irresistible to insects."

He frowned at me in the gathering shadows. "Got some beauties there, Alex. You're worse than I am."

He was not exaggerating. I could only blame myself. Even if he was fool enough to lie around in the bush, bare arse, begging to be eaten, I should have remembered. Being on holiday makes no difference. We would be lucky, I thought belatedly, if we did not get malaria. The hills were clothed in rainforest, pools and streams – a breeding ground for mosquitoes.

I drove on the way back. We found a little druggist's in a tiny, shabby railway town called Anchovy. It was a shed with a modern frontage tacked on, some plate glass and plastic shelves. We were dubious about the stock but desperate enough by then to try anything. Every ant in Jamaica seemed to have made tracks for my backside. From Greg's animated fidgeting, he was not much better.

The shop was lit by naked bulbs, its shelves stacked with patent imports on one hand – Disprins, Bandaids, Dettol – and on the other with potted local cures. Folk medicine? Herbal lore?

Speculations about voodoo in my mind, I loitered at the door to watch Greg saunter into the shop as if he had lived on Jamaica all his life. The man serving behind the counter looked a hundred years old, smoked like a kipper and still smoking. He was stoking a pipe with what we recognized as a mixture of tobacco and marijuana.

Marijuana is one of Jamaica's big industries. They smuggle a couple of thousand tonnes of the stuff into the USA every year, which makes it a staple crop even though it is illegally grown and the law will ostensibly be down on the growers like a load of bricks. Ostensibly – the diplomatic face shown to the Americans, who manipulate the Caribbean states for reasons of local security.

The truth is, the police will rarely interfere in the "ganja" trade. They share in its profits, and they have their spies in the business, there to run surveillance on the Rastafarian community, whose religious rites use marijuana. Rastafarians are not merely a moral voice, but a political one. The doctrine of black solidarity could conceivably rouse the rabble, and the police are wary. Then, the ganja trade has set up a pecking-order, a Jamaican caste system where the "haves" repress the "have nots" without the need for the police themselves to wield the big stick. The rabble has locked itself in its own shackles, and keeps them locked.

There is also the pacifying effect of the ganja. Doped and docile, who has the energy to get up and struggle for justice? The old man behind the counter was slack-mouthed and vacant-eyed with some mixture of drugs, and, for what it was worth, content.

"Evening," Greg said to him. "What have you got for insect bites?"

A pot of thick brown ointment was forthcoming. Odourless and of the consistency of wallpaper paste. It was evil-looking and we frowned at it as the man threw a few coins into an old fashioned drawer till. I frowned at the shelves, hunting for some patent label I would recognize, but found no such luxury.

Anchovy was almost deserted. I saw a few children playing with a bucket of water, and a knot of old women standing to gossip outside of a grocer's. As Greg went in search of something cool to drink, I ambled around the druggist's shack. In the lengthening shadows at the back was a light commercial flat bed, loaded with wooden crates. The name stencilled on the cab door read "Goldmark". Idle curiosity took me closer.

Tomatoes, bound for the tourist traps, filled the top crates. I saw the colour of them through gaps in crates that were old, battered and starting to break up. I had turned to go when I saw stems escaping from a lower crate, one of those on the bottom of the stack. I could not resist teasing one out.

So they transported the stuff from hills to harbour dressed up as tomatoes for the hotels. I smiled at the token gesture. Just enough to keep up a legal front for the sake of the tourists. This cargo would be headed for Falmouth or Lucea, one of the smaller ports, and from there to the Mexican coast for transportation straight over the border.

A can of lemonade was waiting for me back at the Jeep. I put the strand of herbage into Greg's waiting hand. "What's that look like?"

"Where d'you get this?" he snickered. "That old goat at the druggist's isn't selling the stuff under the counter –?"

"No. But there's a van 'round the back loaded with it. That, and tomatoes." I started the Jeep. "Cute, no?"

"Predictable. Not exactly original, as smuggling goes." He held the weed to his nose to inhale its distinctive smell and puffed out his cheeks.

"Doesn't have to be clever, the police won't get into it," I said as I pulled back onto the road. "All they have to worry about is keeping it out of the way of the tourists."

"Yeah." He twirled the stalk under my nose and laughed. "How long since you smoked this stuff."

I could answer that to the day. "'81, at a press party in Lebanon. I was so dim afterward I didn't see the trouble coming, got shit kicked out of me by a gang of young bucks who didn't like yesterday's UPI releases. I never used it again. I'd like to stay alive. You?"

"Oh, about the same." He considered the weed and then threw it into the road. "Pull over, will you?"

We were not far north of Anchovy. Greg began to roll up the legs of his slacks. I watched him rub the ointment into some of the worst of the bites. He had scratched them raw already, and muttered in surprise as he smoothed in the ointment.

"Stops the stinging at least. Doesn't hurt." He studied the contents of the jar in the gathering dusk. "Cross your fingers, this might work."

Ten minutes later he was rubbing the evil-looking ointment into every bite he could decently reach, and muttering in contentment. I reached over for the pot. "Let's have it. You're not getting all the joy."

Relief was minutes in coming, then I too moaned in comfort. Greg laughed at my beatific expression. "If that's voodoo, I'm all for it."

I kissed him while the road was deserted, dropped the Jeep into gear and headed us for home. I was ravenous, eager to clean up and eat. The roads in Jamaica are eccentric at best and there are not many of them. Your kidneys are tested to destruction, driving anywhere at all. Speeding is infeasible, even if your kidneys could survive. Not even truck suspension would take it for long, metalled surface or no.

We parked in the deep, mauve shadows by the floodlit Grand Hotel. Sunset blazed out over Montego Bay. The view was spectacular from the Grand's bar, and we stood to admire it, drinking Black Douglas and looking forward to a shower.

Greg had the keys. He went ahead of me into the room. Everything was tidy, almost as we had left it. Almost. Then we noticed that the wardrobe door was ajar, and my suitcase was on its side rather than on end, as it should have been. I swore lividly.

"Someone's been in here," Greg said quietly. "Cleaners? In to change the linen, wash the windows?"

"That doesn't give them the right to muck about with our luggage!" I was angry enough to pick up the phone and shout. Five minutes later the assistant manager was in the room, a young blond with a contrived accent, flustered and very British as he tried to smooth us over. "Who's been in here since noon?" I wanted to know, and I must have sounded nasty. Greg just rolled his eyes to the gods and turned his back on me.

"No one, sir." The young blond flushed scarlet. "The girls changed your linen, but that was this morning. No one else has been in."

"Then I suggest you tell your girls to stay out of your guests' personal effects," I snarled. "And if we find our belongings missing, there'll be hell to pay!"

"I hardly think our staff would do any such thing," he protested.

"No? Well, someone's been in here, and the room was locked." I gestured at the open wardrobe and disturbed baggage. "You telling me you have thieves in this hotel?"

"No, of course not!"

"Then what?" I watched his flush deepen. He was at a complete loss.

"Alex." Greg stepped forward. The calm tone of voice wooed the young assistant manager after my anger. "Someone has been in here, no doubt about it. We're not imagining things. Now, we'll find out if anything's been taken, and in the meantime, I suggest you see about your house security. If we've been robbed, we'll claim. And we don't expect this to happen again." His tone sharpened with the last remark.

I slammed the door behind the man and threw my shirt into the laundry bin. "Christ. Thieves, is it? Employees on the take?"

"Or something to do with that Dodge that tried to smear us all over the road?" he asked as his clothes followed mine into the bin and he headed for the bathroom. "I'm liking this less and less, Alex."

Such thoughts preoccupied me as we showered quickly, dried off and took turns to stretch out and be rubbed with the ointment. Already most of the damage had subsided. The massage was more for pleasure than necessity. I love having Greg under my hands, even platonically. When he jumped the tendons in his back I spent happy hours rubbing it for him. Greg indulged me with an amused look.

The dining room was crowded. We waited for a table,

drinking Camparis at the bar until a young waiter, with those gazelle-eyes black boys sometimes have, summoned us. It was a sumptuous affair, a delight of chicken and apricots, some house speciality, complimented by white wine and topped off with a lemon meringue that was lighter than air.

The dining room opened onto the wide, breezy area of the big patio and dance floor. We were on the very fringe of it, almost outside under the Chinese paper lanterns. Fairy lights nodded in the breeze and couples danced to the music of a Creole band. I wished I could have danced with Greg, an absurd impossibility in the West Indies, where homosexuality is deeply frowned on, barely tolerated. They have gained one kind of freedom, but not yet complete freedom.

The night was very soft and warm, but we were still on edge with a hunted feeling, after the run-in with the Dodge and the intrusion into our room. I had that feeling of being watched but put it down to edgy nerves until I saw Greg looking around, and realised I was right.

It was just a child watching us. He stood under the big frangipani bushes at the edge of the patio, his face illuminated by the lanterns. At first I assumed the boy was hanging about looking for a handout, a meal or money. Some of the time the beggar children are employed, begging as a job. They front for a greasy adult who takes everything they get. It's a fact of life in so many impoverished countries where tourism has invaded. The time I collected a bullet, in the shacks outside of Bangkok, it was over a crippled beggar boy. God knows what happened to him. I was in hospital for a month.

The little waif was looking right at us, and Greg said softly, under the band, "I know that kid's face. I've seen him somewhere." His brow creased in a frown. "Where? At the boatyard, Conway's place, this morning. He was working there, polishing, remember?"

"I didn't see him," I said, helping myself to another coffee. "I wasn't taking any notice. Too busy looking at you, if you must know."

He flashed me a smile. "I only noticed him because he was whistling a tune I knew. He's looking at us like it's business." Before I could stop him or object, he beckoned the boy to our table. I bit back a groan, fully expecting to be taken to the cleaners. "You looking for us, son?" Greg asked.

The boy was ten or eleven, thin and dark brown, with big

doe-eyes and skin like satin. He would grow up into a real beauty, given six or eight years to mature. His clothes were patched but clean and he wore shoes, which is unusual for poor people's children. The boy edged warily toward the table, shuffling, hesitant. Nervous? He pushed a scrap of paper at Greg. Greg took it, unfolded it.

"You is Connor and Farris, I seen you at Conway's," he said in an accent so thick the words were slurred, hardly seeming like English at all.

And then he ran. Greg blinked after him in surprise before he turned attention to the paper. He held it to the light and frowned again. "It's a note. 'Come to The Maroon at ten in the morning, I must talk to you. It is very important. Please come'. And it's initialled, 'S.H.' He passed the slip of paper across the table to me. "What the hell does that mean?"

"It means somebody with nice handwriting and good taste in notepaper wants to talk to us, urgently," I said glibly. "I might be wrong, but I'd say this is a woman's writing." I held the paper to his nose. "What's that smell like?"

"Jasmin, is it?" He took it back to scan the message again. "S.H."

"What's The Maroon?" I knew I was missing something.

"That pub, the waterhole up that way," he told me. "The place with the muskets and spears and drums tacked up around the door. It's the locals' bar, strictly blacktown. Could turn nasty if they don't like tourists with white faces shoving in where they don't belong."

"You kidding?" I gestured out at the bay, at the yachts and pleasure craft rocking at anchor there. Rampant wealth, displaying itself like a whore flaunting his beautiful arse for the fun of it. "This place runs on tourism. If all we white buggers decide to pack up and go, and not come back, there's a lot of people going to be starving hereabouts." Sighing resignedly, I sipped the last of my coffee. "That does in the cricket tomorrow. If we were going to drive it, or fly for that matter, we should have been half way there by ten. Damn." The day's play started at half past and I had been looking forward to it. "Maybe the day after? I'd like to see Dujon knock up a century on his home wicket."

Jamaica was pasting Antigua, despite Viv Richards' best efforts, but it was early days in the series. Everyone and his uncle were talking about the condition of the pitches to be played on, the break-up of the wickets, which was a "batsman's track", or a "bowler's paradise". The bowlers were being hammered all over the Kingston ground. It would have been quite something to see a Shell Shield match in the flesh.

We ordered cognac and listened to the band. It was still early and the sea wind was cool. Greg wanted to walk and we found ourselves on the beach, almost alone under a half moon. We heard the noise of a party from one of the motor yachts offshore, shrill, girlish giggling and hard rock. Who needed it? Greg tumbled me in the soft, warm sand, straddled me, pinned both my hands out at my sides as if I was crucified on a feather mattress. We had shaved before dinner and were still smooth. His mouth covered my face and throat an inch at a time.

We walked for miles as the tide turned, held hands in the dark, and headed back for the hotel when it was late. We were lulled by the sound of the sea, by the fine meal in us, and the solitude. We walked right into it.

Four men, big, heavy – shadows against the darkness just short of the hotel. I knew instinctively they had been waiting for us. Lights spilling from the hotel windows caught the uplifted blade of a knife in one big fist and my throat dried. They must have been watching us since we drove back, just waiting to catch us alone.

Who the hell were they – what did they want with us? Good questions that I banished the moment I saw the knife. All I could imagine was that fish-gutting blade, hilt deep in Greg. If they had shooters we were done before it started. The four of them had been hidden in the rhododendrons. Before we knew they were there, two were behind us, two in front. We stood like statues and my eyes never left that knife.

One of the men behind us spoke in a whisper, whisky-hoarse: "It's them, Logan, like Conway said."

Conway – at the boat ramp? I glanced at Greg, saw his face dimly in the same light that gleamed coldly on the gutting knife. "Look, what is this?" I levelled my voice, tried to speak reasonably. It was like trying to reason with a white pointer.

"Shut your mouth, white boy." The tallest, heaviest of the two before us spoke out of the darkness.

Greg found a low, quiet voice. "At least tell us what we've done!"

A snicker answered him. "Can tell you what you's gonna do, boy," Logan said with a rich, satisfied sound. "You's gonna die, right here."

And he took a pace toward Greg. The blood pounded in my ears. Standing still would have taken sanity, and in those moments I was certifiable as he brought that knife a step nearer Greg. My knuckles split on bone that felt like concrete. I heard a gutteral cursing as Logan stumbled, down on one knee, his bells probably ringing. I thought I had broken my hand.

Off to my right I heard a grunt, a winded "oof", but not Greg's voice. Somebody had taken a fist in the gut – Greg's. I prayed to any soldier's god that might be listening as I swung my foot into the well of shadow where Logan's bowed head must be. As I felt the jar of impact, heard him go sprawling under the shrubs, arms closed around me from behind.

They held me like steel bands, to a chest like a barrel. I used what leverage I had, both feet kicking off the ground, and the man stumbled backward. Logan remained down but his companion was only looking for an opening, and all I had between me and the gutting knife was my feet. I could hear the sounds of a scuffle behind me – Greg was still on the loose. But Greg is light, not in the heavyweight bracket. It could only be a matter of time.

A grunt, and Logan was up again. Sweat prickled my ribs and the arms about me cut off my breathing. I wasn't getting air and my struggles were finishing me. "Greg?" I wheezed. "Greg!"

And then, giggling, raucous singing, loud American voices, the Stones hammering out of a ghetto blaster. A voice close by my ear hissed, "Shit, Logan, whassat?"

It was a gaggle of American tourists, right on top of us as they came out of the hotel's side lobby, headed for the beach and a moonlight beach orgy. As suddenly as the assault had begun it was over. I was thrown face down on the asphalt. I rolled over, winded but not hurt, frantic until I saw Greg on his knees under the bushes.

We found our feet together and moved, fast, into the lobby where the night staff were on. Floor polishers and vacuum cleaners whined, boys were polishing the acres of plate glass. Greg had a hand to his side but did not look back at me as he punched up the lift. I held my tongue till we were in its seclusion, and then grabbed him by the shoulders.

"You hurt, Greg, for Chrissake?"

"Let go, you're breaking my shoulders," he hissed, and I realised I was gripping him with all the strength I had. I eased up and he leaned back against the lift's chrome panelled wall. "I took one," he said, still holding his right side. "It's all right, I'll live."

"Sure? You sure? You want a doctor?"

"Oh, Alex." He fended me off as the lift opened, and limped along to our door. Key in his hand, he stopped and looked up at me. "Shall I go in first, or will you?"

I had my breath back, and I had not actually been hit. I also have three inches and a lot of muscle over Greg. I swiped the key out of his hand and motioned him back, well out of the way. The door slammed back on its hinges, kicked open as the key turned, but the room was empty. In a moment more I gave him the all-clear.

He limped past me, sprawled out across the bed as I locked up. He lay still, let me take his shirt off. I peered at the livid mark that would soon become a beauty of a bruise, just below the line of his ribs. I shook my head over him and kissed it.

"Well, you'll live."

"As I told you." He sat up. "What in God's name is this about? You think we're safe here? In the hotel? They've been in the room once – it must have been them! They know right where we are. They can come for us any time they like."

"I know." I rubbed my face hard, trying to think. No, we were not safe there, but where could we go to be safer? I reached over him and picked up the phone. "Is there a manager on duty tonight?" I asked when the switch-girl answered. "You've got trouble, love. Big trouble. You could end up with some very dead guests. It's room 84."

The blond young man lived in the hotel, we discovered ten minutes later as he hurried down from the penthouse level with demands to know what was going on. Greg was starting to hurt, the way blows wait a few minutes before the aches set in. There could be no mistaking what had happened outside.

Paul Curtis was shocked. He closed his mouth and listened as I said, "I don't know what's going on, but someone's marked our cards. They were in here earlier, and now this. Have you got somewhere we can stay tonight? Or, can you give us some kind of security?"

"Yes – of course." He raked his fingers back through the short yellow hair, leaving it tousled. "I'm sorry, we don't usually . . . That is, nothing like this has ever . . . ." He cleared his throat. "You can stay in my suite if you like. It's got a private lift access that's lockable, you'll be safe there. I'll call the police. Believe me, Mr Connor, nothing like this has ever happened in this hotel. Would your friend like a doctor?"

Greg was pouring a brandy and just shook his head. "No need," I said, though his hands shook just a little. "I think we'll have to move out in the morning. I don't see that it's safe to stay. Is there any chance of you pulling some strings, get us a switch with someone else, to another hotel, with different names? Smith and Jones or something," I added drily.

"I'll try. I should be able to manage something," he muttered.

I realised I had misjudged the young manager earlier. He was on the level, shocked and flustered by the trouble. "I'll pack us a bag," I said quietly, shepherding him to the door. When it was closed behind him I opened my case on the bed and watched Greg begin to slam odds and ends of personal effects into it. Every movement betrayed anger.

"It's that plane," he said at last. He looked up at me with grey eyes that glittered. "It has to be. Police again, tomorrow?"

"Or tonight, if Curtis gives them a bell. They might come looking for us. You've got enough there, honey, we can finish packing tomorrow, when Curtis has found us somewhere to go." I took him against me for a moment. "You sure you're all right?"

"Just bruised." He leaned heavily on me. I luxuriated in the press of his spare, solid body before he fended me off again and picked up the case. At the door he turned back and arched a brow at me. "If they've got shooters, we're in real trouble. Wonder if we can get one in town?"

The thought sobered me. Curtis hovered beside the service desk to wait for us. He went up in the lift with us, unlocking a mechanism that allowed the car to pass on, above the normal floors, to his own level. "You can lock it again, so no one can get up here," he told me as he ushered Greg through into the plush penthouse suite. "I've already spoken to the police. They want to see you in the morning, if you can go in to the station – ?"

"No problem." I glanced around Curtis' rooms: very nice, done out in pastels and antiques. I wondered what he was making as a junior manager in a place like this. A lot. "We'll see you at breakfast then, and if you can find us somewhere else to go, we'll be out of your hair."

"Mr. Smith and Mr. Jones," he said ruefully. "It'll probably be a single room again, I'm afraid. There isn't much unbooked, and you'll be exchanging with a couple. I mean, a married couple."

"I know what you mean." I hid a faint, wry smile.

He flushed, the way blonds do. "Um, it's the same here. My bedroom . . . my facilities are . . . "

"It's very pleasant," Greg told him. "Thank you." He stood at the bedroom door, surveying a big double with mauve sheets. I wondered if Paul Curtis had any idea what I intended to do to Greg in his bed.

"Well, I'll leave you to it." Curtis was on his way out. "You'll find everything you need. Till breakfast, then."

I followed him out, locked the lift access and returned to find Greg standing under hot water. He was just angry, and I left him to soak his aches away. I turned down Curtis' sheets and found a bottle of dark rum. I commandeered it and took it to bed with us. A few glasses, and we settled, spooned together in the dark, too tense to sleep although we were tired.

Our first stop in the morning must be the police. Would D.S. Payne evince some twitch of interest at the attempted murder of two island visitors? We had a name for him. Logan. And I was guessing that Logan must be known from past episodes. The threat of sudden, casual death came too easily. He was no amateur. And, I realised as I courted sleep with my face pressed into Greg's soft hair, there had been the anticipation of pleasure in Logan's voice. As if spilling blood was one of life's little satisfactions. .

4

MORNING sunlight was filtered by lowered venetian blinds. I peered at my watch, surprised to see it was already seven thirty as I stirred. And I realised what had woken me in the same moment. Greg had my cock cradled in his palm. He was stroking me from root to tip with his thumb, watching my face as I came to and closed my eyes again with helpless pleasure.

He kicked the bedding out of the way and straddled my

chest. I moaned something inarticulate as his beautiful mouth closed over me. His own cock throbbed, hot against the middle of my chest. I couldn't reach it to suck it, and took him by the hips, pulled him back till his knees were buried in the pillows on either side of my head.

We turned Curtis' bed into a disaster, rolled from this to that contortion, and I had his whisker burns from breast to crotch before we let go and finished. I swallowed his cum, felt his throat twitch against the blunt tip of me as he swallowed too.

His head lay on my thigh. I reached down to stroke his face. My nails raked through his stubble. "That was nice. What got you going?"

A vast yawn ambushed him before he could reply. "Watching you sleep." He sat up, stretched thinly muscled but astonishingly strong arms above his head. For one so slim, Greg is sometimes alarmingly strong. He can hurt me, and I'm not too macho to admit it. He leaned over to kiss me, sharing the last traces of our semen, and went to set the shower.

His bruise was blue this morning. I fretted over it till he lifted two fingers at me, and then palmed his arse while his head was a mass of suds. He gave a yelp but humped back into my hands. I caught the sluicing shampoo, used it to lather him up, fingers inside him until he was absolutely clean. Then I knelt behind him and spread those buttocks, kissed between them, rimmed him until I knew his bones must have been liquid. I pulled him down into my arms. The shower stall overflowed, the bathroom flooding as we knelt on the tiles and kissed luxuriously.

Curtis was waiting for us when we made it down to the dining room. He had been a busy boy. "I've got you a booking at the Marina. It's just a small hotel – the best I can do on such short notice. But they don't know your names, and I can send your luggage over there surreptitiously. Well, with the laundry van, actually."

"Thanks." I accepted the coffee and croissants. "If the cops pick up Logan and his mates we might still get a holiday out of this. Otherwise . . . " I looked at Greg, one brow up in speculation.

He made a throat-cutting gesture. "Out. All the way out, before it gets any nastier." He gave Curtis a smile, and his keys. "Thanks for last night. It was good of you."

"The least I could do. Detective Sergeant Payne is expecting you at nine, and you can use my car, my driver. You should be safe that way. I'll send the boy along at ten minutes to. And I'll see to your luggage, if you would like to return to the room and pack. I really am sorry."

I sighed into my coffee. "It's not your fault."

Curtis made a face. "No, but our house security is supposed to look after our guests. Robbery, rape and murder happen in blacktown, not on the hotel premises!"

"But robbery, rape and murder do happen?" Greg asked shrewdly.

"I'm afraid they do." Curtis looked out through the big dining room windows, toward the beach and green sea. "Jamaica can be very violent. And very lawless. But we don't beat up our tourists. Well, not usually." He stirred, forced a polite smile for our benefit. "My car will be waiting for you."

"Kind of you." Greg reached for another croissant as Curtis ambled away toward the reception area.

The day's newspapers waited for us on the trolly. They covered European and American tales of woe. We found a copy of last month's *Perspective*. Greg's story was on Chile, then one vast, nation-sized concentration camp, accompanied by my pictorial.

We had not been sent to hell on assignment, but to a small, discreet hotel that had hosted a number of refugees. They escaped over the border into Bolivia, which in itself is damned dangerous. Our Chilean runaways came to London as narcotics couriers and brought the whole lot to *Perspective*. Greg and I walked out of that private hotel with several kilos of uncut heroin which had come through the docks undetected, and with a story for Matt Lansing that crisped the paper. The runaways went into police custody for their own protection. I had pulled every professional trick I knew to produce shots and yet disguise their faces.

We read through yesterday's news from London, pleased not to be there, despite our troubles here. A bomb had blown the insides out of a bus station. Jews were the target and several political groups had claimed it. A near collision in the "stacks" over Heathrow. And there were new AIDS horror stories. There always are. The dining room was empty now. I reached across for Greg's hand as we read the headlines and viewed the photographs of a rally at the funeral of a prominent gay personality. Often, I think how lucky I am, to have found someone to love. To be faithful to.

He smiled at me, but it was a sad smile. Two of his old

lovers are ill and one has died already. There is such sadness, even for those who have, like us, escaped by the skin of our teeth. I wanted to hold him, but the waitresses were bustling about, clearing away, and instead I tossed the paper back onto the trolly and gave him a push to his feet.

We approached our old room cautiously, but the door was open and we heard a vacuum cleaner inside. The maid was in, cleaning for the new occupants. We gave her a smile and packed quickly. Curtis was on the phone in reception as we left the baggage for him. He pointed us at the staff exit, which was through at the back of the building.

A Jaguar stood outside. Its bored driver read the paper as he killed time waiting for us. We slid into the back, and he knew where he was going. The big V8 was silent as we left the Grand Hotel. We skirted several commercial vehicles that serviced the hotel. I grunted in amusement as I saw the name "Goldmark" on the side of one of the vans. I wondered if Curtis and his boss knew the market gardener who supplied their salad smuggled ganja on the side. They probably did. There is little point getting excited about these things with the police being deliberately blind.

It was still cool, quiet, and the station was deserted. Payne was on duty. He ushered us into the same office and took notes with that same infuriatingly bland look on his face. I felt anger begin to kindle in my gut and shot a glance at Greg. He was tight-lipped. I knew that expression. An eruption was due, and the longer he controlled it the more explosive it would be when it escaped.

I cleared my throat, levelled my voice and leaned across the desk. "I don't think you understand, Sergeant. Someone is trying to kill us. There was the Dodge that nearly pasted us all over the road, there was someone in our hotel room – "

"Was anything stolen?" He looked at us disinterestedly.

I took a breath, wanting to hit him. "No, nothing. I think they were looking for us, not our belongings.

"If nothing was stolen, we can't charge anyone."

And then Greg got to his feet, his voice a sharp bark. "It could have been two dead bodies you were finding, Sergeant, either in our room or on the beach last night! Four heavies, big guys, two of them with knives, one of them answering to 'Logan', and telling us straight, we were dead meat." He glared at Payne. "The name means nothing to you?"

We saw the flicker in Payne's dead fish eyes at this. "Not to me, sir, but we'll look into it."

"You'll look into it." Greg snatched his jacket from the back of his chair and marched to the door. "That's enough, Alex, come on. Alex!"

I gave Payne a disgusted look and followed. I stopped at the door for just a moment. Some sixth sense had my hackles rising. Payne watched me, unblinking, as if he was just waiting for me to leave the room, get out of his space. My nerves crawled. I slammed the door and pulled my sunglasses from my shirt pocket. Greg was already in the Jaguar.

We said nothing on the way over to the Marina. Curtis' driver dropped us at the staff entrance at the back and left us. We should have made it over unobserved and be relatively safe, and our baggage would be waiting for us in the room, so Curtis promised. As the Jag pulled out Greg took a look around, wary as a one-eyed old wolf.

"What?" I asked. I've learned to trust his instincts.

"I don't . . . Just paranoia, probably," he said quietly, and went ahead of me, in through the kitchen entrance.

In the big cold store, through the open doorway, I saw a tall stack of battered wooden crates, each of them branded with a name, for collection purposes. "Goldmark". Goldmark; ganja smuggling; criminal wheeler-dealing; police who don't give a shit when the knives come out and blood starts to spill; and the two of us, rumbled twice – for what?

I can't bear mysteries. I can't even bear to read them, let alone be part of them. Annoyed, I followed Greg to the manager's office to meet an obese little man with thinning hair. We went up in the staff lift to a room at the back. It was small, plain, uninspiring. Greg took the key. Our bags were already there.

We could have stood grumbling, but instead he took the folded sheet of notepaper from his backpocket and reread the message as I threw the cases into the little wardrobe. "The Maroon, at ten. Blacktown . . . You thinking what I'm thinking?"

"That we could get our arses booted off?" I slammed the door on the wardrobe and shoved my hands into my pockets. "Public place, broad daylight. Better than being caught out at night. Just stay where there's people, and don't get suckered."

He waved the note under my nose. "This could be a set up."

But I shook my head. "No way, my son. That was delivered

by a kid – sneaking into the hotel to find us. And it was after that when Logan tried to make bait out of us. He hasn't got the brains to send scented notepaper and set us up. And even if he had, he wouldn't fix us up for a ten o'clock knifing today, and then jump us last night." I gave the paper a frown. "I'll buy this one. What worries me is the location. Blacktown pub. And we haven't even got a pocket knife between us."

"We can put that right at least." Greg winked at me and locked the room up behind us.

We left by the rear again and he turned along the alley toward the market place, back along the way Curtis' company car brought us. We were as anonymous there as we could be, just tourists. I hoped. Greg was shopping for fishing tackle. I watched him purchase the same kind of gutting knives Logan and his friends had sported. The kind of blade that will take the fingers off you if you're not careful, and turns cod into sushi at a stroke. If Logan's people had guns we were on a one way trip home in body bags, but with the gutting knife in my back pocket I felt just a little less naked.

The Maroon lay downtown, away from the hotels. Greg knew the way. He had taken an interest in the muskets and drums, African tribal oddities, as we ambled by on our way back to the hotel from a swim. My eyes were everywhere, raking the milling market crowd for some reason for my crawling nerves and lifting hackles. But I saw nothing and had begun to breathe a little easier when we came upon the pub.

It was a few minutes before ten. The street was dusty, glaringly bright, not far off the waterfront. The Maroon lay in the heart of the local quarter and there would be no tourists. We bought pineapple and crushed ice at a stall on the edge of the market, sat down on white-painted tyres fifty yards from the pub and scouted the place before committing ourselves.

Nothing appeared suspicious. A barman was sweeping out the yard, there was a clatter of crated empties as a lorry serviced the pub, and the smell of frying onions. I tossed away my empty paper cup as Greg made moves in the direction of The Maroon. We went in under the tacked-up collection of antiques, musketry, drums and spears. After the sunglare it was dark and green inside. A polished cherry-wood bar, red leather upholstery, a man polishing glassware, obviously surprised to see two white faces in the establishment.

Greg ordered a couple of beers, discovering to his displeasure that they served only the American variety, freezing, bitter lemonade that packs all the kick of your aged, maiden aunt. How anyone gets drunk on it is a mystery. Heaven help them if they try the European beer. Still, we needed clear heads that day and accepted the Budweiser without comment.

We had finished the beer when we heard a woman's light voice. "Mr. Connor, Mr. Farris – ?"

She was in the pub's lounge, small and very pretty, perhaps thirty, I guessed, dressed in a pink sun frock and white sandals. She had been there for some time, watching us as warily as we had watched The Maroon from across the road. The voice was deep and husky with something of Greg's sexy timbre about it. It made me smile. I gave Greg a nudge with one elbow. "Our 'S.H.', I believe."

"It's Shirley Hamilton," she said politely. "Malcolm came to me yesterday with a story I didn't dare believe."

We strolled into the lounge and slid in behind the corner table. She sat on the other side of it, both hands about a tall glass of something cool. "You have us at a disadvantage, Miss Hamilton," I said. "You seem to know us. I wish I could say the same."

"Oh, no, not really. Malcolm saw your names on ṳie boat hire slip – that's all I know, just Farris and Connor. I don't know your first names, or even which is which . . . Which *is* which, incidentally?" She tried a smile but it was a skittish expression.

I offered my hand. "I'm Connor. Alex Connor. This is Greg Farris." Her hand was tiny, soft, cool, but the palm was sweating a little. Nerves?

She shook Greg's hand briefly across the table. "As I said, Malcolm came to me yesterday with a story I just didn't dare believe – "

"Malcolm is the boy who brought us the note?" Greg wondered.

"Yes. Malcolm Dennison. He told me – well, he said you saw a light plane in the water just offshore. Was . . . Is the pilot still in it?"

Greg looked sidelong at me. "We found a plane, Miss Hamilton." Red leather squealed under him as he moved into the corner of the contoured seating. "We reported it to the police yesterday."

"And the pilot?" She leaned closer, intent on him. She had

the biggest, brownest eyes I have ever seen, and they were filled with some mix of sadness and fright.

"Well, what's left of him is," Greg said carefully. "Or, should I say, what's left of someone. It's been in the water a long time, almost a year, so Fat Conway said."

"Malcolm told me you mentioned it to Conway. You ought to be running. It's why I asked you to meet me today, as soon as I could get to you. Malcolm watched for you to come back all afternoon. I've got a chart here – " She rummaged through her handbag, brought out a fisherman's reef chart and folded it on the table. She uncapped a felt marker pen. "Just mark down where the plane is for me, and then get out and run. Get off the island before they fillet you."

Greg and I looked at each other as she pushed the chart across the table. "Why?" I asked. "Just tell me what in Christ's name we're running away from! Running's not our style, and if we're going to do it, we want to know what for."

Her mouth opened, closed, like a fish out of water, and I saw her eyes flood. "Please, just go. You're lucky they haven't caught up with you already. They'll gut you! There's been enough killing already."

"You mean Logan and the boys?" I asked. Her eyes widened. "They've tried twice already. We've told the police. They don't seem interested."

Shirley Hamilton's lush mouth twisted, a bitter expression. "The police. Did you speak to Detective Sergeant Payne? Or was it Inspector Williams?"

"It was Payne," Greg told her. He reached across the table for her hand as she fiddled with the marker. "Why don't you just tell us what this is about? What have we done to make Logan want us dead? Is it the plane? Conway said it went down almost a year ago."

Her eyes closed as if she was in physical pain, then opened again, and the tears spilled. "It disappeared on April 14th last year, at eight o'clock in the morning."

Grey eyes probed into me and then Greg looked back at the woman. "You're very sure of your facts, Miss Hamilton."

"I ought to be." Her voice was roughened with emotion. She returned to the present with an obvious effort and scrubbed at her eyes as if angry at the tears. "It was my father flying that plane. And I think . . . I'm sure he was murdered. The plane was never found, nothing could ever be proven, and then Malcolm came running to find me yesterday. I work as a receptionist for Doctor Clarke. Uptown. White doctor for white tourists. I could hardly believe it." She shook herself, hard. "Malcolm works at the boatyard for pocket money, Conway's odd jobs." She looked from Greg to me and back again and her face had that hunted look. "My father was murdered. I know he was."

I groaned soundlessly. Not again, not here, not while we were trying to have our first decent holiday in years and all I wanted to do was swim and eat and sleep and get fucked, then do the same to him until I was incapable. But we were already in too deep to back out. I schooled my face, pinned on what I hoped was a lucid expression.

"And what makes you so certain of this, Miss Hamilton?"

She gulped the dregs of what must have been a lemonade. Greg waved for the barman to fetch another, and a couple of beers for us. She seemed to struggle with her thoughts and tongue for a moment and then got a grip on herself. I knew the feeling, so did Greg. Any journalist is used to watching human beings under duress, and you learn patience.

"My father was a pilot for Shell as long ago as World War II. He was the best damned pilot on this island," she said fiercely. Aggressively. "He was English, in case you're wondering. I'm half caste." She looked up at us defiantly, as if challenging us to make something of it. There is still a lot of bad feeling about mixed marriages in the Caribbean states. She need not have troubled herself. We did not even lift an eyebrow at her and she seemed to relax. When she found her voice again it was calmer.

"My father was too good to make mistakes on a stupid little shuttle flight over from Haiti." Her mouth compressed to a thin, defiant line. "And he was not drunk or stoned!"

"Who said he was?" Greg prompted, shrewd as any journalist.

"The investigating authorities. Civil aviation, the law. They said he must have misjudged his refuelling in Haiti. I said John Hamilton was too good to screw it up like that, and they agreed – sober, he was. Which meant he was high. Or drunk. He just ran it out of fuel, didn't make the island."

Uneasy silence followed as our drinks came. I leaned forward over the table to take my beer from the barman. "There's no chance that could have happened? Pilot error – not the drunkenness. Mistakes, even lethal ones, are easy to make."

Shirley's eyes shot daggers at me for that. "By plebes, maybe, not by career pilots who flew Spitfires with the

RAF!"

Silence again, till Greg observed, "You were very proud of him."

"I still am." She drew her hand across her eyes. "I haven't sold the business off. We don't have a plane, but we have the field. It's Hamair, south of the town. Little white hangar with the blue sign on the roof. I can't bring myself to sell it off. One of these days, if the insurance ever pays out, I'll buy another plane. I've got a licence. I can fly, he taught me. Get a girl in to do the paperwork." She was on the point of tears again, and blinked them away savagely. "He was well insured, but they won't pay out – the investigation's been on 'hold' for six months. I'm punching a typewriter to keep the bills paid."

I saw her frustration and grief, and sympathised with both. "How old was your father?" Greg asked, obviously adding up dates. The Battle of Britain is a piece of history.

"Sixty-four." She took a sip of lemonade and looked up at me. I saw a real intellect looking out of those chocolate brown eyes. Soft, very beautiful eyes, deep and sad. My throat tightened and I looked away.

"He was the right age to have a heart attack," Greg was saying quietly. "It happens, Miss Hamilton. The authorities may have been unjustified in bringing alcohol or drugs into it – you probably knew your father better than that. But a heart attack would have been just as fatal. He could have been dead before the plane went in."

She shook her head slowly, stubbornly. "He was a fitness enthusiast. Amateur boxing champion thirty years ago. Didn't drink, didn't smoke, wouldn't touch red meat. That sound to you like a man who's going to have a heart attack out of the blue? He was as healthy as a horse – Doctor Clarke has his files, I've seen them. It was the first thing the investigators looked at, and why they said he must have been boozing or smoking something, since he was as fit as a man half his age. He ran three miles a day to keep fit, played tennis twice a week with his partner, Jeff Mathers." Her face twisted again. "The late Jeff Mathers. He drowned in a fishing accident two weeks after the plane disappeared."

"Sporting accidents do happen," I said quietly.

She leaned back, looked into her glass as if it was a crystal ball. "The last time Jeff went fishing was before I was born. And nobody who has lived thirty years on an island goes out in a little boat when there's a Force Eight forecast. Jeff was

... making trouble. Asking questions. And his big mistake was dropping names."

"Logan?" I finished my beer.

"Logan's just a gorilla." Her hands fidgeted, like those of a smoker trying to give it up, dying for a drag. "Get out of here while you can – you'll go the same way as Jeff. At least his insurance paid out. His widow is living high in Kingston. Big American insurance company. The plane was registered in Miami, Jeff had a private field over there too. They used to shuttle from Florida to Venezuela, right through the islands." She looked up at me, and then at Greg. "You want to be dead? You get on Oliver Rolland's shit list, and you'll be fish bait – 'like saying good morning', as my father used to say. Get out of here while you can!"

Oliver Rolland. I took the name in, digested it, but before Greg or I could speak again there was the sudden slam of a door, a dimming as the pub's lights were doused, and every hair on my head stood on end.

The woman caught her breath audibly, glanced over her shoulder and crossed herself, all one movement. Greg slid out from the corner seat, swept her with him and held her by the upper arms. I was on my feet, heart beating against my ribs as I saw four of them. Very big, very black. And angry. The largest of the four sported a swollen eye. I did not have to be told my foot had delivered the blow last night. Logan.

The fish gutting knife was in his hand again, and the trio behind him stood back as if instructed to. He wanted to settle his own accounts. Greg steered the woman to one side and gave her a push.

"Get out, girl. Get out and keep going. Go!"

She was scared enough to bolt. As Logan came forward, Shirley Hamilton scrambled away. One of the baboons made a grab for her but I moved, fast. Catching his attention, I swung a brass table lamp at his head. As he ducked under it the woman ran. We heard squealing in the bar, sounds of a struggle, but we could do no more for her.

The knives we had bought only half an hour before were like razors. Logan's eyes narrowed on the blade in my hand as I moved up to cover Greg's shoulder. There is something in the way a man's hand holds a knife that tells you in the first half second whether he knows how to use it.

We learned the hard way. Sydney by night. The docks, the Rocks, the Cross. Sydney has its own wild side, and I have run it. For Greg, the learning came even harder and earlier.

London's gutters, waiting to swallow the "nancy" who ran from the government home, waiting to rape and brutalize him. Greg has had hell beaten out of him, more than once. And has returned the bruises while I've watched.

The knives lay in our hands as if they belonged there. Logan's teeth bared in a grin, closer to grimace than smile. Then it was on.

There is a saying about fear lending wings to one's heels. I don't think I ever moved faster, slippery as an eel, Logan's knife never more than a hand's breadth away as I twisted and wove. Trying to watch Greg would kill me, I knew. I turned my back on him, tried to buy him at least one safe angle.

Blood spattered from a nick along Logan's forearm. Behind me, someone howled as Greg drew blood at almost the same moment. A lamp hit the floor, glass shattered. I heard a blow land hard as Logan came again and this time the gutting knife was close enough to go through my shirt. It missed the skin beneath by a whisker.

A body fell heavily, upsetting a table, and curses grunted at us. The whole scene played out in no more than seconds, but to me it seemed as if time elongated, stretched till it could have been an hour. I saw the knife in Logan's fist as he tried to eviscerate me. I twisted my own knife, and the razor edge sliced along the line of his triceps, cutting muscle-deep, a wound that would need doctoring. Blood gushed, and in the fraction of a second when I had the advantage, I stamped my foot into his right knee.

He went down, fell awkwardly between the table and seats where we had sat with Shirley Hamilton. Logan grunted like a sow in labour, wedged in tight, and I did not dare watch him for long. Greg had put one of the others down but there were two more, and both nasty.

Tearing my eyes away from the squirming Logan, I cast a glance after Greg. He was back against the plastered wall, sliding to and fro, nowhere to go, a bar stool in his hands. Somehow he had lost the knife. The gorilla he was up against was twice his size. If that stool was taken from him, Greg was dead. My heart was in my mouth, choking me. Logan was half way to his feet and the fourth of them was just waiting for me to lose a second's concentration.

The eruption of ear-splitting noise in the next half second took all six of us by surprise. Shotgun pellets spattered into the ceiling, plaster rattled down, and all of us ducked. Then, a woman's voice, high and sharp with fright: "Run, for Chrissakes, there's only one barrel left!"

We ran like startled rabbits. Shirley Hamilton was standing at The Maroon's rear door, outlined against the sunlight falling in through the exit into the publican's yard. She could have slammed it behind her and just fled into the alleys. A twelve-gauge wobbled around in her frail, thin little arms. She had the kind of guts you would admire in a man twice her size. The barman was laid out on his face, the beer bottle that had put him down dumped nearby.

"Out!" I hissed at her and Greg. I gave Greg a push toward the back door. He lifted the rabbit gun out of her hands as we hurried by, and I slammed the door hard. It bolted from the inside, there was no way to lock it behind us, but they knew we had one barrel left and would already be hurrying for the pub's front. They would have to go around several shops. How long did it give us? A minute? Half that?

"Which way?" Greg hissed at Shirley. She knew this town like the back of her hand. To us it was just a labyrinth of snares.

No need to ask. Shirley was off like a greyhound, leading us on a sprint into a maze of twisted galvanised iron and rotten timber fences. She put a dozen corners between us and The Maroon inside the minute's grace the shotgun had bought us, not even stopping to breathe until Greg and I were completely lost. Then we crouched behind the bins at the rear of a street cafe, and listened.

Voices, far off. Angry shouting. Pounding feet. But I realised in a moment more, the feet were heading away. Now, Shirley was crying as sheer fright got the better of her. She trembled, head to foot, and I put my arms around her. I marvelled at the tiny body. It was like handling a child. I think of Greg as slight, slender, but the woman was disturbing, as if I would break her if I held her as I hold him.

"Come on, love," I cajoled. "Time for this later. Where can we go?"

"You? You can't. White faces." She heaved herself to her feet and wrenched out of my grasp. "I've got family in Kingston. I'm out, and I'm not coming back." She was moving as she spoke. One hand clenched into her skirt. She turned back for just a moment, looked at us with wild, feral eyes. "Get off the island! They'll kill you too, or worse! Rolland'll have the pair of you!"

That name again. Rolland, Oliver Rolland. Greg and I stood

behind the reeking bins to watch her out of sight. I looked him up and down, still concerned that he might be hurt. I saw no blood on him, but his face was set in stoic lines. What had happened to his knife?

"I sank it into a big, fat bum," he said tartly. "The muscle must have grabbed, I couldn't get it out again. Buy another one." He raked his hands through his hair, leaned back against the painted brickwork. "What now?" Grey eyes glittered at me. "She's right. The intelligent thing would be to clear off the island. Home."

But I shook my head slowly. "You think they won't expect us to do that? They'll be waiting at the airport, Greg. Show our faces there, and the only way we'll get on the plane is in boxes." I rubbed my face, hard. "We need breathing space. Time to think. Come on."

I had seen a tumbledown shed as we ran through the alleyway. I marked out shootholes and hiding places in case we needed them. Greg had the shotgun. He had propped it against the wall, and now crooked it into his left arm as he followed me back to the shed, and in, out of sight. The place reeked of petrol and oil, but we were lucky for the moment. The vehicle usually garaged here was gone. After a brief, but thorough check around, we pulled the door closed behind us.

Greg sat down on one end of the cluttered workbench and rubbed his palms together thoughtfully. "Rolland. Who the hell is Rolland? Logan's just a gorilla, she said. A minder, working for Rolland?"

"Bound to be. Running around, doing the boss's dirty work, part of which is to get rid of us. Bury us. Question is, what for? If we knew that we'd be halfway home."

"It's that plane, and her father," he mused, on his feet again, restless, unable to be still. "Trouble is, we've got nothing to go to the police with."

"Even if we had, the local police wouldn't bat an eyelid if we turned up on a slab." I broke the shotgun, took out the spent round and snapped it shut. "This is better than nothing, if we can get some more ammo. A bait and tackle shop, maybe. You can get sharks in these waters." A lot of folk lore surrounds sharks, but the truth is, a twelve-gauge in the right place, around the fish's tiny little brain, makes a mess of the average shark. A lot of boat owners keep a shotgun around.

"What about the police in Kingston, then?" Greg hazarded. "They can't all be bloody corrupt! If we went to them with a strong story, enough to put a lid on this, we might at least get off the island alive." He looked at me with the same wild, feral eyes as Shirley Hamilton. "It's the only chance we've got, Alex. What do you say? Give it a go? Or they'll be sending us back to Lansing in body bags."

I leaned against the creaking timber wall. It was hot, the sun beating on the outside of it. I gazed up into the steel spars holding up the roof, absently noticing the cobwebs there. Greg and I have seen a lot of action, the real thing. Cities that have become war zones. Beirut, Belfast, Tehran. By comparison, the local action was strictly Toytown. Greg was waiting, and I found a smile for him. "Why not? Do the job we're paid for. Again. The Argie *Buzo Tactico* didn't take us. Must count for something."

"Right." He hooked his thumbs into his pockets. "What have we got? A plane in the water, coming home from a milk run to Haiti. Girl says the flight was sabotaged. We see it, suddenly we're on someone's shit list, and the name is Oliver Rolland. I'd like to take a peek at Hamair's paperwork. What did she say? Little white hangar with the blue sign on the roof? South of town?"

"We need some wheels," I said thoughtfully. "Proper ones. Something that'll give us some horsepower." I had seen a hessian sack under the work bench, and appropriated it, to wrap the shotgun. It would not do to be seen carrying it through the streets of a tourist trap, back to the Avis agency. "How much money have you got on you?"

"The lot," he said at once. "I never leave cash behind in hotels. Next time you look it isn't there."

"Good. Because we can't go back to the room, honey." And we had nothing, not even a change of rags. I leaned over and kissed his cheek, on my way out of the shed. "Come on."

But before I had set my hand on the door I heard a van engine. I stepped back, peered warily through the dirty window glass. I was sure it would be the shed's owner returning to garage his vehicle, but moments later I muttered surprised obscenities as I saw a light commercial flatbed come grinding along the narrow alleyway. The name on the door was "Goldmark", and leaning out of the passenger's window was a face I knew, with an eye still swollen from the impact of my foot. Logan.

I ducked out of sight before the vehicle stopped. Greg and I squeezed into the cover of a stack of empty Castrol drums. The vehicle stopped. We heard the squeal of an opening door, and then sunlight shafted into the dim shed interior as they checked. They searched with the carelessness of anger and frustration. Spanners rattled out of a toolbox, a petrol tin rolled into the wall, and then the shed door slammed shut again. I let down the hammer on the shotgun's single remaining barrel. As the vehicle pulled away, Greg and I got moving.

We headed away from The Maroon, uptown, skirted the marketplace and hurried back to tourist country where we would be less conspicuous among faces as white as our own. The shops were crowded as I shouldered in to buy a few odds and ends. A bag, shirts, shorts, jeans, underwear, shaving tackle. Enough for a few days' living hard and sleeping rough.

Greg stayed on the street, eyes peeled, and I made one last stop on the way across to the Avis yard. I blew less dollars than I had expected on a cheap camera and multipurpose film. Too much emphasis is placed on the price and sophistication of camera gear. In fact, a bad photographer won't get good shots with the best camera in the world, and a good photographer will get onto the cover of *Life* with a Brownie. I bought a cheap SLR that gave me the option of eight apertures and six shutter speeds. It was a toy by comparison to the Canons and Nikons I was used to. But the high-tech cameras just make my job that much easier. The toy would serve its purpose adequately, with a little professional trickery.

Then we strolled along to the Avis yard to check out a modest Ford. It would be nippy enough to get by and yet small, light enough, to handle well through tight spaces. Greg was driving. He dropped the mousy grey sedan into gear and took us out of Montego Bay, heading south. I kept my eyes peeled for a bait shop and gave him a nudge when I saw nets and spearguns hanging around an open doorway.

"Pull over for a tick. I'll see if they keep twelve-gauge."

They had buck, rabbit and birdshot. I bought the heavy stuff, a box of fifty rounds. I looked like a holiday sport fisherman, probably over there to slaughter anything in the sea that would give me a fight. The young girl behind the counter handed over the cartridges without comment, much more interested in the radio cricket commentary.

Greg had kept the engine running. As I slid back into the car he pulled out fast, taking the most direct route out of the clutter of the town, into the hill country where woods and distance bought us the freedom to think. Stalls along the way sold an assortment of food, and a little after noon, we sat on a fallen, rotting log beside the car, eating bananas and sweet rice. We looked down on Montego Bay from the vantage of a few hundred feet.

We were safe for the moment. Even if Logan and his gorillas managed to get a look at the Avis paperwork, which I signed with my own name when they required identification, Rolland's minders would not know if we had hit the road to Kingston or Timbuktu. He would probably stake out the airport, I thought, assuming we would try to get out, fast. The kind of knee-jerk stupidity a man of Logan's mentality would expect.

"You reckon it's ganja smuggling?" Greg asked as he licked his fingers clean after the sticky, sweet rice. "I mean, Hamilton and his American partner, flying between Venezuela and Florida, right through the islands. Light plane on milk runs could carry a lot of the stuff in and out under the noses of the police, disguised as legit cargo."

"Maybe," I mused. "Although Shirley would argue. Her dad was a hero, according to her. Spitfire pilot. Best damned pilot in the islands . . . Did you see the flat bed outside the shed? Goldmark. The same van was parked behind the druggist's in Anchovy. Loaded with tomatoes, and ganja. And there were Goldmark fruit boxes in the cold store at the Marina. I saw them on the way in. So if Logan's running around in a Goldmark van, same van as smuggles ganja out of the hills, and if he's minding for Rolland, that puts Rolland in the ganja trade."

He frowned deeply. "Black or white?"

"Come again?" I finished off the Coke.

"Rolland. Black or white?" He speculated.

I puffed out my cheeks. "Hard to tell when you've got a baboon called Logan, and a beached whale called Conway! Does it matter?"

"It might," Greg mused. "If we're trying to hide out among white faces, and he could be anywhere." He tapped his nose. "A little research, my love, goes a long way." And then he hopped off the log and lay down in the grass, head pillowed on his forearms. "Get some rest. I slept about half an hour last night. We can't make a move till it's dark. Then I want to look at old man Hamilton's paperwork. It should be in the hangar office. If it isn't, we're sunk – Shirley'll be miles away by now. But she wants to kickstart the business, so I'm betting she locked the door on the whole works, and it'll still be there."

Resting was not easy. My nerves were strung up, tight as piano wires. I stretched out beside him. Grass tickled my neck as I lay on my side to watch the dappled sunlight cast patterns across his face. I shuffled closer, nuzzled his ear, and he turned his head to kiss. His tongue slipped easily into my mouth. I sucked it in, made love to it, and he tugged me over into his arms until I was lying on him.

Greg is solid, muscular. Strong. Nothing there to snap when I hold him. Holding the woman had been like handling a child. It was a man against me now, male and beautiful. I buried my nose in his hair, combing through the silky mass of it. He sighed. His breath scudded across my cheek, and I held him tighter.

After a while we dozed. We needed sleep. The shadows were already long when we woke, and I was hungry. I slid in behind the wheel of the Ford to drive down to the stalls where we had bought lunch. He chose seafood, fruit and crushed pineapple. We ate well, lounged in the car and watched sunset blaze across Montego Bay. The tourists would be set for the night's entertainment and I envied them.

Our night's work would be less than pleasant – less than safe.

The headlights probed along the south road as twilight thickened into night proper. The Hamair hangar was not hard to find, a galvanised iron structure in the midst of an open paddock in need of mowing. The strip itself was overgrown, the whole field unkempt. I pulled the car in at the fence under a stand of trees that would help disguise its presence, and turned off the lights.

"You realise we'll be breaking and entering?" Greg asked ruefully.

"Tough," I said drily and swung open the door. The night air was starting to cool. My damp shirt stuck icily to my back in the breeze.

We went over the fence and ploughed through the grass, lush and knee deep, toward the strip and, beyond it, the hangar. The building was locked up, as if no one had been out there in months. If Shirley was chained to a typewriter to keep the bills paid, she would be too hassled to spend fruitless hours there, haunted by the past.

The door was secured, but a window broke and Greg

knocked out the jagged glass with the same rock. He lifted himself in and onto some surface just under the window. It was a desk. My knees found it as I followed him. Moonlight streamed in, enough to see by if we did not need to make out fine details. Greg went carefully through drawers and filing cabinets. The air reeked of old dust and stale oil.

He was looking for the charter records, and I joined him. A ledger, I guessed. Computers are rare in the islands and competent operators rarer still. It would be a book or file, probably in the form of a professional appointments journal.

And there it was, jammed into the filing cabinet under "C" for charter. Shirley Hamilton had made things easy for us. We did not have enough light to read the text. A flick of the desk lamp's switch demonstrated that the power was off. Greg tucked the journal under his arm and hoisted himself back out through the window.

The world was quiet, nothing moved for miles, and I turned on the light in the car. Greg leafed forward through the book, checked a listing here and there.

"According to this he ran light cargo as a rule. The occasional passenger. Most of these are business names. Market gardeners – an orchid grower, see? A doctor. A pharmaceuticals importer. Perishable prescription drugs, at a guess. Passengers for Barbados and Martinique. Probably missed their commercial airbus. Thrilling stuff, Alex."

"Bread and butter work," I agreed. "Makes the world go round. Look at April 12th, 13th. That's when the charter to Haiti would have been booked. And I'm giving odds. Short ones."

He traced the columns of clear handwriting and came to the listing we wanted. "Here it is. April 13th, Hamair chartered to fly to Haiti, pick up a cargo from Geminex Ltd., refuel and shuttle home. A note here says the fuelling fees were paid by cheque. And the charterer was Goldmark Enterprises."

"Which means Logan, which means Oliver Rolland, since Logan's just – a gorilla, as she put it."

"I'd like to prove that out," he mused. "That Rolland owns Goldmark. The local Chamber of Commerce could verify it." He closed the book and pushed it into our bag. "If she wants it back, she only has to ask . . . Just borrowing it. Right now, I want to look at the manifest file. An organised little mind like Shirley Hamilton's probably left it filed under 'M'."

We ploughed back through the thigh-deep grass, and

searched the filing cabinet in minutes. The records for a one year period were in the current file, the rest of them code-numbered and boxed, with the library sheet in the cabinet. Greg pulled the thick manilla folder and returned to the cabinet when I had turned to leave.

"What are you after now?" I hissed. The place made you whisper when in fact there was no one in miles.

"Paid accounts. The fuelling and service checks on the plane. Just in case we end up chasing this to Haiti, it'd be nice to know where to go . . . Here we are. Bless her, it's under 'Accounts-Paid', and the slips are filed chronologically. Thank God for systematized minds." He slammed the drawer and went through the window before me.

"We ought to report the break-in," I said, grudgingly amused. "Someone ought to come out and nail a board over it."

The manifests made interesting reading. Most of Hamilton's cargoes were mundane stuff. Orchids, tropical fish, pharmaceuticals, antiques, the kind of goods that must be transported quickly, or very carefully. There was the chance, even the probability, that Hamair had been shipping narcotics on the side – there is always that chance. But the manifests were strictly legit and the accounts paid up on time, in full.

"Everything's on the up and up," I mused as I scanned the bills. "The plane and business reggo are still current a year later. The property's on lease till '92. The insurance on plane and pilot is up to date, for what that's worth. You found the manifest for the Haiti charter?"

"Yeah." He spread the folder on his knee and turned the top sheet toward me. "The charterer is listed there, Goldmark. See the signature, Alex. The man signed for the job in person, and that's not surprising when you take a look at the cargo." He lifted the topsheet. The manifest was stapled to it, along with a document from AGF, the insurance underwriter, in Houston, Texas.

The policy was a monster. The cargo was gems. Diamonds, emeralds, each piece only small, with the exception of an emerald that must have been the size of a pigeon's egg, but the aggregate value was worked out at just over four million dollars, US federal currency.

"Something," Greg said tartly, "stinks in the state of Denmark, and you smell it from here." He shuffled papers again, produced a receipt from a contractor in Haiti. "Ever-

73

arde Aviation serviced the plane and loaded every litre Hamilton specified."

"Enough to make Jamaica?" I was trying to work out what the fuel consumption would be on the home run.

"According to the paperwork, yes," Greg mused, "but that's iffy. You buck a head wind, have carburation trouble, detour around a storm front, you can run it right down to fumes in half the distance."

"Right. The day's papers would give us the weather forecast. We want the archive in Kingston for that."

"If you think it's worth the bother," he said drily. "Look, Hamilton's operation was straight up, no monkey business. Shirley's paperwork is clean as a whistle. They've been in work constantly, the whole year, and Hamilton's spent more time in the air than on the ground. The more I look at this, the more I believe Shirley. He wouldn't misjudge his fuel load, and if there was heavy weather in front of him, he'd know better than to try it. Detour to another island, put it down, start again with full tanks or sit it out till the weather clears. Everarde looked at the plane, said there wasn't a damned thing wrong with it in Haiti, and I don't believe in gremlins."

I sat back, watched moths batter at the outside of the windscreen. "So you're ruling out pilot error . . . You trust an aircraft mechanic in a place like Haiti?" I asked acidly.

Greg puffed out his cheeks. "Hamilton did, and he's the Spitfire jockey. Christ knows, but I'd bet Hamilton wouldn't trust fools, not when his life was at stake every time he took off."

"Okay, I'll buy that." I looked down at the manifest. "There's still the age of the man to think about. Sixty-four is just right to have a heart attack. And the plane could have developed engine trouble on the last leg, just short of Jamaica."

"You'd have to salvage it to find that out," Greg said darkly, "and I think that's what this might be about." He looked at me levelly. "We know where it is. We're the only ones who know where it is. Why get excited about it if there was no double-dealing? Rolland's insurance paid out on the jewellery, he couldn't lose, not with cover like this."

"Right." I stirred, shuffled the paperwork together and stuffed it into our bag along with the charter journal. I started the car and pulled out onto the unmetalled road. "Where to? We don't dare try for a room in Montego Bay, even if I thought there was one."

He jerked his thumb over his shoulder. "Falmouth. There has to be a pub with a room going spare."

"Optimist," I accused as the Ford began to shudder over a surface that could not have been graded in six months.

$$5$$

*F*ALMOUTH lies twenty miles from Montego Bay. Nowhere in Jamaica is very far from anywhere. The brochures claim there are several hundred hotel rooms to be booked, but the best we could do was a broom closet sized cubicle at the back of a pub called The Crown. The bathroom was on the floor below, and the noise from the shed out back went on till dawn. Local lads were gambling, cockfights and two up, or the regional equivalent. I did not push my luck to find out, but I heard the jingle of coins.

The two single beds were soft, the linen fresh. It would do. At the very least it gave us the anonymity we needed. Greg went down to shower and I spread Shirley Hamilton's paperwork out on one of the beds to study the details of what had all the makings of a classic con job. You choose a nothing air company that nonetheless has a solid rep, you get an underwriter to insure a king's ransom in light cargo, and then you lose it, accidentally on purpose, and cover your tracks, fast.

Conway's voice whispered in my ear. *It vanish jus' before a storm, an' by de time dey lookin' for it, it was gone.* I could imagine the panic, as Rolland discovered it was impossible to erase the evidence.

I could imagine the panic, eleven months later, when a couple of sport divers stumbled over the plane, and suddenly the damning evidence was just sitting on the sea bottom, waiting to be salvaged. It was gut reaction to recognise the truth when I saw it, but in fact all we had at that moment was the basis of a slander suit. Rolland had to be very wealthy if he traded in gems of that value. The ganja trade is nothing if not lucrative. If the dead, vacant eyes of the local police were anything to go by, he had bought them too.

And you do not go up against the likes of Rolland unless you have enough to tie the noose around his neck, first time. I was glaring at the Hamair paperwork as Greg returned, towelling his hair. He smelt of the cedar soap I had picked up on our brief shopping spree. I caught him by the hips, dumped him down on the bed beside me. I wanted his mouth, and got it as he stripped.

Then he rolled over, let me rub his back and rump while he shuffled papers and grumbled. "There's just enough here to get us killed and *Perspective* sued. You realise that."

"Mm." I licked down his supple spine. "A flash-bugger lawyer would chop the whole case down to a bunch of allegations founded on a hysterical young girl's paranoia, and a couple of tourists' imaginary misadventures. We didn't get knifed or rolled into the road by that Dodge – it's only our word that anything ever happened at all."

"There were witnesses in the market!" he said loudly.

"All looking the wrong way, as bloody usual." I sank my teeth into his buttock to brand him. "We need more. Something concrete. If Shirley's right, Rolland has done away with two men at least. Hamilton himself, and the partner, drowned in a fishing accident."

"You'll have a nice time proving that one out," Greg muttered.

"Can talk to his widow, though. Drive around to Kingston tomorrow. Start early, be there for lunch. Every mile we put between us and Logan is fine by me."

"You're on." He rolled over and rubbed his bare back on the bedspread. "I keep thinking about that kid, Malcolm. Shirley's run for it, but he can't get out. And if he's been working around the boat yard since the time Hamilton went down, I'll bet he's a mine of information. If," he added as I began to graze on his chest, "we dare show our faces around there, looking for him!"

"Tomorrow," I decided. "Worry about it later." For now, I wanted him, wanted to release the day's tensions in the best way I knew. I sat up to look at him, saw his cock lift without a touch as he watched me watching him. He should have looked like a hustler – spread, with a hopeful erection like a lethal weapon arching over his flat belly. Instead he just looked like Greg, smiling lazily at me, letting me look my fill because he knows how much I enjoy looking.

We set the strife aside for a few minutes and his face was

serene, filled with amused affection as I dropped my clothes, lay down on him and made it simple. He wrapped his legs around me, tried to get some friction. My weight held him down as I took both our cocks in my hand and squeezed us together. He cursed into my neck and I felt his own hand snake down between us to hold our balls together. He squeezed the delicate goods a little less roughly than my grip on our cocks. My palm was slick with our pre-cum, his tongue probed my mouth, keeping rhythm with our hands. Climax was slow and deep and easy, not enough semen to brag about. I held my hand to his lips. He licked once, took half of the cream. I savoured the rest myself and had his mouth again, hard.

The noise from the impromptu casino at the back of the pub kept me awake until not long before dawn, and then Greg's stirring woke me as he rummaged for his shaving gear. It was just daylight. Empty bottles rattled in the yard and I smelt the aroma of bacon frying. It made me aware of my growling insides.

We ate well, an English style breakfast. The Crown was owned by a couple who had retired there from Liverpool, finding their way into a backwater where a man's super-annuation payout made a decent investment. His wife chatted us up over the counter as we ate. We gave her names that would mean nothing to Logan, even if he did trace us there, which would be an act of blind fate. She packed us sandwiches and yesterday's pastries, and I slid in behind the wheel of the hired Ford by eight.

The best road – the only one you can make speed on – runs about the perimeter of the island from Black River, leading west and around to Kingston and Port Royal. Names to conjure with. Jamaica is a law unto itself. In patches, paradise and purgatory, depending on your income, your colour and your luck.

We drove through some of the most beautiful geography in the world. Golden beaches, the resorts, the lushly jungled hills. Runaway Bay, Ocho Rios, Port Antonio, Morant Bay, and into Kingston itself, not long before noon. More than half a million people live there and many, perhaps most, do not live well.

The bright lights attract rurals into the ghettoes but there is no work. The dreams are empty, and violence can happen anywhere. There are gangs in the ghettoes, and they are armed with guns. Jamaica can flare into near civil war, and did, in 1980, when almost seven hundred people died in the riots surrounding the election that put Edward Seaga into office. At the time Jamaica's economy was in tatters. Hunger was rife, with a thirty percent inflation rate.

Today, Kingston wears two faces. There is the uptown, modern face – the hotels, the banks, the building projects begun twenty years ago by the same Edward Seaga, then a government minister. Behind the modern frontages are the shacks, the slums, the hardship. Gangs on the streets, ruling their domain with M-16s. If you see a young person, he is probably out of work. Desperate needs demand desperate measures.

Driving westward into Kingston from Bull Bay, and the small ports along the way, we saw the bright face the city shows to tourists, and for once we were content to accept it. Lunch was steak and salad in a decent little restaurant where holiday wallies vied noisily for the attention of a buxom young waitress.

Finished eating, Greg sauntered along to the phone to consult the Kingston white pages, look up the name of Mathers. I leaned back in the plush leather seat, watched him exchange notes for coins and begin the ring-around. Trial and error. How often have I relaxed, waiting for a film subject to show itself, while Greg goes about his methodical, meticulous work?

He rang six numbers, getting a "no" at each, and then I saw him smile, and he gave me a thumbs-up sign. Joining him, I took a look at the book and saw that he had rung seven out of the eight "Mathers" listed in the Kingston telephone district.

"Yes, Mrs. Mathers, it's a friend of Shirley Hamilton's. It's about your husband, and Hamair . . . Yes, ma'am, about the crash . . . I'm a journalist with *Perspective* magazine from London . . . Could we? That would be wonderful, ma'am, thank you. What time suits you? Two o'clock is perfect. We'll see you then, Mrs. Mathers. Goodbye."

He hung up and borrowed the pen from the tin beside the counter's cash register to scribble notes on a paper serviette. "She's angry, she's talkative, and she's screaming to meet us. Two o'clock, at her home on Jubilee Avenue, Tivoli Gardens."

I looked at the time. It was already one, and we had to find the address. One of the waitresses gave us directions, and as Greg started the car I checked my camera. I could only hope

Mrs. Mathers would not recognize a dirt-cheap tourist throw-away when she saw one. A photographer from *Perspective* should have been armed with prime gear, not junk, although it is true, the junk will do the same job in a pinch. Twenty years ago, the best Zeiss, top of the range, had less actual technology built in than the cheap toy I was using out of necessity today. Tim Page did not complain about the Contaflex that recorded the frames I used to marvel over as a young hopeful.

We had spruced up in the men's room before leaving the restaurant and at least looked the part when Greg parked outside of Mrs. Mather's address. A neat little garden separated it from the road. Frangipani and anthuriums grew in ornamental pots about the front door. Greg rang the bell and we heard feet inside at once. She had been waiting for us.

She was an American, we had known that. The surprise was that the woman was a black American, small, plump, perhaps sixty, with blow-waved hair and nice clothes. We were ushered into a comfortable home smelling of polish and flowers. I remembered Shirley Hamilton's remark, that the widow was living high on the insurance payout. She introduced herself as Juliette Mathers, shook our hands and poured jasmin tea as we sat around a fan in her living room. Greg had notepad and pen on his knee, and I went through the motions of setting up to take a few frames before putting the camera safely out of sight.

"I'm Greg Farris," he told her. He should have had ID to present, his press card, if she had known it, but our cards were in our baggage, in a hotel in Montego Bay, out of reach. As it was, Mrs. Mathers was too agitated to think about ID. "This is Alex Connor, my photographer. We're on assignment for *Perspective* magazine."

The diplomatic lie. She knew the magazine. I saw a sharp, vengeful look in her face, as if Matt Lansing's publication was a loaded gun that could be aimed, and she was just waiting to pull the trigger. For the first time since we blundered into this mess, I caught a glimmer of light at the end of the tunnel. I pricked up my ears as Greg leaned forward to ask his shrewd questions.

A framed photograph stood on the mantel. I would have placed the man at fifty, but guessed he must be older, sixty-plus. He looked half cast or Creole, not-quite-white, healthy and attractive. He wore his age well, Jeff Mathers. He sported the blue and white crew cap with the Mustang

Club's prop-fighter logo. Had he flown P51s for the USAF at the same time Hamilton flew Spitfires for the RAF? Greg would find out.

But I was surprised to see the bunch of red, gold and green ribbons on the corner of the photoframe. The Rastafarian colours. Greg had noticed them too, and gestured toward them as he began.

"Your husband was a Rastafarian, Mrs. Mathers?"

She looked at the photograph. Eleven months after his death, she would still flood with tears. "We came here on holiday, ten years ago. Just never went back. Jeff met an old buddy. Airforce buddy. The War. Christ, it was like coming home! Jeff put what money we had into Ham's business. We had a farm in Florida, and a plane. The Piper Ham was flying when . . . Anyways, Ham had his own crate at the time, Cessna, getting along in years. He retired it, flew the Piper instead. Jeff didn't fly much. Trouble with his ears. He had a busted eardrum, altitude made him sick. Sure, he was a Rastafarian. Good people, Rastas. Bobo Ashantis." She looked away and scrubbed at her nose with a tissue. "I'm sorry. I don't mean to blubber, but I can't hardly think about Jeff without . . . I'm sorry."

"Miss Hamilton said he was drowned," Greg prompted. "A fishing accident was the official story. You don't agree?"

Anger replaced her grief as she turned back to us. "Fishing means water! My Jeff wouldn't go nowhere near water in case it got in his ears. Never had nothing but trouble with 'em. Used to plug 'em with cotton waste to get in the shower. Jesus Christ – fishing? He wouldn't go in a boat if you paid him to do it. They said he went out without listening to the storm alert on the radio. Jeff Mathers could read the sky like you and me read books. He was a flyer."

Greg looked sidelong at me and arched one brow. "Then you're saying there were suspicious circumstances?"

"I'm saying he was murdered. Damned right," she said angrily. The Florida vowels thickened with her agitation.

"And if you had to put the finger on the culprit?" Greg asked shrewdly.

I knew what she was going to say. "Rolland. That asshole, Oliver Rolland." Mrs. Mathers scrubbed at her nose again. "He chartered the trip to Haiti. He collected the insurance on the cargo. You bet your ass Rolland wasted my Jeff. You're here to prove it." She paused, looked from Greg to me and back again. "Aren't you?"

"We'll certainly see what we can dig up," Greg promised. "You want to tell us about Rolland? Your own observations. The official info we can get anywhere."

She settled against the stuffed cushions of her armchair. "He's a New Yorker. Big, flash, likes his cars and his women black. He's a plantationer. You could call it that."

"Marijuana?" Greg asked. We already knew.

Mrs. Mathers nodded. "Oh, he grows cash crops to keep up a legit front. Market garden produce. But the ganja's money, and screw the government. He's a big noise around Montego Bay. I moved as far away as you can get, after . . . Anyways, Jeff went to the police, but they don't care squat about what a guy knows, what he's seen. Then Jeff drowned and it was all over."

"Growing ganja is still illegal," I said. "You could at least get the man up on narcotics charges."

She made a face. "You can tell the police a thousand times where the crops are, the vehicles. It's like spitting in the wind."

"What about the police here in Kingston?" Greg asked reasonably. "You've put the whole island between you and Rolland's enterprise, and this is a decent sized town. The whole police department can't be corrupt."

She gave a short laugh, a bark of bitter cynicism. I heard no humour in it, but a lot of scorn. "Nobody's got that kind of a death wish, man. People have been known to turn up dead, you know? There was this one old boy . . . Wait."

We looked speculatively at one another as she got up, went to rummage through a drawer and returned with a photo album. She opened it on the coffee table beside the jasmin tea. In it we saw not snapshots but newspaper cuttings. I leaned forward, craned my neck to read them as she turned them towards Greg. Now we were getting somewhere.

They made grizzly reading. A man had hanged himself in his own backyard. We saw a paragraph from a local paper, a photograph of a young buck with a cigarette in his mouth and zealous eyes. Another death was a hit-and-run. The car belonged to Oliver Rolland, but a "chauffeur" had been driving it. The name quoted was Leroy Logan. We guessed it could only have been a black monstrosity out of Detroit. Chauffeur? That was a witticism.

"Do you know the man, Leroy Logan?" Greg asked blandly.

The woman's face could have soured a gallon of milk. "Not

socially. But the ghetto knows Logan, even here in Kingston. He's shit, take it from me. If you've got Leroy Logan behind you, you're dog meat."

"True?" I attempted a smile. "He's had three goes at us, so far. Tried to smear us all over the road, jumped us above the beach one night. Cornered us in The Maroon, in Montego Bay yesterday."

Eyes widened in surprise. "And you're still on the island? Why don't you get out while you can?"

She was right. Kingston's Norman Manley Airport could fly us out as soon as we could arrange bookings on a flight to Barbados or somewhere safe. We could get out from here. I looked at Greg, but his face was bleak, and I knew he was thinking the same thoughts as me. The world is a small place. London is just a few hours away, a phone call away, from Jamaica. If Rolland was the kind of operator Mrs. Mathers believed, Greg and I would be little safer in London. We had one shot at living the rest of our lives out. To put a lid on Rolland, here and now.

I lifted a brow at my lover and Greg nodded. "We've got an assignment," he told her. "And as someone once said, they only ever tackle the one with the ball. If Rolland's after us we're at least on the right track." He looked down at the press cuttings in the album. "What makes you so sure Logan is responsible for these."

"Ghetto gossip." She folded her plump arms, glared at the album. "You hear things. And there's more. Did Shirley Hamilton tell you about her cousin, Peter?"

Greg turned over a leaf in his notebook. He had taken down a compacted version of every word she said. "No. She didn't get the chance."

Her eyes closed. "Peter was a beautiful kid. Twelve, thirteen, something like that. He worked for Rolland, polishing cars. One day he went to work, never came home. Rolland swore he'd never turned up in the morning, but I watched him go in through the gate, I know he was there." She flipped a few pages in the album and turned it back to us. "They found his body eight weeks later, face down in the river. He was a mess of needle tracks down both arms. And they'd fixed him."

"Fixed him?" I had to ask. I wished I hadn't.

"Fixed him," Mrs. Mathers elaborated bitterly. "Castrated him. Gelded him like a horse. Like a child whore."

Greg scanned the newspaper copy. "It doesn't say that

here."

"I identified the body," she whispered. "They didn't print nothing about the whip scars, neither, and the rest of it. Peter was tortured. I saw the marks. They did everything to him, the motherfuckers."

"They?" Greg asked quietly. "They who? Names, Mrs. Mathers?"

"Oh, somebody who got hold of him after I saw him go through Oliver Rolland's gateway," she hissed, the fierceness back in her voice after a few moments' grief. "Addicted, castrated, a pretty black kid would be worth a fortune on the market down south. Paraguay. Wherever." She looked tired and ten years older.

"So the kind of people who would castrate and sell boys wouldn't think twice about nobbling a plane and killing the pilot to get the insurance money on a cargo of gemstones." I looked over at Greg's bleak profile. "Had Hamair carried this kind of cargo before?"

"Oh, sure." She rubbed her eyes hard. "Usually we carried perishables, joy-riders, lost luggage, pets the regular airlines won't touch. There's a rabies problem all over the islands, you know? Orchids for the rich bitches in those goddamned hotels. But we'd carried valuable cargo before. There has to be a man to guard it. He sits in the plane with a .44 magnum. The cargo's as safe as it would be on a commercial jet. Maybe more, because it gets babied all the way, not stuffed into a hold and left. It was supposed to come over on one of the regular airbuses but Geminex, the dealer in Haiti, missed the connection. Some hold-up with customs. They know how to make your life hard. The stones were going to auction in Colombia, the whole thing was on a tight schedule. Haitian customs took responsibility for the hold-up that put Goldmark – Rolland's company – on the spot, and recommended a local carrier. Us. Good, cheap, reliable service. Jesus."

Still, why choose to fly a precious cargo with a sixty-four year old pilot in a single-engine plane? Single-engine aircraft inevitably have a high failure risk. And this one was owned and operated by a small business without any weight behind it, or the money, to fight an insurance case against high power American lawyers. The whole thing was classic.

"Pretty good set-up," Greg said bitterly. "Alex?"

I shrugged. "Grease a few palms in Haiti. Customs get in the way, the airbus leaves on time, the rest of it falls right into place. It was only a matter of sabotaging either Hamilton or the plane."

"Sabotage?" Mrs. Mathers leaned forward.

"As easy as making sure the fuel lines leak slowly," Greg said sourly. "Or contaminated fuel. Sugar in the plane's tank. The only way to find that out is to salvage the aircraft."

So the plane ditched, and a storm blew up and suddenly it was gone for good. Rolland was left holding the insurance payoff, but with a timebomb sitting just offshore, waiting to go off. No way to cover his tracks. Then Greg and I happen along, two sport divers, and suddenly the panic sets in. I liked the way it was going together less and less.

Mrs. Mathers picked up the tea tray and went out to the kitchen to brew another pot. I turned to Greg with a bleak look. "I'd say we're in a lot of trouble, my lad."

"Understatement," he muttered. He leafed on through the album and gave a grunt as he came across a colour magazine photo. "This is the man. The feature is on a boat race. Powerboats. He sponsored it."

I saw a yachting cap, a fat gut and a large cigar. Of the same species as Alan Bond, but not as salubrious, nor as amicable as Perth's beer baron. "So?" I prompted. I watched his expression harden.

"Three choices," he said quietly. "One. We forget the whole thing and get out. Hope Rolland doesn't pick up a phone and have us mauled at home."

"Fat chance," I said drily. "Two, we can take what we've got now to the fuzz here in Kingston, tell them who we are. *Perspective* ought to be good for a few pulled strings. They may listen to us where they ignore the locals."

"Which leaves us ducking bullets from Rolland's kill-happy private army," Greg said cynically. "And then a New York defence lawyer will make mincemeat out of the case when it finally gets into court, about three years from now. Alex, we won't live to read about it." Unconsciously, he rubbed at the shoulder that had collected a 9mm round from the rifle of a Klan youth. I know the scar with fingers and tongue and was sick to my stomach.

"And, three?" I prompted quietly as Mrs. Mathers' kettle boiled.

"Three." He steepled his fingers on his knees and frowned at them. "We take a crack at them. We've got a shotgun, plenty of ammo, a decent car, and we know where that plane is. Nobody else does. When we go to the police in Kingston there has to be enough to screw the coffin lid down on

Rolland, or it's *our* coffins. If the plane was sabotaged we might be able to see it, and all fingers'll point at Rolland. Christ, no wonder they're keen to bury this down deep – and us with it. I'll bet they had kittens when that storm blew up and covered the plane before they could dispose of it!" He spoke quietly as Mrs. Mathers worked in the kitchen. "The gems must still be on it."

"If they were ever on it in the first place," I hazarded. "Salvage will blow the whole thing sky high, but it'll cost a fortune. To get the police excited enough to bother, there'd have to be some concrete information."

"Which dumps the onus right on us." He looked up with a sham smile as the woman returned, offering us shortbreads.

Mrs. Mathers could not tell us much more. We drank another cup of tea for the sake of politeness. I took a few photographs – Mrs. Mathers, the room, the portrait of her late husband with its Rastafarian ribbons. Greg continued to study the album, and as I snapped the case shut about the cheap little camera he asked, "Do you mind if we borrow this? It saves us a lot of leg work, Mrs. Mathers. We'd have to plough through the archives to get this stuff, otherwise. I can return the book to you later, when we've put the story together, also, we'll need releases from you before *Perspective* goes to press. Is that a problem?"

"If you put a noose around Oliver Rolland's neck," she said tartly, "I'll sign anything you want."

"Then we'll be in touch in due course." He stood, gave her his hand, and she shook it. "Thanks for your help, Mrs. Mathers. And for this." A gesture with the album. "I can't tell you where you can get in touch with us – the truth is, with Logan looking for us, we don't dare stand still long enough to have an address."

"Be careful," she said as she showed us to the door. "For Christ's sake, be careful. You can go the same way as the others if you don't watch your asses."

Out in the car I made him an offer. "I'll watch your arse if you'll watch mine."

"Deal," he agreed with a wink at me. He started the car but sat looking at the plastic dashboard. "Where now? It's back to Montego Bay isn't it? The bloody lion's den."

"Where the action is." I looked at the time. "It'll be dark by the time we get back there, which suits us. I want to find young Malcolm Dennison. He must have seen everything, heard everything. That kid could probably hang Rolland all on his own – "

"If Rolland didn't have the balls off him, and ship him to Paraguay as a boytoy first." Greg dropped the car into gear and put his foot down with sudden annoyance. "This is the kind of thing that turns my stomach . . . I want Rolland, Alex. Tied to a queer-looking chair, with his head shaved!"

I sobered, watched him drive. We headed out of Kingston as afternoon became oppressively hot. I rolled down the windows, eager for any breeze off the sea. I popped a few frames, looking for good back-up material, now that I knew I was shooting on a freelance assignment. Time was when freelance work was all I could get. I would take a punt, get my shots and sell them where I could. My work appeared in everything from *Woman's Weekly* to the *Sun Herald*.

We had dinner in beautiful Port Antonio. White fish steaks in lemon sauce, by candlelight. It would have been romantic if we had not been as strung up as sprinters under the starting gun. I drove the last leg, back into the world of highrise hotels, glorious, floodlit beaches and lapping sea. Montego Bay's public face smiled for the tourists.

Under cover of darkness I prowled along behind the hotels to come up on Conway's boatyard. It was eight o'clock and the place was still open for business. A boat party was in progress. They were loading crates of beer onto a motor launch, and I saw Conway at the wheel of it. He would take the goods out to the rich man's toy, a big yacht on the bay where an orgy was in full cry. We could hear the acid rock across a quarter of a mile of water.

We did not dare let Conway see us. I turned off lights and motor and waited till the boss had taken the launch out before I got out of the car. Greg had one hand on the shotgun and slid in to drive as I went in search of the boy. Everything we owned, and every scrap of evidence, was in that car. I kept to the shadows, skulking and watching. With Conway gone I saw only two above the ramp. One was a woman, enormously fat, dressed in a tent of a frock. The other was the boy.

He was cleaning odds and ends of gear in a bucket of detergent water, unaware of my presence until I tossed a pebble into the bucket. He looked up, saw me pressed against the side of Conway's shed, and I beckoned. Malcolm took a quick look after the fat woman, and slipped silently out of the glare of the floodlights.

"I thought you's dead!" he said in that thick, slurred

accent. "I heard about the fight in The Maroon."

"We got out." I shepherded him to the car. He got into the back of it and Greg pulled out into the anonymity of the night. Away from the hotels, the beaches and glitter. Out past the ghetto, away from people. Any people. We had no idea who we could trust – white faces, black faces, all had begun to look dangerous.

Greg turned off the engine and offered Malcolm a bar of chocolate. He took it, devoured it as if chocolate was a novelty. "What do you know, son?" Greg asked. "We've got to know if we're going to make sense of this."

At first he clammed up tight, afraid to say a word – afraid, I knew, that he would go the same way as Shirley's cousin, Peter. It could happen. I wished we could offer the boy some kind of protection, but the best we could do was hustle him back to his pocketmoney job fast, so no one noticed he had gone.

I think it was anger that got the better of Malcolm at last. He had known the Hamiltons and the Mathers. Oliver Rolland's private army, as Greg called it, had accounted for no less than three of them, with an option on a fourth if they could get their hands on Shirley. The only thing keeping Mrs. Mathers alive was that it would be too ludicrously transparent if she also turned up dead or missing.

The Jamaican accent thickened the boy's speech until we struggled for his words, and half of them were regionalisms, Rastafarianisms. The gist of it was, several young boys had vanished out of the Montego Bay area, that Malcolm knew about. Peter Cole, Shirley's cousin, was just one. Another had been a budding spin bowler, supposedly destined for a touring career, a third was a bible blues singer. Jamaica releases more vocal tracks in any one week than any other country. The music industry is one escape route from the ghetto, if you sing well and write your own material.

Malcolm was running scared. He was right at the age where a boy becomes jail bait. There was enough of the man about him to make you take an interest, yet enough of the boy to get you locked up. Greg took down a few notes, deciphering what Malcolm said with care. "And what does the – the ghetto gossip say, son? Where do the boys go?"

They went south, to some state in the great, grey chaos of South America, but it was only gossip. Malcolm had heard talk between Conway and Leroy Logan. Had seen money changing hands. Faces vanishing. The boy was scared. I wondered why he would hang around here, working, but the answer was predictable enough. It was all he could get, he was on his own and he needed money to get out. He worked when and where he could, stashed away what he got, and soon he was out of here.

From him we learned that Oliver Rolland had a mansion on the river, owned powerboats and entertained guests who came in and out of Montego Bay not by plane, which would be noticeable to whatever authorities bothered to check, but by boat. He spoke of the millionaire's fantasy, the motor yacht on the bay. A rich American was on it, and Rolland would be along later, after midnight, when the guests were too stoned to know him.

Malcolm had little more to give us, and Greg closed the notebook. "What will you tell Conway? You've been gone half an hour or so."

Boredom, friends coming by, a bottle of moonshine. Conway would buy it, it was typical of boys anywhere. Greg started the car and swung it around to take us back to the boatramp. The party was gearing up out on the water. The music was louder, the screams of laughter and outrage more piercing. I took a quick look around but saw no one close enough to worry us before I got out of the car to let the kid out of the back.

Where the battered old red Pinto came from I do not know, but suddenly Greg was yelling at me, Malcolm was struggling to get out of our underpowered little grocery-getter, and there was no time. I shoved him back in again, slammed the door, and Greg put his foot down as the battle-scarred old Detroit Ford came barrelling up past Conway's yard.

Our luck stank. It was a hundred to one shot against us chancing along when Rolland's "rude boys" were there, and then being seen when we were parked in the shadows and deliberately skulking. Our luck runs true to form every time.

At that hour of the night we met no vehicles on the road, only a few pedestrians, most of them on their way to or from the scanty nightlife. The restaurants, drinking places, the cockfights. Greg was in third, weaving his way around the obstructions, never more than a shave away from disaster. The Pinto rode our rear fender. We had no chance to pull away from it in the chicanes and tight places before we got onto the open space of the graded south road.

And when we were clear to make speed, the Pinto had us disgustingly out-horsepowered. With Greg's foot flat to the floor, we were violently shunted. Malcolm hung onto the back of my seat, muttering continuously. It was some time before I realised he was praying – and with reason to. The Pinto slammed into us and Greg cursed as we put a wheel into a hole and the steering wheel jumped out of his hands.

The report of a gunshot was muffled by engine noise and windstream, but I heard the round whang off the bodywork. Greg changed down and punished the little motor for everything it would give. I rummaged under my seat for the shotgun. It was loaded, and I ran the window down, let them have both barrels, one at a time. It would only be luck if I actually hit the Pinto, but there is nothing like the sight of a double-barrel rabbit gun for making anyone think again.

They dropped back, which gave me a chance to reload, but also gave the sharpshooter a clear shot at us. If he was aiming for the petrol tank – and gut instinct said he must be – we were on thin ice. I had both smoking barrels loaded again when Malcolm began to shout.

"Sit down, kid! Sit down and hang onto something!" I yelled at him.

But he ignored me, tugged at Greg's shoulder. "Go that way – that way! Go that road, man!"

"Take a right?" Greg glanced at me and I shrugged. "What's there, Malcolm? Malcolm!"

But he made the right, drifted across the loose surface, marbled with gravel. The tyres spun, losing traction for a moment before they began to bite again and we fishtailed. In a moment, I was sure we had made the last mistake of our lives. The road was so bad, the grader must have bypassed it for years. If we did not break an axle or just bottom out in a hole so deep we would never pull ourselves out, we were the luckiest pair of fools on the island.

Cursing fluently, Greg did his best. Not far behind us, the Pinto wallowed on its broken suspension. Every jerk bounced it flat to its belly, and we began to make distance on them. "Malcolm!" Greg shouted, "what's down here, for Chrissakes?"

And then we saw it. Lights up ahead, a shantytown in the foothills above Montego Bay as we ran south-east toward Cockpit country. Greg braked down as we came into the midst of the clustered shacks. In the back, Malcolm scrambled to get out, clawed at me to move myself, as if I was not already moving as fast as I knew how. I took cover behind the open door, hoping for a double-barrelled shot at the

Pinto as Malcolm began to scream for someone called Isaac.

The Pinto pulled up, nose to the dirt road, fifty yards behind us, just inside the shantytown. The driver revved its battered engine but came no closer. I saw the gun, waving out through the passenger's window, but no shots were fired. I wondered why, and then suddenly I understood.

They came out of the darkness like wraiths, several around our car, and several around the Pinto. I saw red, green and gold shirts, and the unmistakable shape of Eugene Stoner's automatic rifle, the ubiquitous M-16, in the hands of several of them. The Pinto stood for a second longer, then its tyres scrabbled on the gravel, throwing pebbles and dust into the air as the driver slammed it into reverse and pulled out, fast.

As its engine noise faded down I began to breathe again, and belatedly discovered that I was shaking, head to foot. Adrenalin overload is like coming down off a high, without having had the pleasure of the trip. I stood, let down the twin hammers but kept the rabbit gun in both hands until I knew what these people wanted of us.

"Mr. Connor?" The woman's voice astonished me. I shot a glance at Greg, saw the same surprise in his face as we turned to see Shirley Hamilton coming out of one of the shacks. Malcolm was with her, and a big man, six inches taller than me, easily, and not much under twice my weight. He wore a mane of dreadlocks that gave him a surreal look, but his face was passive, as if he was merely waiting for explanations.

The kid babbled, his high-speed volley making sense to the Rastafarians, and to Shirley. While he spoke to the big man – Isaac, the headman, I guessed, he must be – I said to the woman, "I thought you were heading for Kingston."

"So did I," she told me ruefully. "I got to the railway station. Logan's men were there. So I came here. I've got friends here."

"So has Malcolm," I observed as Isaac took the scared kid under his arm. "Look, keep him here if it's safe, till this is over. His card's as marked as ours now. I wouldn't want him turning up like your cousin, Peter. Or just vanishing off the face of the earth, like the others."

"You heard about that?" She sounded surprised. "Malcolm told you?"

Greg had come about the car and was standing in the wash of halogen glare from the headlights. "Some of it. We found Jeff Mathers' widow in Kingston. She gave us a lot more.

We've got enough to hang Rolland, but we can't prove any of it, and his lawyers'll cut what we have got down to allegation and slander."

Her mouth twisted bitterly. "Yes. I thought it would come to that. I just don't know where to go, what to do. And now there's Malcolm to think about. He's not going to end like Peter!"

"Hey, just give us a chance," Greg said with a faint smile. "Are we safe here tonight?" He glanced doubtfully at the Rastafarians.

"It's just about the only place you are safe," she said tartly. "Logan won't make trouble here. There's too many, and they've got guns."

I counted a dozen M-16s. "So I see. Can we stay till morning? We'll get out before daylight, but we could use some rest. Tomorrow's going to be hairy."

"You can stay with me," she said, looking up at Isaac for approbation. He said nothing, but nodded that head maned with twisted dreadlocks. Malcolm chattered constantly. I could not get a word of the strange Rasta language. English it is not.

She led us toward a shack built from corrugated sheets and brushwood. This settlement was not on any map, might not even exist in a year if the Rastafarians chose to pull up stumps and go. There was no permanence, as if we had wandered into the midst of a band of gypsies, or tinkers. We were safe for the moment, which was all we needed to know. On Shirley's threshold, I turned back to watch three strapping youths push our abused car out of sight.

"They're not going to loot our gear, are they?" I asked pointedly. "If they are, tell them to leave the paperwork and the camera, or the whole case against Rolland goes down the gurgler."

"They won't steal," she said scornfully. "They've got a little faith, a little pride. They're not criminals, but they won't be pushed and shoved. You're safe here." She showed us to a corner, where spare blankets were stacked against the cool nights and chilly early mornings Jamaica can produce. "I can't offer you much, I'm sorry."

Pumpkin, corn and rice to eat, tea, and a few hours of sleep before Greg shook me awake again. I peered at my watch and saw five o'clock. My back was aching against the dirt floor. The shack smelt of smoke and paraffin and sweat, and for an instant I had that dislocated sensation of not knowing where the hell I was. Memory came back with a flood, I groaned and looked over at the bundle of blankets that was the sleeping Shirley Hamilton.

"I want to check the car out," Greg whispered. "We hammered it last night, and I don't want to get into hot water with a motor that's going to go west. Give me a hand?"

I got both elbows under me, reached up and kissed him while I had the chance. Whiskers rasped on whiskers. Shirley did not stir as I got to my feet and followed him out into the cool of the night. Dawn was a couple of hours away.

A shape stepped out of the darkness as we appeared. The eyes of a zealot gleamed in the starlight. Isaac. Beside him, Greg was like a child. "Got to look at the car, man," my lover said quietly. "If Logan's right behind us we don't dare take chances."

The headman stepped aside. They had pushed the car in between two shacks. Greg turned on the headlights, working in their reflected light. He examined the hired car, flat on his back under it, while I looked at the motor. It is a tribute to Ford that half a litre of water in the radiator was the total it was begging for. Soon enough Greg was satisfied and we returned to Shirley's shack to find her making tea.

We shaved in hot water, ate sweet potatoes and bananas with the Rastas. Dawn was still half an hour away v.nen we spread the roadmap out on the bonnet, looking for a road that could not make a casualty of the car. Jamaica's roads are not unlike Australian backcountry roads. If they get the grader once a year they're fortunate, and wheel ruts can be deep enough to stop a tractor. Until recent years Australian cars were built like tanks – suspension, axles, bodywork that would take the pounding, since the rural buyer expected to muster sheep in the old Holden, rather than amble to the shops and back.

By comparison, the Detroit J-car we had hired was a toy, but the cars Rolland was running were little better suited to the conditions, with their sloppy suspension and sheer obesity. I traced out the road we were on with one fingertip to draw Greg's attention to my schemes.

"We'll connect with something decent in a couple of miles if we stick to this. The road down from the plantations. There's a town called Deeside."

"Okay. And after that, where?"

"Well, if we're going to dive the wrecked plane again," I mused, "we need gear and we need to hire a boat. And we don't dare try to hire stuff in Montego Bay. They'll be expecting us. There's always Falmouth, it's only about ten miles the other side of Deeside."

"Makes sense." He folded the map. "We'd better push off before it's daylight. Can't afford to be seen."

I knew Isaac had been watching us since we left Shirley's shack, and I looked over my shoulder at him. "Any of Rolland's men around here? We need a head start on them, if we can get it."

He smiled, all large, white teeth and flaring nostrils. "Dat's de only road through, man. And dey not followin' you. Count on it."

"Thanks," I said honestly. "Look after Shirley and Malcolm, will you? If we can put Rolland's head into a noose for you, we will."

The smile dwindled and Isaac's brow furrowed. He thrust his hands into the back pockets of faded jeans. His shirt pulled tight across a chest like a heavyweight boxer and I could not help looking at his groin. Fantasy or fright, depending on your personal predilection. "Why?" he asked flatly. "Why you bothered?"

I looked at Greg. "Rolland's kind make us sick. Users. Then, it's been us or them since the day after we got here . . . And we don't like the idea that kids like Malcolm and the others could be standing on an auction block. Good enough?"

Isaac said no more. He stood stroking his jaw as he watched us slide into the car and leave the shanty town as the first glimmers of light began to show. I drove first. I took it very slowly, very carefully, trying to pick a way through the rucked surface.

It was half an hour before I saw the connection to the better road, but the car was in one piece. The road down out of the hills was kept in good order for the trucks that shuttled between the plantations and the towns. Corn, papayas and coconuts come down to the markets. The road was newly graded and after the last few miles it was sheer relief.

We ran through sugarcane country, headed for the coast, and it rained lightly. Water streamed across the road, the hills misted out. In the east, clouds were banking up, and I turned on the radio for the news and weather. The forecast was for fresh winds and moderate seas, and the rain would clear by noon.

Just after nine, we drew near Falmouth, and I parked under

the trees. I turned off the motor and stood beside the car to enjoy the lingering coolness. Rain still pattered in the leaves above. An occasional drop made its way through to my face.

Greg came to lean on the rough bark of the tree beside me. "The question is," he mused, "are Logan and the boys looking for us this far afield?"

I slung my arm around his shoulders. "I'm not clairvoyant. You want to chance it, honey, or keep going? They can't search the whole damned island for us. Falmouth might be safe, if you want to try pushing our luck."

"What I want? God, what I want." He rubbed his eyes with the heels of his hands, leaned back against the rough bark, kneaded his shoulders on it. The mist was lifting from the hills as the patter of rain stopped. The air smelt of humus and decay, of earth and water. "All I wanted was to lie in the sun and get laid a lot," he said almost defiantly.

"It was your idea to dive." I traced the long, clean lines of his gullet and collarbone.

"I know." He looked at me, angled up a little, the hand's span I have over him in height. "And I'm sorry."

"Did I ask you to be sorry? It's just our luck. Bloody predictable, every time." I leaned both hands on the tree, on either side of him. "You look debauched. Delicious. We can't lie in the sun, but as for the other thing – "

"Getting laid a lot?" His arms went loosely about me.

"Yeah. We aim to please. Soon as we're safe. If you're that way inclined."

"I'm . . . that way inclined," he admitted, and gave his mouth to me. He wanted to kiss deeply and for a long time.

I surfaced from it with tender lips. "You want to try Falmouth or look elsewhere?"

He frowned at the waterfront town, which still lay several miles away. It had a couple of hotels, nothing special. The highrise buildings stuck out like sore thumbs above the Jamaican quarter. The river cutting down from Deeside and the Cockpit country emptied into the sea on an estuary that shone in the early morning sun, as the rain cleared.

"Try our luck, keep our eyes open, and one hand on the shotgun," he decided. "Chances are, Logan will assume we've gone to ground with the Rastas. It would be the intelligent thing to do." He winked at me. "Since when did we ever do the intelligent thing?"

I was about to contest that, and then closed my mouth. I could have been on good money, photographing fashion shows. Highly paid models wiggling their cute little arses at the camera while Fabergé and Gucci paid my handsome fee. I could have been shooting skin shots for the porno glossies, bums and cocks and bronzed chests. As I slid in behind the wheel for the drive down into Falmouth I fantasized Greg into these scenarios and decided he was right. Intelligence must have deserted me at an early age.

6

IT was going to make a rich, meaty story. American millionaire businessman trades in the bodies of beautiful, castrated black boys, smuggles drugs into the US and scams an insurance underwriter out of a king's ransom, killing at least two pilots in the process. The kind of story Matt Lansing was going to make a meal of – if we lived to file it.

Falmouth was still just stirring when we drove down, and we slunk into the town, nothing to draw attention to our presence. I parked on the outskirts and we walked in, took the back streets, passed through the accretion of shacks like tourists. I bought us another breakfast of bananas and rice and we sat on a fence between woodland and river to watch men at work among the crops of corn and yams.

"We're going to get away with it," Greg said quietly as he threw away the debris of his meal. "Rolland is probably making trouble for the Rastas, or turning over Kingston – makes sense. Either we've accepted protection or made tracks for the police in the nearest thing this island's got to a city with a proper police department." And then he made a face. "Damn. We paid for a high time, and what are we getting? Shantytown!"

I could only agree with him. "But look on the bright side. We might work this out in a few days."

"We might." He hopped down off the fence. "I make it ten o'clock, and I think we're safe to poke about. We need a boat, lover. A good one."

We needed something powerful under us if we were going

to go up against Rolland. A motor cruiser, I thought as I framed a few shots of Falmouth, pictures that might accompany Greg's text. Lush forest, blue-green sea, the highrise towers jutting over the rural town like bourgeois obscenities, labourers smoking as they worked along the river, the hills still misted with the morning's rain.

And being loose on the water would give us a kind of freedom that was impossible otherwise. I could spread him wide and have him in the sun, eager and panting for me. I said so as we strolled to a halt under the palms just above the beach. I was exciting myself with these whispered nothings and he gave me an amused look.

"You're a berk, aren't you, Alex? Must be why I love you." He punched my shoulder, as close to an expression of affection as you can get while observed by a crowd of geriatric Jamaicans, with geriatric morality.

Falmouth is just a fishing town, very rustic and in its own way appealing. Waterbirds flocked over the estuary and mud flats, hunting for shellfish turned up by each tide. A dredge lay rusting at anchor. We felt a drowsiness about the place that was soothing, and I knew complacency setting in. I shook myself hard. The fact was, any face we saw could have belonged to an informant of Rolland's.

We ambled along the beach toward the deep water where the boats were anchored. A ramshackle shop sold us Coca-Cola. Fishermen, working with nets and lobster traps, watched the white intruders suspiciously as we sat on coiled hawsers and looked over the available boats.

The choice was limited. None of the vessels was anything special, and the powerful inboard cruiser I had hoped to see was absent. "So it's sail or swim," Greg said acidly as he drained his Coke. He looked out at a white-hulled vision of loveliness. "What's the transom say?"

I narrowed my eyes against the glare of the sun on the water and made out the lettering. *Spirit of Jamaica*. The owner had a sense of humour. It was a play on the rum commercial.

"If she's for hire, she'll do," Greg mused. "Two could sail her, and I'm game."

"Famous last words," I muttered, disenchanted by the proposition even while I admired the boat.

My experience of boats to that point went as far as yachting, and a single outing in the crew of a Sydney To Hobart contender. I went along with the *Ruffian* crew to get a colourful documentary for the *Daily Mirror*. It was damned hard work in mountainous seas, constantly wet, cold, my stomach queasy if not downright nauseous as the maxi rolled, pitched and yawed, seeming simultaneously. On corrected handicap time, we came in seventeenth, but at least we arrived in Hobart afloat. There had been times when I was sure the Police Rescue helicopter would be pulling me out of the water, and my insurance company paying out on a thousand bucks' worth of camera gear, lost at sea.

The craft Greg decided on was no yacht. His own experience went far beyond mine, and I deferred to that knowledge. At twenty, too beautiful for his own good and dangerously naive, even after the knocks life had dealt him, Greg accepted an older man as his lover. He could have been the ball-less kid found floating face-down somewhere, but the Farris luck held and for two years he was the pampered plaything of a man old enough to be his father. He traded sexual favours for the good life, the first good living he had ever known. I have never blamed him.

The man owned a schooner. He showed Greg the Aegean, the Adriatic, Monaco, Naples, Alexandria. He paid for Greg's scuba tuition, and after two years on the schooner what Greg does not know about sailing craft is not to be known.

Still, he was asking me to trust him. It was one of those occasions where I discover to just what extent I do trust Greg with my life. "If she's for hire," I agreed. "We'll never know till we ask."

The *Spirit of Jamaica* was a converted pearl lugger. Broad in the beam and with two masts up, she was beautifully restored, not a blemish on her that we could see from the forefront. I wondered if we would be able to afford the price of her charter, even supposing her master would allow her out of his sight.

An old fisherman with a face like a pickled walnut sat working on the quay. I watched his gnarled but still nimble hands mending a lobster trap. Five dollars bought us the information we wanted. He pointed us in the direction of the shacks above the tidal zone, told us to look for Jake.

The day's heat had begun. It was going to be a scorcher. We could smell the wrack, rotting in the sun. We kicked through drifts of it, driven up on the beach by the storm that churned up the sea bottom to exhume Jeff Mather's Piper Navajo. Sea birds wheeled noisily overhead as we came to a dilapidated shack.

The thatch was ruined by the storm. No attempt had been made to repair it. The morning's rain had sluiced in through the rents and the dirt floor inside was still muddy. I peered into the near darkness and smelt a peculiar mixture of coffee, rum and sweat. Vacant eyes looked back.

He was young but raddled, sitting on the side of a rumpled bed, wearing red bikini underwear that suggested lax, modest genitals. How old? I wondered. Eighteen? Twenty? The boy had a serious problem. He lived in the drugged stupor you get tired of seeing on the faces of London's homeless and hopeless youth.

Greg leaned on the doorframe, rapped on it. "Is Jake here?"

The words were slurred. "Who wants 'im?"

"We'd like to charter his boat." Greg stepped into the unpleasant interior of the shack and took out his wallet. I saw the boy's glassy eyes fasten hungrily on the money. Another look you get tired of seeing in the young. Was there anything he would not have done for that money? I doubted it. Greg waited for a reaction.

"I's Jake." He shuffled to his feet and the haggling began.

He did not care about the lugger, that much was clear at once. The boat had been someone's pride and joy, but not this pot-head's. Greg let him set his price, sky-high, and offered next to nothing. It took them half an hour to come to an agreement, a figure we could afford to pay, and which did not actually rip the boy off.

Half a bottle of Appleton rum appeared. If we expected glasses we were disillusioned, and swigged it out of the bottle as money changed hands. The hire fee agreed on was something similar to Fat Conway's asking price. Jake took the money, pulled on a pair of cutoff denims, stuffed the folded notes into the back pocket of them and left the shack without even having sense enough to get our names on a piece of paper. We could have made off with the lugger and never returned. I wondered if the kid would have noticed. Or cared.

"Kids like that worry me." Greg shook his head over the young fool. "Who's to say we'll bring it back? What if we took it out and sank it?" He put away his wallet and gave the wet, smelly, dilapidated shack a look of disgust. "I feel in need of fumigation."

I echoed the feeling. "Five gets you ten he makes tracks for his supplier, blows the lot and is high as a kite in half an hour."

It was a safe bet. "It's his life," Greg said, and put the young fool from his mind.

A leaky little rowing boat lay beached just below the shacks. I assumed it must be Jake's. No one challenged us as we appropriated it and rowed out to look over what we had hired. I tied up alongside and hoisted myself over the stern, reached back to pull Greg up.

She was beautiful. Every fixture was practical and either new or reconditioned. Everything polished, still immaculately clean. Inside, the lugger was as painstakingly restored, with walnut and brass fittings. Greg murmured in appreciation.

"Jesus, will you look at this? You reckon pot-head inherited it or won it playing cards?"

"Search me," I said, similarly impressed as we looked her over from chain locker to rigging. She was a real working boat rather than a simple pleasure craft, which was exactly what we needed. She did not have the turn of raw speed a powerboat offered, but she made up for it in style, old world elegance.

"We can shove off tonight," Greg decided, head cocked as he listened to the sound of the water on the hull. "Better see if there's anything to eat on board."

But there was not. A tin of powdered milk and a sack of sugar was the sum of her stores. Greg made a shrewd list of groceries, items that would keep in the heat. It was noon as we beached the rowing boat and headed up toward the main street.

It led up from the waterfront, and if one of Rolland's informants was going to spot us anywhere in Falmouth, it would be there. My eyes were everywhere, suspicious of everything, as we scouted the facilities. The shotgun was in the car. My fingers itched for it.

The only place to hire tanks was a fishing tackle shop, and it was not a PADI affiliate. The equipment was very basic, suicidally so for the rank amateur. The tanks were old, steel rather than aluminium, and battered. At least they were numbered, which meant, old as they were, they were sound. No service station in the world will fill an unnumbered tank for you. They love to explode when they get old and worn.

They kept no BCDs, no octopus regulators, just basic regulators and steel weights. Greg slung a belt about his hips, guessing and adjusting. He would be somewhere near right. I followed his example as I paid for the hire of the gear.

We would be roughing it, but we were well trained, which was a matter of sheer luck.

The dive was only in thirty feet, and that was sheer luck also. It could have been a hundred and thirty, which would have made it infinitely harder. At that depth it's cold and dark and your bottom duration calculations are imperative. It's your life you're gambling, and you can "get bent" all too easily.

The woman in charge of the tackle shop, which was no more than a shed stuffed with every conceivable oddment from tinned maggots to spearguns, had fishermen's tidal charts of the reefs, intended for those adventurous types who slaughter game fish for sport. I ceased to see the sport in it when I photographed a story of the Sea of Cortez for *National Geographic* . Everything over three feet long is on for extinction.

We could only guess the draught of the lugger, but we would need the charts or run the risk of hanging her, keel first, on the reef. Even with the charts there was still a very real danger. Again, I deferred to Greg. We laboured back to the beach with tanks and weight belts that were heavy enough to tax me, remind me of how long it was since I had done any solid manual work. I was getting soft, and knew it by the time the tanks had been hoisted over the lugger's stern and thumped onto the decking.

Our second priority was to conceal the car, which was not too great a problem. Half a mile inland from Falmouth the woods began to thicken, and became quite dense. After half an hour's deliberation we shunted the Ford between two massive trees, locked it up and stood back on the road to look at it. Its mousy grey colour was adequately camouflaging. It should be safely hidden.

I had the shotgun in its sacking and Greg slung our bag over his shoulder. In it was every sheet of evidence we had. If we were jumped now, the whole enterprise was in the lap of the gods.

It was hot as we ate a late lunch in a cafe in tourist country. No one seemed to recognize the shape of a shotgun at my feet as we enjoyed seafood and salad, fruit cocktail and a light white wine.

"I want to go over the boat before we shove off," Greg said quietly under the noise of the street. Our table was on the pavement under a shade umbrella. A handful of tourists sat lunching nearby. "Check her bilges for a start. Don't want to get into heavy weather and find out she leaks!"

"You know best," I deferred. "What about the engines?"

"Keep your fingers crossed," he said drily. "One thing we cannot afford is to start loading diesel oil. I'm just about down to traveller's cheques. Paying off pot-head cleaned me out. You?"

"I've got plenty for odds and ends, but not for loading diesel," I said flatly. "We could phone home for money from Kingston."

"Shall probably need to," Greg mused. "Keep the receipts. When Lansing prints this, everything ends up as expense chits." He scraped back his chair and got moving as the shadows began to lengthen with mid-afternoon.

We shopped for groceries as we headed back to the waterfront. Bread, jam, eggs, ham, condensed milk, cereals, anything that would survive the climate for a few days. I bought several rolls of multipurpose film to replace what I had used, and then we pulled back out to the lugger in Jake's leaky rowing boat. We loosed it, left the tide to take it in.

The same tide would be running out at 18:45, so said the charts' almanac notation. We had a few hours to go over the lugger. While I stowed the groceries and film, Greg began. Despite his grumbling at the suspension of our holiday, he was thriving on the activity. Greg is a doer who likes to be busy, enjoys the exhilaration of danger so long as he has a fair chance of winning through.

These are the qualities that made him a battlefield journalist rather than the pampered pet of a rich man. If he wanted no more than the rich, idle life, Greg could still have been living that way. His looks have matured like fine wine rather than ruining with age. He could have moved from lover to lover as one man grew bored and wanted something new.

But it was Greg who grew bored. He's been there, done that, discovered what he wants and needs. We share the same taste for excitement. It's what made me who I am, and what. People have no understanding of what a photojournalist is and does. I'm often dismissed as "Greg Farris' photographer". Such ignorance makes me smile.

I heard the squeals of blocks and tackles working, the rattle of anchorchains as he checked them, and the electric motors that pulled up the lugger's heavy anchors, port and starboard of the bow. Everything was working. I took the sails up and down, found that even the winches had been serviced. The sails were not new, but patched thoroughly, and dry. They unfurled, ivory-white, and fell with a billowing of heavy canvas. Satisfied, I reefed them again. We had a breeze out of the east, and as Greg dislodged the anchors in trying the winches, the slightest movement of the soupy air was enough to set us drifting.

Evening thickened out over the estuary. The birds were silent as we finished examining the lugger, and I felt the run of the water begin to rock the hull as the tide turned. It was time to go.

Greg took the wheel as I made short work of setting sail, just enough canvas to move her a few miles offshore. Far enough for us to be quite anonymous, so that when Logan or his "rude boys" made it this far, and Jake told him that the *Spirit of Jamaica* had gone out on hire, he would not know where to start looking for us.

We needed safe space, time to sleep, relax, let go the tension that knotted my insides up like baling wire. The big anchors splashed into the water. The tide charts said the bottom was sixty feet down, and we waited to feel the pull on the boat as they began to drag, and then the sudden stop as they bit into coral or boulders and pulled us up.

I took the sails up, made fast for the night. Greg had turned the bow into the wind and with the sea smooth as a pond under us we knew we would enjoy a pleasant night. Before we dared go anywhere we must study the reef charts in detail. We could pick the shape of the reefs at low water by the colour toning of the sea – which was how it was possible to pinpoint the plane down to the last few metres. But as the tide rose the reefs became harder to distinguish. One towering coral spire could rip the bottom out of the lugger.

Greg put together a hasty meal as we listened to the radio for the fishermen's forecast. Eggs spattered in a skillet full of safflower oil over a propane burner. He fried bread, slapped the eggs onto it and smothered the whole lot in tomato sauce. "There," he said, handing me a plate. "Give your arteries a fright on me."

I was ravenous and couldn't have cared less about my arteries. We ate on deck in the coolness of evening as sunset blazed in the west. Greg was silent as we ate, smouldering. His eyes glittered with suppressed anger as he looked out over the sea. Eyes less grey than silver, very beautiful, albeit with a deadly kind of beauty, like the cobra about to strike.

"We could hop over to Barbados," I said quietly. "Logan won't catch up with us there and we can phone London, tell

Lansing to pull some strings. Give him the full story."

"And then Rolland makes a phonecall, and in a week's time – if we live that long – we collect a couple of bullets in the street in Islington." He shook his head. "Daydreams, loverboy. We either get the information that screws the lid down on Rolland – "

"Or we get screwed," I finished. I watched the corner of his mouth tug upward in a reluctant smile. "Look at it as a busman's holiday. We've done tougher jobs."

"We must have," he agreed, setting his plate aside. "Just now I can't seem to think of any, but doubtless you're right . . . Ah, damn."

"What?" I shuffled closer, took him against me. He turned his head for me to nibble his lobes, tongue inside his ears.

His arms went around me. "This isn't what we booked for," he observed ruefully.

I wriggled my tongue into his left ear, felt him shiver against me with a sense of smug satisfaction. I know what gets to him. "Maybe not, but we'll come out ahead."

"If we don't come out dead," he retorted with surprising vehemence. "Or worse than dead."

I let him slip out of my arms and looked at his face in the last faint mauve of twilight. "What's on your mind?"

"Pretty boys with their balls missing, listed as 'goods various', and shipped to eager buyers. What do you call that?"

"Slaving, is it? It's the only word I know."

His face darkened. "Yeah. Difficult to think it still goes on. First World complacency – the Third World is riddled with this shit."

Slaving still goes on in many countries. There is a great demand for dark meat. And white, if it can be supplied. I took Greg under my arm again, both of us leaning against the side of the wheelhouse. The woodwork was still sun-hot. "If this is what we've blundered into, it could get nasty."

He looked at me levelly, unblinkingly, the kind of look that can be unnerving. "Say it."

I took a breath. "All right. You'd make a very nice toy. Very marketable."

"Too old," he argued. "Thirty-two's over the hump, Alex."

"You don't look it by a long shot," I said tersely. "You'd make a very nice toy indeed."

"So would you," he retorted. "Marketable, did you say?"

Was he mocking me? For once I was unable to tell, and it

troubled me. I took him by the upper arms, abruptly more aware than usual of how whipcord-slender Greg is, how much the difference in our height means. The slim body and boyish face would put Greg at risk if we ran Rolland's gauntlet and lost.

"I'm too big, too heavy, too old," I began.

He tried to make a joke of it. "You trying to tell me I've got bad taste all of a sudden?"

"No." I tightened my grip on his arms. "I'm trying to say you don't have the same tastes as the creatures that buy slaves. They wouldn't look twice at me."

His eyes darkened, just rims of silver-grey about vast, black pupils, as if he was tripping on something. He shook his head. "You're wrong, Alex. There's the kind that only want them big and tough, so they can have the delight of breaking them. I've seen it."

I relaxed my grip on his arms, rubbed them. I guessed he would wear my finger-bruises tomorrow. He has bylines to his credit that have shocked and sickened me. Greg is – tough. Sometimes I forget how tough. "All right, so we could both end up on an auction block," I admitted, "just not paraded for the same customers. The object is not to let that happen." He leaned over to kiss me. "Be careful," I told him when I was permitted to speak again. "You bloody promise me that."

"Promise," he said dutifully, lightly, but it was not a quip.

He went to clean the crockery but I remained where I was, brooding as I looked out over the sea. I heard the throaty roar of a powerboat, miles away, churning out of the west, but was so preoccupied with our bleak remarks as to Rolland's business that I was slow to react. It took half a minute for me to snap to, and hiss at Greg to douse our lights.

It could be one of Rolland's boats. If we had been followed as far as Falmouth, a phonecall back to Montego Bay would have Logan out on the water and we could be in dead trouble. Greg plunged the cabin into darkness, and I went for the shotgun.

Logan or no, the powerboat passed by us a mile seaward and its noise faded again. I began to breathe, speculating about paranoia. The lugger was held tight by her anchors, deep in the coral spurs below. It was like being rocked in a big cradle. A gentle, soothing rhythm that was difficult to resist as the old timbers creaked and groaned, as if she was speaking.

I always loved the sea. A childhood dream was to run away and be a merchant sailor, beloved by the skipper of a square rigger in the China Seas. I had been reading Joseph Conrad. I would be the helmsman of a tea clipper, and gently fucked in the skipper's feather bed. I shared that daydream with Greg once, years ago, expecting him to laugh. Instead he played it out as a fantasy for me while we were yachting in Norfolk. It was bloody marvellous.

He brought a bottle of rum back on deck, and we ate nuts and chocolate as night fell and the stars began to blaze. So far away from the lights of any town, the whole sky seemed bright. City dwellers don't know what they're missing. Even today's Australian cities are so bright at night, the stars don't blaze as they did when I was boy.

The sea was almost smooth. The lugger seemed suspended in a kind of silvery half-world, half sky, half water, as the lines slapped against the masts and we lay on sun-warmed timbers.

If we had begun by resenting the situation, we changed our minds. It was wonderful beyond description to lie in Greg's arms an hour after sunset, when the air was shifting and fresh. I indulged my imagination in that childhood fantasy, square riggers and the love of a merchant skipper. Did Greg guess?

That first night aboard the lugger it was a siren luring me to my doom. Greg was bewitching, beguiling. I never saw him more seductive, as if our unreal surroundings had seduced him as they had me. The sleeping arrangements were comfortable, if narrow. The bed was bench-type, with a thick foam rubber mattress and a heap of woollen rugs. I wanted him fiercely – not teasing and playing around, but a real, thorough session. No wasting time, just pure technique, long ago perfected, lavished on one another as we like it best.

We could have stepped back centuries in time, that night. The lugger had been built in the eighteen hundreds, only its Gleniffer engine dated from this century, and we were riding nose-to-the-wind off jungle-clad hills that are steeped in history. It would not have been much different if we had been the youngest son of nobility eloped with the master of horse, paid a remittance by a scandalised family to go far away and stay away, and keep our mysterious and unnatural tendencies to ourselves.

I chuckled over that scenario without sharing it and Greg lifted his head from its pillow of bundled-up clothes on the deck. The wind stirred in the lines as the boat began to yaw under us. The timbers were still warm.

"What's so funny?" He wanted to know. I told him. "Youngest son of nobility," he mocked gently. He let me turn him over, and over again, so I could go over him an inch at a time.

"You could be peerage." I nipped at his chest with my teeth. "Not the ordinary looking lad, are you? There's always something different about gentry, isn't there?"

"You mean their horsy faces and big teeth and jug-handle ears?" he demanded, describing a good many of England's titled. And one or two in particular.

I was suckling on his left nipple, and bit down hard enough to make him yelp. "No, I don't." I kissed the nipple I had hurt a little and sucked for a long while. I lifted my head at last to see his face. Dreamy, eyes closed, as he revelled in pure sensation. "I rather fancy myself as a master of horse," I admitted, and patted his bony hip meaningfully. "I like riding."

His eyes opened, gleaming in the light of the paraffin lamp he had lit at dusk. "I know you do. Just so long as you don't start mistaking me for a bloody horse."

I knelt astride his legs to consider the suggestion and shook my head. "Not a chance, mate. No way in the world . . . What would you like tonight?"

He shrugged sinuously, drew a deep breath of fresh sea air and stretched, head to foot. "Anything at all."

So I took him to bed and sucked him, loving the taste of him. I murmured in delight as he pulled me around so he could suck me too. As his mouth closed over me I gasped and froze, suspended in that moment that is as close to agony as pleasure. It was some time before I could go on. This time he led, I followed, taking up his example the next instant. Greg is nothing if not thorough and it was exhausting. A little cum tingled in my throat as he came, then I spent myself too. Limp, adhered sweatily to him, I dozed with my head on his thigh.

The roll of the lugger woke us as the wind picked up close to midnight. Caresses were tickling my back and legs. I rolled over to watch as he returned the pampering he had received from me, charting my body, feature by feature, scar by scar. He drove me back to arousal with methodical deliberation. He knows me better than anyone else ever did.

I wanted him desperately, and wanted him to kneel for me.

He has the most alluring arse I ever saw, and he knows he has. To see it uplifted and spread takes my breath away – and he knows that too. Knows what I want, what I need. Although he likes to lie on his back he never refuses me when I turn him over.

He was utterly relaxed, already open as he knelt up, cheek on his forearms. I paused, just to look at him for some time before I put my hands on his buttocks and kneaded them to make him shiver. I was weeping enough pre-cum to do. He sucked in a breath as he felt my cock press up behind, let the penetration expel the air from his lungs, wriggled until the sudden fullness was comfortable. Then his breathing rhythm settled, deep and even as he relaxed, and I was sheathed to the balls in him.

The roll of the boat made us shift slightly, rocking sideways, and both of us groaned at the involuntary stimuli. He whispered soft, half-formed curses. His musk was sinfully erotic. A lift of his hips brought me alive with delight. I closed my fingers around his tender scrotum and pulled, hard enough to stave off his climax. He cursed me, clenched like a fist and bucked back onto me. The heat turned up full. Our skin glistened like patent leather in the lamplight as I took my pleasure from him, gave him back an equal measure.

Or more. He was flying on the dual sensations of my hands and my cock, caressing him inside and out, and he was wild. I lifted him into my lap. The boat heaved under us and he tensed, gasped as I felt my own control snap. We fell forward onto our knees. Feverish then, I drove us hard, knowing how the spasms in his arse would finish me.

Climax destroyed me. Did I scream or was it Greg? Then I collapsed on him, muscles like rubber, senses swimming. He was out, dead asleep while I remained buried in him. I rested on his back until I had strength and wits enough to grope for a handful of tissues. He stirred as I mopped us up, turned over and pulled me down, imprisoning me in arms that crushed me. We lay in a tangle of sticky limbs and slept.

It was not yet dawn when we woke, but the first powdery light of dawn had begun. We had slept jammed into the narrow bed and Greg was twisted. He swore as he tried to move, "Jesus, my bloody back's broken."

"Just your back?" I asked groggily. I slid off the bed. "We were a bit wild last night." I spread his buttocks to look at him. It was too dim to see properly, but I was sure he was just tender. It's years since we were rough enough to hurt each other, and it was never deliberate, just youthful enthusiasm paying the price for its own lust.

He purred as I rubbed his tailbone, coming awake as daylight brightened. He blinked at his watch. I turned him over, dropped a kiss on his soft, warm cock. It twitched against my lips, smooth and musky, making me smile. "Good morning to you too," I told it. "I trust you had a nice time last night?"

"He enjoyed himself," Greg assured me drily. "He told me so."

We laughed and I got my feet under me. The deck yawed deeply, made me reach for a handhold. The cabin still smelt ripe as I went through to the neat little galley to make tea. Neither of us bothered to dress. He was on deck when the tea was made, sitting on the side by the stern to look at the distant coastline. I could still feel the phantom thrills of pleasure from last night's antics as I handed him a cup. His whiskery face smiled at me. One grey eye winked.

"We're safe here," I judged. "Even if pot-head Jake spills the lot to Logan for a fiver, the sea is a damned big place. They'll run themselves ragged if they even try to look for us. For all they know we could have headed for Barbados!"

He yawned, worked the kinks out of his shoulders as he watched the gulls swoop low over the water. The sun showed the first bloated, glaring wedge of its face over the horizon. The sky was like a pink and powder-blue abstract.

"We can dive the wreck today," he said, sipping his tea. "Fast."

Fast, before Oliver Rolland's people could get out there and destroy the evidence that would have them on charges, put a lid on this farce, and secure our own safety. That meant making a thorough study of the reef charts before we dared move the lugger, and measuring the depth to the keel with some degree of accuracy.

Greg went over the side to do that with a rope tied to the stern. I watched his pale form quiver and distort, deep under the surface as he went down. He came up half a minute later with a hitch tied in the rope to mark our depth under the waterline. Knowing that, we could work out which channels through the reef we could navigate, and which were suicide.

I had done work that was similar, but not in more years than I cared to remember. I knew the Barrier Reef charts well, that summer when I was desperate for the affections of the master of the dive boat *Dreamtime*. He was a big, bronze fantasy man. And as straight as a bunch of rulers, with a wife and four kids at home. Unrequited lust was like an acid burn.

As Greg made us a breakfast of scrambled eggs, rough-sliced bread and black cherry jam, I spread the charts out on the bed. He handed a plate to me and we pored over them for an hour, marking them up. The reefs are not too chaotic a tangle, but more than a few Spanish galleons went down laden in these seas, blown onto the coral spires by hurricanes and tropical storms that can whip up without warning. The *Spirit of Jamaica* did not draw much water, which was fortunate, as neither of us has studied for a marine pilot's licence, and the tuition we did receive is long in the past.

"Be best to cut straight out to sea and approach Montego Bay from the north," Greg mused. He was making sense. "That way we can use the channel they keep dredged for the cruise ships and we haven't got a worry." I heard his joints crack as he stretched. "We'll need a weather report too. You know the tropics. Capricious."

I slid my arm around his waist to rub his bony shoulder-blade. "We'll get the best case we can and call home, what do you think? Lansing can call the Kingston fuzz direct, make them aware of who we are and that we've got something bloody important for them. Even if the insurance scam doesn't get them excited, the marijuana plantations might."

"Or the stories about the trade in bodies," Greg added quietly.

I threaded my fingers into his damp hair. "Right. You know what bothers me? Rolland only holds the reins. His minders are Jamaican. Black predators selling black boys. It's obscene."

"Bastards come in all colours," he said bitterly. "There's a lot of poverty here. A lot of the poor sods don't eat regularly. The only option they've got is crime. Ganja. Grow it, smuggle it."

"But Oliver Rolland isn't a poor sod," I said drily. "He's a flash American bugger who's got a kick up the arse coming that's richly deserved."

Greg set his empty cup down with a clatter. The stub of a pencil ran over the charts as he planned our way through the reefs. "It's only seven, we've got time on our side. Turn the radio on. We might as well get the weather bulletin."

A calypso band played reggae songs as I cleaned up the galley and checked the lugger's fresh water tanks. We had enough for drinking, but I decided to bathe in seawater. I boiled the kettle and we sat in the shade on deck to shave before Greg announced he was going over the side again. "I want to take a good look around the hull under the waterline. She's been scraped, I saw that when I measured the keel, so I expect she'll be sound."

He pulled on the diver's facemask. The tragedy is, the Caribbean is one of the most polluted seas in the world, and you must protect your eyes. I stood watching, listening to the radio as he duckdived several times, bare rump breaking surface for a moment. I gave him my hand to haul him back over the transom, and he was satisfied.

"Swam around the whole hull," he panted. "She's been somebody's pride and joy."

"So how did she get into pot-head's clutches?" I was aware that my shoulders had begun to tighten and pink in the sun. I would have to dress soon.

"I should think he won her," Greg guessed as he rummaged for something cold.

"Or," I added, "somebody's been using this sweet little lady to run ganja into America, and got caught."

He shot a hard look at me. "Oh, Christ. You don't suppose the police are looking for this boat?"

"Don't even think it," I told him. "We're in enough trouble as it is." I took a swig from his can and we pricked up our ears as the reggae ended and the radio news came on. The weather report would follow.

Rampant political strife, a murder in Kingston overnight, a new building project and the cricket results. Then, the important information. Fresh winds, rising in the afternoon, slight to moderate seas, a strong wind warning out for eastern and southern coastal waters. Quite decent sailing weather so long as you were not out in a dinghy. And then the bad news. I groaned as the weather man read off the details of Hurricane Rita, which was gathering out in the Atlantic, moving steadily northwards, not expected to arrive in Jamaica for a couple of days.

Greg swore lividly. "That settles it. We put a lid on this before the big wind, or we get out. I don't know about you, but I've never handled a boat in a Force Ten."

I had come close. The year I crewed the Sydney to Hobart contender, the weather was rough. But that was a maxi ocean racer, not an old lugger with antique hull configuration, and there had been nine of us on that yacht, not two. Greg was right. We did not want to get caught at sea in a hurricane. We might as well hand ourselves into Rolland's custody and take it as it came.

The biggest blow I ever experienced at first hand was Christmas of 1974 – Australia will not forget Cyclone Tracy in a hurry. One moment Darwin was there, the next, it was gone. Utterly. The wreckage looked like the aftermath of a bombing raid. Nothing standing, no power, no water fit to drink. Looting in the ruins and a legion of the injured and homeless. I was up in the Territory by a fluke, doing a pictorial on tourism. Most of the country knew something was very, very wrong when the notices began to appear on television. It was Christmas Eve, and among the seasonal commercial jingles there would be a frame of an RAAF helicopter, and a read-over of new standing orders. All crews of this and that ship to report back to the dock, pronto. It must have looked to the casual television audience as if we were at war, not quite out of the blue. Indonesia has been casting avaricious glances at the northern coasts for some time.

But it was Cyclone Tracy. I stood on the docks once savagely bombed by Japanese aircraft, roped myself down and blew all the bulk-loaded film I had. The pictures were phenomenal but they did not even suggest the sheer fright, the adrenalin high, of standing in the teeth of it. I don't think I shall ever forget the mountainous seas, the wind like a giant hand, crushing the breath out of my chest, the lightning and driving rain.

Greg has had all the stories from me. "The worst blow I ever saw was off Hong Kong," he was saying as I returned to the present. "A typhoon – and that was aboard a container ship. I was doing a story about export fraud. It wallowed like a pig. This little tub would swamp in five minutes."

I pantomimed a cringe. "You trying to scare shit out of me?"

"I'm not so crazy about inhaling salt water myself," he admitted. "I think we'd better take a look at the engine. If we get into trouble, we'd better be able to pull ourselves out. Look, you take a dip, freshen up, I'll check out the situation. And Alex." I had one leg over the side. "Keep an eye out for fins, won't you? These waters have been known to have sharks."

He had to say that. I gave him a glare and dived over the side anyway with the abandon typical of my countrymen. They can be warned out of the shallows by the shark spotter's siren, and then go back in again ten minutes later, knowing there are bronze whalers not far away. I stayed close to the boat and kept my eyes peeled.

The water was cold and invigorating and I took the opportunity to look at the hull. She had been scraped and patched, there were no barnacles, and a lot of white lead. Cold and prickling with gooseflesh, I pulled myself back into the sun.

The engine hatches were up, a cavern in the decking, and Greg was clucking like a broody hen, his back to me as he doubled over the old Gleniffer. "Hatching an egg, are you?" I teased. "Got you pregnant at last."

"Good news and bad." He completely ignored my wit. "We've got about a third of a tank of oil. That isn't going to go far but it might pull us out of trouble if we save it, run on sails until or unless we get into strife. That's the good news. Look here." He stood aside, beckoned me to the hatch beneath which was the diesel. "This hasn't been looked at since before we were born, if I'm any judge. There's fifty years of grease on it. They probably intended to get to the engine last and didn't get around to it before whatever went bad happened, and landed her in that numbskull's hands."

I peered into the engine hatch and echoed his disgust. "Turn it on, let's have a listen to it. These old engines often look after themselves so long as there's plenty of lubricant in 'em." I winked at him. "Same as us in that respect."

But the Gleniffer started only with great reluctance and a belch of greasy smoke, and we were listening to the bearings. They were not much short of dry. Much work asked of this antique, and those bearings would seize. They are made to run hot, but they are also supposed to be packed in oil. It was possible that the last time these were serviced, there was a king on the throne.

Would the engine hold together long enough to haul us out of trouble if we were on the water when the hurricane hit? I remembered Tracy and could not help shuddering. Greg wiped his oily hands off on ragging pulled from a box in the corner of the engine compartment.

"It's a matter of blind faith," he said drily.

"So we run on sails," I mused, "and make bloody damned sure we're out of the way of the storm."

"Suits me." He threw away the rags and leaned over to kiss me before hoisting himself out of the hatch. We were still naked and my shoulders were growing pink. He tickled them deliberately to draw my attention to them.

"Give me a second to dress and I'll make sail," I offered.

"Don't dress on my account," he called after me. "But for Christ's sake put some sunblock on yourself. Something to do with the Ozone Layer, isn't it?"

I could feel his eyes on my backside. He would want it later. Both of us still savoured memories of last night's indulgences. Thoughts of the rematch filled my belly with a delicious thrill. I put on a lot of sun oil, slacks and a shirt. Delicious anticipation or no, I had to dress or become a broiled lobster.

I was up on deck in moments to find him clad in shorts, waving at a pleasure craft. A gaggle of young women were shouting at him, invitations to a boat party. I wondered if he had got the shorts on in the nick of time, or if the invitations were the result of a glimpse of my beautiful bare-arsed and well endowed lover. The powerboat roared off and I laughed, swatted the buttocks in question.

Setting sail was an elaborate game. I enjoyed myself with the lines as Greg weighted his charts, double-checked the depth notations and brought up the anchors. The sails were in excellent repair, an acre of cream canvas as I set them. The tackle was well oiled, lines ran smoothly through their blocks.

The compass was a precision instrument, fluid mounted, and very accurate. Greg brought us about and held us forty degrees off the wind. He was loving it. She handled like an angel. I could fall in love with this boat and knew from the rapt look on Greg's face he shared the feeling. He made love to her, the wheel cradled lightly in his palms as she answered every caress. I almost envied her.

A dome of blue sky made the water just as blue but we saw the cloud front coming up in the east. Hurricane Rita was out there somewhere, playing in the Atlantic. I had my eye on the horizon and my ear on the radio as the broadcasters took a break in the cricket to give updates on the progress of the storm.

Rita bounced around like a rubber ball, one hour moving out to sea imperceptibly, the next moving back inward, and growing every minute. When she arrived in Jamaica we would see the blow of the century. Our luck was running true to form.

$$\boxed{7}$$

*T*HE *Spirit of Jamaica* made good speed, running before a fresh wind. Unless I was trimming sail there was nothing much for me to do and I stood at Greg's back, spooned against him, eating his ears as he wove through his pre-plotted course, between the reefs. The channels were wide enough to admit trawlers and sport fishing cruisers. We were safe so long as we stuck to them.

At midmorning we saw the tall highrise hotels of Montego Bay, white against the jewel green of the hills. We began to scout for the landmarks by which we would pinpoint the correct arm of the reef, where the plane was, but before we sighted the second marker Greg gave me a nudge, pointed at a big, yellow cabin cruiser with a winch and enormous Evinrude outboards.

"What the hell is that? You're looking at a hundred grand's worth there. More." His eyes narrowed against the sunglare. "Hello, divers."

He had seen the "divers down" flag, a blue and white flutter on the cruiser's mast. "Rolland's dive boat?" I wondered.

"Has to be. I never did believe in coincidence." He made a face at the display of wealth before us and gave me a punch in the shoulder. "Trim, will you? We'd better get out of here fast, before they see our smiling faces. It proves out Shirley Hamilton's ideas, doesn't it? We didn't give the details to Conway, we gave them to D.S. Payne at the copshop. We might as well have phoned Rolland and told him where it is – not," he added acidly, "that they're diving in the right place. Unless I'm vastly mistaken they're about half a mile too far west, aren't they?"

They were. "Round about." I trimmed to accommodate a sharp tack that took us away from the cruiser. The lugger ambled away, seaward, and I returned to Greg's side to take a glance at the compass. "That puts the kabosh on us for the time being. We don't dare dive till they've pulled out, and they won't shove off until their divers are out of air."

"They might have a compressor aboard," Greg speculated.

"Then they'll work till the divers get into hypothermia and exhaustion on repeated dives," I mused. "And in thirty feet that's going to mean several hours. Then they'll either finish for the day and let the same divers go again tomorrow, or switch to a new crew. Either way, they head home in a few hours."

"So we have time to kill." He looked at his watch. "You want to sail up to Lucea? You can buy me lunch."

"Nice idea." I stroked the wheel, making subtle hints, and he released it to me.

"Have a go. Just stay in this channel – " pointing out a pencilled line on the reef charts " – and you can't go wrong."

It was the deep-dredged channel the cruise liners used, wide enough for a novice to handle easily. Greg hopped about, trimming as we tacked. Brown, lithe and agile, he managed the work like an old seahand. But the simile made me frown. Greg would not survive long at sea among the kind of predators who crew some of the tramps.

He might not mind being screwed into the deck, might endure being made to do it when he would rather not, but the games can get rough and nasty, and ten against one makes it hard. Too hard, when you're still hurting from round one, and they're ready for more. Greg is the kind who'd drive men wild, three weeks out of port when everyone is getting twitchy and the sight of a tight little rump in a pair of cutoff Levis is like ringing the dinner gong. I had a mate on a tramp out of Amsterdam. I heard all the stories.

Lucea is much like Falmouth. Small, shabby, inhabited by rustics, and as far as we were concerned, safe because of its obscurity. A rotting jetty probed out into the little bay. The tide was low as we hitched up below the stepway between a creaking old trawler and a hulk that must have been rusting there for years. It was past noon and the sun was blazing, like a heavy hand pressing down on top of my head. Greg was getting darker every moment while I worried about my fair Irish skin burning.

Despite the heat they were serving beef stew with dumplings and soft apple pudding, which we washed down with warm beer. We took a table in the shade outside a ramshackle pub, ogled by the locals. "Better buy in some more food while we're here," Greg decided as he cleaned his plate. "Going to get tired of eggs on the boat. Or silt up our arteries with cholesterol and save Rolland the bother of doing away with us!"

We bought fruit, corn, potatoes, ham, cheese, anything we could use quickly before the climate had its way. The tastebuds can become jaded with French dressings after a while and we looked forward to simple fare. I like to cook, as does Greg. Not that we get much opportunity to.

The sky was still blue in the west but in the east we saw the building weather front. We were not looking at Rita yet, but at the masses of cloud-laden, humid air pushed in front of the hurricane as it bounced around out to sea. Greg frowned at the mass of cumulus, sunglasses perched on his nose. "That's going to beat us to it if we're not careful, and if she rearranges the bottom again we might never find the plane."

I glanced at my watch as he spoke. "I make it half past one. Time to shove off?"

It was only a short run back to Montego Bay. We had been gone a little over three hours and I reefed in well out so that we could scout the area in safety. The yellow cruiser was just leaving. We had timed it to a nicety. The divers would be heading back to exchange with fresh men, or get the tanks filled, or both. They were still a long way off target but working their way slowly in the right direction. They were probably watching the sky as we were, knowing they were on a tight schedule.

We would get one chance. Greg brought the lugger through the last long tack. "They didn't get anywhere near it," he observed with fat, smug satisfaction. "How long, do you reckon, before the boat's back out?"

"An hour," I guessed. "Depends if they have tanks to rotate, or need those filled – or have a compressor on board, as you said. Bet you a fiver the boat crew stops for a beer and a meal. They've been roasting out here since who knows what time this morning. And the divers'll be dry. Tank air."

"Which gives us long enough to scramble through." He put the wheel over to bring us up to the outmost arm of the reef. I dropped the sails as the anchors hit the water. They bit into the coral heads and pulled us up with a little jolt. Thirty feet below us was the wreck of a Piper Navajo, with the remains of John Hamilton, Spitfire pilot, ex-Shell pilot, still at the controls.

We knew where we were down to the last few metres. We

could see our old hotel, an enormous white concrete tower, we could see the headland in one direction, an orange marker buoy in the other, and the reef pointed away at right angles beneath us.

In our favour was the fact that Rolland's divers did not yet know they had competition. Working against us was the fact that the gear we had hired was not the best. I wondered if Rolland had associates in the hotels. If Goldmark vans supplied them, it was probable. They must be scouring the island for us, and they must have learned we had hired the lugger.

Greg's brows knitted in a frown as I said as much, then he shrugged eloquently. "With any luck it won't make any difference. They'll be running around like blue arse flies." He grinned, an impish, urchin expression. "If they've got people in the hotel they probably know we share a bed, you realise. You don't have to be Sherlock Holmes to work it out, not after the condition of some of our laundry. It could be to our advantage."

"How's that?" I looked up at him over the tanks and regulators I was checking out.

"They'll peg us as a couple of 'pansy poofters', as they say over here. A couple of fairies who can't take the pace and have run at the first sign of real trouble. They won't expect us back."

I snorted with laughter. "Never thought it'd be advantageous to be pegged as a fairy."

He echoed the humour, posed with one hand on his hip and the other wrist dangling limply, batted his eyelashes and pouted. "Oh, darling, do you really think we ought to get involved?"

"How too, too camp," I lisped, and bowled an orange at him. He fielded it deftly, like Viv Richards in the slips, and tossed it back into the basket.

It never bothered me, after my father died, what people said or thought of me. There was always that throb of guilt while the old man was alive – filial responsibility shirked. I was his only son, I was expected to marry, perpetuate the name and the bloodline. His brother, my Uncle Allan, had three sons, I reasoned. There are Connors galore in Sydney. More, from me, were an unnecessary luxury, and my two sisters had handed him several grandchildren before I flew the nest. Still, that pang of guilt persisted. He disapproved. I ran the wild side briefly in my late teens and early twenties, and it got back to him who I was running with. *Hey, Jack Connor, do you know that nong of a son of yours is balling boys in Surfers?* There followed stern, disapproving glares, but he said nothing to me. Most likely he realised that to lay down the law would be to drive me away sooner rather than later. I was twenty, already freelancing. Only some sense of duty kept me in touch.

Then my father died, which was no surprise to me or my mother, since he had smoked fifty a day for thirty years. The mystery was how he lived so long. I felt no further guilty pangs. If people liked to call me a faggot or a fairy, I could live with it.

But Greg was tortured when he was a boy, and was touchy for years. I have the Connor genes, my grandfather's VFL-hero stature. I escaped the viciousness. Greg is as tough as they come, masculine, very strong; his eyes, his hair and his arse make him a prime target for the vitriol, and he suffered a lot. It bothered him, even years after he and I got together, as if he had his manhood to prove. Slowly the aggression and hot temper eroded. I like to believe I dispelled the painful identity crisis. Whatever he had to prove to himself, those days are past. He can camp with the best of them and enjoy it now.

The battered old diving gear had been stored inside, out of the sun. You cannot be too careful when the equipment is old. You're handling potential bombs that have enough kick to blow a boat out of the sea. It was hot and the cold water was a shock. Greg's weight belt was incorrectly balanced. It gave him trouble, and as he had no BCD, he worked hard. I hung in midwater under the boat to watch him duckdive, kick hard and haul himself down the starboard anchor chain, hand over hand, to compensate for the bad weighting.

The world was blue-green, shafts of sunlight striking at a steep angle, bright by the surface and not quite making it to the bottom. The reef opened up beneath us, colourful in the filtered sunlight, populated by its dancing rainbow of fish. The water was much clearer than it had been on our last dive. Visibility was more than sixty feet, which is unusual in today's polluted seas. We were looking for the geometric shape of the plane this time, and we saw it in minutes as we swam along the tapered arm of the coral outcropping.

The storm that had churned up the sea bottom was a cousin of Rita's, a harbinger of the big wind to come. We were working in the lull between upheavals and for the moment it was tranquil, serene. Perfect holiday conditions, I thought ruefully as I caught sight of the plane and drew Greg toward it.

The windscreen had shattered away. Jags of broken glass were still affixed to the frame, but a rock knocked them out, made it safe for us to wriggle inside the cabin. It was Greg who noticed the first oddity – it could only be seen from inside, so we had missed it on our previous dive. The hatch mechanism that locked the door on the left was in its "unlock" position, while the pilot was strapped into his seat.

There had certainly been a passenger. I remembered Mrs. Mathers' remark about a precious cargo requiring a minder, a guard with a magnum pistol. So the man had got out. Before or after she hit the water? A safe guess was that he had jumped for it when she touched, or moments before. After the plane began to submerge the water pressure on the outside of the doors would hold them closed, like getting trapped in a car underwater. There is almost no way to get out, and the deeper it sinks, the more the pressure.

The next item was left for me to discover, and it was crucial. There would have been obscenities if I had not had a regulator jammed between my teeth. I had wriggled into the cabin and turned around in the cramped space, which gave me a view of the back of the pilot's skull. It was smashed in. John Hamilton had been hit with something hard, elongated, just once. The shape of the punched delve suggested the butt end of a rifle – the dimensions were consistent. I drew Greg's attention to it and he nodded. His fingers fished for the chain that still hung around the skeleton's twisted neck.

Dogtags, World War II vintage, British variety, RAF. He took the tags off the heap of bones as I backed out of the cramped space. Our bubbles cascaded across my facemask. The cabin's roof section was filling with our exhalation, pockets of air trapped in the corners. If Rolland's divers found the plane before Rita rampaged through and buried it again, the air pockets would be a dead giveaway. They would know other divers had been before them, which could only mean us, the "pansy poofters" who had not run for their lives after all.

Greg investigated the compartment where the pilot's papers and log would have been kept. It had filled with water, but legal quality paper is very tough, designed to survive a century out. With luck, if it was not disturbed too much, Kingston's forensic squad would be able to make something of it.

We searched the cabin for anything that was odd or incongruous and had given up before some small thing caught my eye. I thought at first it was glass, just a shard of the windscreen, shattered inward and trapped in the padding of the passenger's seat, beside the remains of old man Hamilton. But it had a shape, and no piece of broken glass ever took that shape.

I wormed it out of its cranny, fingers starting to grow a little numb with the cold, which is accumulative and insidious, even in warm waters such as the Caribbean. I waved to catch Greg's attention as he sized up the way the skeleton was slumped in its seat.

It was a diamond, beautifully cut, big, priceless, like a piece of ice. Utter perfection. My heart gave a thump against my ribs. For it to get loose there must have been a struggle, the same struggle in which Hamilton's skull had been smashed. I paid attention to what Greg was trying to signal in sign language.

The skeleton was seated awkwardly, jammed against the bulkhead with its legs crooked. And one of them was broken. Had it been snapped in the impact of the crash? Or had there been a desperate fight? Certainly there had been a struggle that culminated in a murder and the loss of a single gem in the seating. The man who killed Hamilton did not have time to retrieve the lost stone before he jumped as the plane went in.

Going over the plane itself would have been pointless. Sabotage, if it had been performed, would be a matter of fuel lines and engine adjustments – nothing visible from the outside, or a veteran like Hamilton would never had missed it. There was plenty of air left in the old tanks but we were getting cold and we wanted to talk. Greg signed that it was time to go up and I agreed. What we needed now was information.

A phonecall to Lansing would sort out a good deal. He could chase up the insurance company without us putting our necks on the block. A diamond like this one would have been photographed from every angle, catalogued, listed by its dealers as it changed hands repeatedly. Give Interpol half an hour, and they would be able to quote us the owner, the dealer, the cutter, perhaps even the mine it had come from. We had enough to give to the police in Kingston, enough to hang Oliver Rolland, and Leroy Logan with him.

Greg had the plane's log and Hamilton's papers pressed flat to his chest. They would go into a plastic bag, kept wet with seawater, till they were handed to a forensics technician for treatment with a fixative, to prevent further deterioration as they dried. He had the dogtags and I had the strongest claim to a case we had, short of the specific location of the aircraft and its murdered pilot. The diamond was hard against my palm.

We broke surface, jubilant at our results. Greg was talking the moment the regulator was out of his mouth.

And then I heard that unmistakable sound of a gun cocking. A double click that makes you sick to your stomach, makes your heart skip a beat and the blood hammer in your ears. I looked up, squinted against the sun. Three intruders waited for us. They stood in the stern of the lugger, silhouetted against the sky, all of them armed. My heart turned to a brick in my chest as one of them spoke.

It was an American voice, cultured and educated. "Get into the boat. Move slowly and carefully, or you're dead men."

I looked at Greg. His mouth was a thin, compressed line of fury. I looked back up at the men above us. "Mr. Rolland?" I asked, throat dry and rasping after the dehydrated tank air. "We might have been expecting you."

"You might have," he said indifferently as we struggled up over the side and dumped the tanks.

Under gravity again we weighed like lead and it would be sheer suicide to make a move. We stood still as the sodden papers, the dogtags and diamond were taken from us by the largest of the three men backing the American. I knew the face. The swelling about his eye had subsided now. Leroy Logan was the size of a Camaroon gorilla, and he had a score to settle with us. My heart was in my throat, choking me.

Rolland held the diamond to the sun, very satisfied. "You might," he said acidly, "have had sense enough to remove your little fannies from this island. But it's too late for that now, isn't it?"

I was looking at the Webley in his hand, and thinking he was very likely right. Oliver Rolland was forty, so I had read in the caption to his photogrpah, in that magazine feature on the powerboat race he had sponsored. At first glance he seemed older. He was obese. A large paunch strained the front of his designer shirt. He was balding beneath the white yachting cap, and green shades disguised a network of crisscross lines about his eyes.

Overfed and oily, like a greasy upmarket pimp, I thought. The competition in New York would have been over his head, so he lorded it in Jamaica where American dollars and connections are enough to found a lucrative, if illicit, enterprise. Greg looked him up and down with thinly veneered disgust. I knew he would not keep his mouth shut for much longer and prayed to any god who might be listening that he would at least speak warily.

His tone was conversational, very offhand. "The insurance must have paid out a bundle. The man who killed John Hamilton got out of the plane okay, did he? So Hamilton took the can back for you. You collected the gems and the insurance, and all you have to do now is destroy the wreck, or wait for the next storm to bury it again."

"Very smart." Oliver Rolland seated himself on the side of the boat and looked us over. "Too smart. Mind your mouth, boy. You could find a fist in it." Greg clamped his teeth together. A muscle in the side of his jaw twitched. "You're pretty things," Rolland went on. "I wouldn't have taken you for faggots."

"I wouldn't have taken you for a tarantula," Greg said glibly, running stupid risks. "That makes us even." He regretted the remark in the next half second as a large, black fist doubled him up, left him winded, gasping.

The man was not impressed by the insult, but satisfied by the blow. "That was lesson number one. As for you, Logan, for Christ's sake be careful. We don't want them broken. They're shit-all use to me broken."

I watched Greg slowly straighten. A scarlet patch the size of my palm blossomed just below his ribs. "We're not worth money, Rolland, if that's what you're thinking," I said. "He has no family and mine isn't worth bothering about, if you're thinking ransom. Took us a year to save to come here, just to get into this mess." And how I wished we had stayed at home and played out our fantasies on the hearthrug.

The American smiled at me. Polished porcelain teeth winked in the sun. "Ransom? It's a possibility. I know who you are. I've been doing some checking up on the two of you. You're Farris and Connor, of *Perspective* magazine, there's a London editor who might pay to get his queers back. But not as much as you're worth to me elsewhere. You're – how shall we say? Marketable commodities."

My throat tightened. The nightmare was coming true. Rolland was weighing us up as if we were horses. "There's not much market for men your age," he admitted. "What are you, twenties?" Greg actually laughed. The backhand compliment was that funny. You beat the calendar and land in the crap, where a face full of accordian pleats would have saved you the aggravation. Rolland ignored the chuckle. He spoke levelly, speculatively, like a dealer discussing the merits of an antique chair.

"There are buyers in Paraguay and Ecuador who will still pay for white meat even if it is a little ripe, and one in particular who likes it ripe. There's not much of a thrill overcoming a boy, so they tell me. Too easy. A man – now, a man has a pride about him, a man will fight, which makes the winning so much more satisfying. In your case, you'll be a little harder to market, being faggots and broken in. But we'll see. We'll see."

Every nightmare I had entertained since we blundered into this mess was about to play itself out. Rolland waved his minders forward, gave Logan his head to perform. I saw lengths of wire and was merely cynical as we were turned, our wrists secured behind us, tightly enough to restrict the circulation in my hands. I kept my mouth shut and prayed that Greg would hold his tongue.

"And now, to review the merchandise." Rolland relaxed as we were bound but the Webley remained levelled on us. "Strip them," he said offhandly to Logan, as if the man needed any encouragement. My blue shorts ripped down the side seam and were tossed onto the deck with Greg's red ones. I stood still. How far would it go?

Rolland wanted his "merchandise" undamaged, which set certain limits on it, but there is a lot that can be done with a man before he's damaged. We were shoved against the side of the boat, arched backwards, and pumped erect by a squeezing fist. The son of a bitch eye-measured us. My back ached on the woodwork. My cock stood up to attention in the sun as Logan's hairy fist squeezed my balls.

There was only one way to cheat them of their fun. I wonder if any other guy ever shot so prematurely or with as little fuss? Like a disappointed child deprived of a toy, Logan was angry. As if he had wanted to see me writhe and squirm, beg to be allowed the luxury of orgasm. He turned his attention to Greg. And, artfully manipulated, Greg paid for my small victory. It went on until Logan misjudged his prey. Greg had no control over it, only waited for the man to make his first mistake. The spattering of semen on Logan's chest was mocking.

Behind him, Rolland laughed. "So much for your nasty, peculiar little perversions, Logan. Do you mind if we get practical now?"

We were not surprised when Logan's understudies turned us belly-down over the side of the boat and spread us. Rolland disapproved as we were roughly probed. "You're not very virginal, are you?" I had three of someone's fingers in me, and they hurt like hell. What did the man want, a grip like a clenched fist? "No matter, the price is negotiable." The fingers pulled out of me, left me sore and smarting, and we were allowed to stand.

As I tried to work the kinks out of my spine, I saw the cruiser coming up alongside the lugger, the boat that had brought Rolland out. It was red, and I smothered an oath. We should have expected the likes of Rolland to have more than one boat. It was an error of judgement that was going to cost us dearly.

The second boat, with a crew of fresh divers, must have been on its way out over the reef when we went down. All they had to do was put Rolland and his minders aboard the *Spirit* and pull the cruiser away to a safe distance, so we would not look up, as we climbed the anchor chain, and see a second hull.

I was hurting after the mauling and guessed Greg was too. But it was only what we had expected, and less than could have happened. They hustled us across the deck as the red cruiser came alongside, nudging the lugger's stern. Logan dumped us over the side into the pleasure craft. Wrists wired up behind us and uncomfortably naked, we fell heavily. The cruiser was manned by three big, brawny Jamaicans, the smallest of whom made me look like a kid. There was nothing to do but wait and watch. Greg's face drew into taut lines. I gave him a warning look but he did not need me to tell him to keep silent, keep still.

We could not even see where we were going. They shoved us face down in the well of the boat, which hurt. The deck was roasting on my genitals. I heard Greg yelp under the noise of the big Evinrudes. "Okay?" I muttered, wondering how hard he had fallen, and on what. His teeth were closed on his lip but he nodded. I guessed his cock had just discovered the heat of the deck. We fidgeted, shuffled from hip to hip as we roasted. Logan watched without verbal comment, but the twist of his mouth must have been a smile.

The man made an art out of being a bastard.

The boat took off fast, headed inshore and then angled through the reefs toward the river. As we approached the shore they threw a tarpaulin over us. The river runs through the residential zone for several miles and having two naked men, bum to the sun, in your boat as you motor along the waterfront might not be such a bright idea.

Under cover of the tarp and the roar of the outboards, I said, "They hurt you, Greg?"

Silence, and then he said, "A bit. I'll survive. I'm just sore. How in hell did we get into this?"

"Got a better question," I said bitterly. "How do we get out?"

"He's not going to kill us, that gives us half a chance," Greg panted. "We could have been dead already if it wasn't for the trade in bodies . . . He might bring the dealers in to see us. Be cheaper than sending the stock out of the country and bringing it back if it's rejected." He paused and added, almost too quietly for me to hear, "I keep thinking about Shirley Hamilton's cousin. Jesus Christ. What about us? Men?"

"That would be customer's discretion," I said quietly while shivers ran down my spine like spiders' feet. "They wouldn't do that to us, not until we'd been marketed." Would they? I tried to think rationally. A customer whose perversions ran to tormenting a man could get a lot more laughs from the plight of a whole man than a eunuch. It made a warped kind of logic and I stopped speculating.

The speed cut back and we felt the wash of other craft going by. It was like a sauna under the tarp and we were suffocating before the boat came to rest at last. It bumped along the tyres cushioning a jetty. Dazzled as the tarpaulin was lifted, unsteady on our feet, we were manhandled out of the well of the boat. I found myself blinking at the clipped lawns and manicured hedges of a private landing stage at the back of a red brick mansion.

I recognized it from the photograph in that cutting given to us by Mrs. Mathers. It was very English, very nice, very expensive. You could smell the reek of money. Logan's heavy boys steered us down a crazy-paved pathway, away from the house. My soles protested the concrete. My primary concern was to find somewhere cooler and softer to put my feet. Before us was an ancient boathouse: timber walls, shingled roof, boarded up window. The side door was unpadlocked, we were shoved through it, and Logan stood looking at his property as momentary blindness overtook us.

"You could use a few lessons," he said – the first time we had heard him speak. The voice was whisky-hoarse, the accent as thick and slurred as young Malcolm's. "And I's the best to teach you how to be good."

"Why don't you go and fuck yourself?" Greg panted.

I held my breath, knowing how stupid it was to provoke him.

"Why don't I fuck you instead?" Logan hissed between bared teeth. "You want my fist in your teeth, white faggot trash? Or you prefer it up your hungry faggot arse?" He clenched his right fist in front of Greg's face. "You's gettin' both, pretty boy. I's goin' to teach you to like it."

The shed's door slammed on us. The padlock rattled as it was secured, and the show was over. Panting, Greg sank down to put his bare rump on an upturned bucket and lift his feet one at a time. "My bloody toes are burned off."

"Same here," I agreed. I sat carefully on the end of a workbench and peered at him in the gloom. "Greg, will you stop pushing."

"Pushing?" He wrenched at the wire about his wrists.

"You know what I mean! You're going to get Rolland or Logan, or both, angry enough to – teach you a lesson you won't forget. You want to be punished? They'd be happy to oblige!"

"I . . . know," he said quietly. "I've said my last. You want the truth?" Grey eyes glared at me in the blue dimness. "I thought he was going to get on and do it, right then. I'm still shaking so hard, I'm seriously considering throwing up."

"Oh, honey." I leaned my head against his. "Let's get this sodding wire off. Turn round."

It took the better part of half an hour for us to tease the wire from our wrists, and they were bleeding after our efforts. I untwisted the last loops, and by that time we had become accustomed to the near-darkness.

A standpipe lay by the wall. We bathed our hands and drank. The water was tepid, brackish. Then we took stock of our situation.

The windows were all boarded up. The double boat doors at the foot of the concrete rampway, fronting onto the river, were locked, and the side door through which we had been shoved was both locked and guarded. A pair of large hiking boots stood by the crack beneath it. Greg stretched out on the ground, squinted through the gap between timber and cement, and signed to me that he could see two guards and one gun.

We turned our attention to the boat doors. They were barred from the outside too, but the wood was so rotten it was splintering away from its rusted old hinges. Boring insects had eaten it away. I gave Greg a wink as I looked around for something to use as a chisel.

Nearby was a bin full of litter. I dumped it, found the remains of an aluminium can. The jagged edges of its lid bit into the splinters beside the hinges. They lifted like the spines of a hedgehog, leaving the rust-red hinge itself grabbing nothing.

"It'll take about an hour, and it'll drop off," Greg said with rich satisfaction. "So we can get out."

"Soon as it's dark, no worries," I agreed. "What time is it?"

Our watches had gone when our wrists were wired. Till that moment, absurdly, I had not even noticed. "About four," he guessed, peering at the lacerations about his wrists.

"So we've got a long wait. Wonder if they'll feed us?" I snaked both arms about his waist and pulled him against me, wanted hard, naked male body the whole length of me. He needed the human contact as much as I did. His arms went around me and held on. He was still shaking just a little. The mental image of Leroy Logan's enormous fist fulfilling various promises was enough to give me the shakes. My grip tightened possessively about the body I considered was mine. "Then the next thing we want's clothes," I said, deliberately attempting levity. "I won't have you displaying your charms for all and sundry."

"Or you," he seconded, and I felt his hands palm both my buttocks and squeeze. He tilted his head, listening. "Sounds like we've got company." He drew away from me and winked. "Don't want to provide them with free entertainment, do we? He'd love to see us together. And he's not going to."

We moved away from the boat doors so as not to draw attention to their frailty or our intentions. We heard the metallic rasp of the padlock, then sunlight blinded us. Rolland stood silhouetted in it. "I see you've got out of the wire. No matter. I assure you, this property is extremely well guarded, there is no way out of here. There is a man on this door who will shoot you down before you have gone three feet, after which I will patch you up and market you as shopsoiled goods."

He spoke levelly, without emphasis, and I felt the terrible certainty that he meant every word. I cleared my throat. "You deal in human bodies often?"

"Often enough." Was he gloating? "There are lucrative markets everywhere, for the gifted entrepreneur. Take care, won't you? I wouldn't like to have you shot."

"It would reduce our market value," I hazarded drily.

He turned back, on the point of leaving. "Naturally. And in the end that merely disadvantages you . . . Shopsoiled goods are cheap, remember. And cheap goods are disposable, used up, broken, discarded and replaced." He looked us up and down. "Cause trouble and Logan will have you. He has a box of the nastiest toys you can imagine. Something to do with leather knick-knacks, clamps and chains and so forth. I'm sure you know all about that." The cultured voice hardened to granite. "Whichever of you makes trouble, I'll give the other one to Logan until they can hear the screams across the river. It will be a pity to break you, but if you force my hand I shall have little alternative, you understand."

The door slammed back into place behind him. Rolland meant every syllable, and Logan was itching for his chance to play. It was like the sword of Damocles over our heads, each of us used to control the other. The man was no amateur. I went down by the door to watch the retreating feet. I saw just the pair of big hiking boots standing guard on us.

How good was the gorilla with the gun out there? Even a rank idiot stands a good chance of coming up the winner with a gun in his hand, but the weakness of guns is that they make a man complacent. And complacency is suicide.

The boatshed was at least cool and there was water on tap. We settled on the ground beside the concrete ramp, from there able to see out through the gap under the ill-fitting boat doors, watch the river traffic and catch a breeze. We were strung up like hawsers but we needed the rest. Logan stayed away until dusk, only looking into the shed to check on us as he went by. On his way out, I thought, going by his gaudy clothes and polished shoes.

Then we were alone again, only waiting for twilight to thicken into darkness. I studied Greg in the dimness, tried to play Rolland's part, evaluating how much a buyer might be willing to pay for such a creature as my lover.

A lot. A young man in the peak of physical condition, with well toned muscles and soft, brown skin, a luxurious head of hair and a beautiful face, large, shapely genitals and long legs, no matter his actual age, would be worth a small fortune. The fact that Greg is well "broken in" would bring the price down. There is a certain thrill about deflowering virgins that haunts us all to a degree. But Greg's spirit, his temper, would bump the price back up again.

He has the cutting edge of anger about him. Those grey eyes can glitter with fury and he can be dangerous. Damned dangerous. They would take a delight in breaking him, I knew. And I knew the awful means they would use to do it.

Sickened, I swallowed hard. I had to touch him then, to make the hideous imaginings go away. It isn't the same as the sex games played out between slave and master, where both players get a cheap thrill and afterward they buy each other a beer, and if the slave is sore here and there he counts it an even trade for his thrills. Genuine, unwanted agony, anguish, despair, the terror of mutilation, castration, death, don't even take place in the imagination of the suburban "slave", who knows it's a tough, sexy game within set limits.

This was different. God help us, this was real, and I was shit-scared.

I reached out and put one hand on his chest, stroked among the soft hair. I woke him from a half-doze he'd slipped into while we waited. It was almost too dim to see his face. Outside it would soon be dark and the daylight making ingress around the doors and windowframes was fading.

"Alex?" He stirred, wondered if it was time to move already. Then he realised I just wanted to be close for a while.

He was tense. I felt the taut stiffness in his sinews as he shuffled closer, against me. Hours of anticipation had made us nervy when there was probably no real need for nerves. I wanted his mouth. I wanted to feel his nipples on my tongue. I wanted to lick down his sides, where his skin is as smooth as silk, and salty, and sink my teeth into the softness of his arse.

He let me, held my head as I kissed the bite-brand on his buttock. I thrust my nose into the warm, musky nest of his groin and took his balls in my mouth. He smelt of Greg, and the sea. I did not arouse him or myself, we were much too tense, too strung out. But I felt as if I had him, owned him, just for a moment. He was mine. Tears stung my eyes but would not be shed. Did I sob?

"Alex?" Greg lifted me off him, rolled me over and held me

down. I was passive under him. "For Godsake, what is it, Alex? What's wrong? Did they hurt you before? I didn't think – "

Wrong? Nothing was wrong. Everything was wrong. "I love you," I told him. How long had it been since I had even bothered to say it to him. Weeks or months. Where is the need to say it? He bent down over me, kissed me hard enough to bring blood into my mouth, fingers knotted painfully into my hair, as if in vengeance.

"Greg?" He had me breathless, captive. His hands were like steel bands about my forearms. I did not have the energy, or the inclination, to resist. "What?"

"You're mine," he hissed in the near darkness. "Mine. I mean that."

I was not about to argue. Slowly his mouth gentled on my own. Our tongues began to twist and thrust, making love while our bodies were reluctant to rouse. There was no time for more. Greg's sharp ears heard the sounds from outside first. He lifted his head, leaving my lips bruised and swollen as he listened hard.

"What the hell is that?" he whispered.

I heard a flap of canvas and a creak of taut lines, the slap of water against the hull of a boat. Greg got an elbow under himself, climbed off me and sprawled beside the boat doors to look out.

"A yacht?" I asked as he wriggled away, blocking my view.

"I can't see," he muttered. And then, only moments later, he gave a fat chuckle. "Well, I'll be damned. Lady Luck's decided to give us a smile after all. Here, Alex, take a look at that."

It was a sight that took a weight off my shoulders. The *Spirit of Jamaica* had tied up at the landing stage. The sons of bitches had decided to have her too. She must have gone around the reef and made slow time up the river, against the current. I slapped Greg's bare backside and pulled him up into my arms.

"All our gear's aboard. They'll have taken the shotgun but there's enough goons around here for there to be plenty of guns. She's our ticket out of here."

"Not without the stuff we took out of the wreck," Greg muttered. "They'll have destroyed the plane by now, bet on it. Those dogtags, and the log, and that piece of ice, are all that props up our story. How would you like to go into court without them? Couldn't even get Lansing to print it, or

Perspective would be in court on libel charges."

"So we take back the goods," I mused. "They'll have the stuff in the house. Where? Safe, maybe?"

"If we're lucky," he agreed. "If we're really unlucky he'll just have destroyed the log and tags and that's the end of everything. We could go to the police but it'd be for the sake of going through the motions. No way they could touch him, and we'd be in deep, deep trouble, with Rolland right behind us with an axe . . . London's only a plane flight away. So," he added in that annoyingly accurate imitation of the accent, "is Australia."

"One step at a time," I told him. "Panic when the time comes. Even if he gets away with the insurance con there's going to be more. There's the trade in human bodies. There's Shirley's cousin, mutilated. That's a matter of record, and Mrs. Mathers ID'd the body. There's the fishy business of Jeff Mathers' death. There's what we know about Goldmark's ganja smuggling activities – if we can't find something in the house to hang that at least on him, Lansing ought to kick our backsides right out of his office. The US government will want Rolland extradited to answer narcotics charges even if the Jamaican government don't hang, draw and quarter him for trading in bodies. White tourist bodies. Ours."

"Like, maybe we're not the first he's dealt in?" He closed his eyes. "Jesus, I didn't think of that."

"Getting slow," I chided, and pulled him hard against me. I loved the feel of him, warm and hard and very naked. In other circumstances we would have turned on faster than it takes to tell. But not that night. My nerves were coiled like an overwound mainspring. I was literally incapable. "As soon as we get this sorted out," I said bluffly, "we'll fax the whole lot back to Lansing for the April edition, and the holiday can start again from scratch. How's that sound? We might work it out tonight."

"You believe that?" He held my head in gentle hands.

"Course I do," I lied. "We'll fax a week's work back to Lansing and ask for bonuses. It's the least he can do since we've worked damned hard this far. Now, kiss me, you luscious creature, and then let's work out some battle strategy. Getting out of this shed's the start, not the end of it."

He savaged my already crushed mouth and I must have left finger bruises on his hips. "The door should be easy," he whispered. "So rotten it'll fall off by itself soon. We could scuttle round the blind side of the shed and belt the goon across the back of the skull. Improve his brains. Lift his shooter. They'll have left the lugger for the night, so we can get some rags. Then, the house."

"Getting in should be no problem," I said slowly. "Searching it will be. The safe will be concealed, and even if we find it he won't have been thoughtful enough to leave it open. It's probably wired to an alarm system. If it is, we're dead."

"Or in Logan's hands," Greg said bleakly, averting his eyes.

"He hurt you, didn't he?" I asked. I knew he had. Deliberately, maliciously, for the fun of it, like a destructive child.

"Like I told you, I'll survive." He touched his knuckles to my cheek, a tiny admission of truth. "Why don't we do this the easy way, for Chrissake?"

"Which is?" I wondered if he was thinking what I was thinking.

"Find another shooter and cover each other, do the SAS act, sweep the house till we find Rolland. Stuff his Webley up his arse till he opens the safe for us and hands us the goods."

"Practical," I agreed.

"Which gets us the stuff, and a hostage," Greg went on. "But we're up the creek here, literally. If we take one of his powerboats everyone within five miles is going to hear it and they'll be right behind us."

"There's the *Spirit*," I suggested. "Quiet."

"Also slow as a tired snail, against the current," Greg added. "We'll get out okay but as soon as they see she's gone they'll be out after us in something that flies, and we're still dead men. Unless – " He stopped and bit his lip. "If you were Oliver Rolland or one of his goons, and your livestock had escaped in a boat, and you had to put your money on where they'd run, what would be your best guess?"

"Open sea," I said with a shrug. "So?" And then I saw his meaning, "Oh, clever lad. Very clever. So we take the *Spirit* upstream, right?"

"And they run themselves ragged checking every cove and cranny on the coast, and miles out to sea," he agreed. "Meanwhile we're upriver."

"And lost in the mangroves," I said thoughtfully. "It could work."

"Could?" he demanded as he stooped after the can we would use as a chisel to get out. "It had better work, lover, it's the only chance we're going to get."

I took the strange tool from him. "And if we've got Rolland, hostage with his own gun in his ear, we'll have some bargaining power. We can tie him down aboard the lugger and keep him out of harm's way. The goons'll run around like halfwits with the boss gone."

I turned my attention to the rotten wood about the hinge. Gnawing insects had done most of the work for me. Outside it was quite dark now. We heard the lap of the river against the boat ramp, the shouts and screams of children playing not far away, the hoarse cries of birds in the reeds. We took turns to chip away the worm-eaten wood, gouging out the rotting splinters around the hinges on the left-side door.

In half an hour Greg had to hold the dead weight of it to stop it giving way with a groan and falling broadside into the water. Being silent was the hardest part of getting out, the actual work was simple. We propped the door against its frame and stepped out into the moonlight.

8

THE night sounds were muted. We heard the bass thump of hi-fi, across the river, the hoarse voices of waterbirds in the marshes, the slap of the water against the hulls of the boats tied up by Rolland's landing stage. The *Spirit of Jamaica* was moored behind the red cruiser that had brought us in. The mustard yellow craft was hitched ahead of its stablemate. I gave the powerboats a sour look as we picked our way by.

Lights shone out of the homes on the other bank, and a few lights blazed from the windows of the red brick English mansion. It was impossible to get along the bank from the ramp to the landing without getting into the water, and we saw a tangle of rusting scrap iron breaking the surface. Greg gestured over his shoulder with one thumb, and we went around the boatshed, close to its peeling walls, barefoot and silent.

From the goon left to mind the door we heard a deep,

regular breathing rhythm. He was either in the process of jerking off or asleep and labouring for breath. Greg peeked around the corner of the shed, relaxed and beckoned me forward. The man was as much fat as muscular. He had a lot of weight to throw around in a fight but most of it looked like lard and he was slumped, suffocating in his own double chin.

The gun was an American police issue Colt revolver, left unattended on his knee. The kind of pistol that finds its way into the hands of the public with distressing ease, manufactured by the million and seemingly available on any street-corner in the rough quarter for a ten dollar pricetag. I reached for it, delicately picked it up in careful fingertips, and then not so delicately rapped it across the side of the minder's head. He woke for an instant in surprise and then returned to sleep. I doubt the fool even knew what had hit him.

No lights burned on the boats and we crept along to the landing. I glanced back at the guard on the boatshed's door. He appeared merely asleep. Anyone looking down from the house would see the same view now as an hour before. They probably thought they had us scared to death, and we would not take much guarding.

They were halfway right. I was certainly scared to death. What we were doing could get the pair of us abused within an inch of our lives, techniques of subtle torment that cynically parody sex, and leave no betraying marks. Logan would have the time of his life playing such games. As I watched Greg hop onto the *Spirit* I bit my lip hard. I recognized the very real possibility we were painting ourselves into the corner that would be our last.

Separated, one of us could be fed any story about the other. Rolland could keep me docile for a month by telling me how Greg had been mauled the night before, when in fact he had been dead for a week, or sold to a dealer in Paraguay a fortnight before.

We had one chance to get out of this with the promise of future survival. The gun was cold and heavy in my right hand and my fingers clenched like talons about it. I have not had much experience with handguns, but most Australians have handled rifles and shotguns, which are very common even in the cities. Allan, my uncle, was a target shooter, and as a kid I never passed up the opportunity to go to the club with him. The members' weapons are, by law, kept under lock and key in the club house. Not even Australians will allow the public to have handguns on the street. Allan had several, including a Luger, a rare War relic probably worth a fortune, and a magnum .44, the original "Dirty Harry" gun. It almost took the wrists off me until I grew accustomed to its donkey-kick.

We had a bright moon as the cloud cover parted for a moment. Pale white flooded the lugger as we went through its cabin for our belongings. As we had expected, the shotgun was gone. Our clothes were strewn over the deck, tipped out of the bag and left there.

The Hamair paperwork was also missing, but the idiots had left Mrs. Mathers' photograph album. They could not even have lifted the cover, just saw an album and tossed it away. My little camera was undamaged but the film was torn out of it. I had only just broken into a new roll, so little was ruined. I had stored the spent film with the raw stock in the coolest place I knew, under the groceries in the locker. Film can ruin in the heat.

If Rolland's minders had known that they would have guessed where to look. But no, my film was still there, out of the heat and dust under the motley assortment of groceries in their cardboard box. I gave a grunt of satisfaction and reloaded the camera.

We found jeans and teeshirts, running shoes – rubber soled, stealthy – and dressed quickly in colours that would merge with the dark. Greg fumbled about in the galley, armed himself with a butcher knife, honed like a razor. His experience with handguns is sketchier than mine. He shot skeets over the stern of his lover's schooner until handling shotguns is second nature to him, but he never actually owned a weapon or a licence. As a boy, however, he ran in the gutter. Knives seem to fit his palm all too easily.

The minder on the door of the boatshed remained still, silent. He was breathing heavily, not quite suffocated by his jowls. I peered at him in the moonlight as we stepped off the lugger. No one noticed us go by as we crept up the crazy-paved pathway to the mansion's rear door. Rubber soled sport shoes were silent. We stood at the servants' entrance for some time to listen.

Lights burned within, a radio was playing, but the kitchen was deserted. We smelt the stale after-odours of boiled cabbage and minced beef. A hinge squealed as I gave the door a push, and we found ourselves in an old-fashioned scullery. The house harked back to days of elegant living, a leftover from the dreams of Empire that made Jamaica into a vast slave labour camp.

We padded through the scullery and kitchen, and stepped cautiously into the lamplit hallway. There were signs of life in a downstairs parlour where the radio played Jimmy Cliff records, soft reggae, calypso with gospel lyrics. We listened at the door, heard the voices of two men, the chink of bottle and glass. Rolland was not one of them.

We found five other doors on the ground floor. The rooms behind them were empty. Like burglars, we went up the stairs. I wished we had another pistol, to cover each other, but nothing moved on the landing or on the second floor. Framed oil paintings of sailing ships drew my eyes as we went through like shadows, landing to landing, room to room.

Most of the men were out for the night, and the servants with them. I expected Rolland to be absent too, and drew contingency plans as we mounted the stairs to the top floor. If the man was gone, we would still have to get into the safe. It came down to the minders drinking in the downstairs parlour. Under the gun, they would be tractable enough. If they had access to the safe was another question. We could be in dead trouble – or just dead.

But Rolland was at home. I took it as an omen. He was in the private rooms on the top floor. Yellow light spilled from around a closed door, and we heard voices, his, and that of a girl. She was speaking quietly, the words slurred with a soft island accent. In the spilling lamplight we shared a tense look. A second person in the room complicated everything.

I brought the gun up, cocked it and set my lips against his ear, not daring even to whisper too loudly. "You grab the girl, get her out of the way, fast as you can." He nodded once, poised by the door as I took the knob in my left hand.

As I went through the door, I levelled the police revolver on the bed. Rolland lay draped over his pillows. The Jamaican girl crouched over him, buff naked, lifting her head away from a fellatio session. She took a deep breath to scream at the sight of the gun. Greg had the naked, writhing little body tucked under one arm before she could scramble away. His hand clamped over her mouth to silence her.

The door clicked shut. Rolland lay there like a dead log, puffing and wheezing. His erection wilted before our eyes. With the door closed, Greg lowered the girl onto the end of the bed but kept his hand over her mouth. "Are you a guest here?" he asked, just above a whisper. Vast, chocolate-brown eyes blinked up at him. She was doped. "Prisoner?" he asked patiently. "You a prisoner, girl?" At last she wagged her head against the gag of his hand. "I'm going to let you go, love," he told her. "Don't make a sound or they'll hear downstairs, understand?"

Another nod. He took his hand from her mouth and she was silent. A pretty little vixen of a creature, pixie-cute and very young. I wondered what price she would fetch at market. It was obscene. "Get your clothes on," Greg whispered at her. "Wait till we've gone, then get out of here. Understand? Get out and go home." She blinked stupidly up at him and slumped onto the bed.

Rolland was dopey too, irises dwindled to thin blue rings about vast, dilated pupils. Greg came around the king-sized bed as I put the muzzle of the Colt into the man's ear. My lover smiled indulgently at our prey. "Tough luck, old horse." He held the butcher knife in clear view and inclined the lethal tip of it toward the American's crotch. "Now, if you're a good lad you'll keep both balls intact, and if you're not, I'm going to take this piece of steel and do something very nasty with it. You do believe me, don't you?"

There is a cutting edge of the survivor about Greg. Angry, he is magnificent. Rolland believed implicitly. He nodded mutely, white to the lips with healthy fear. Had the bastard ever been on the receiving end before? I doubted it. This must be a whole new experience for him.

Greg found his slacks and threw them at him, and I took the Colt from his ear as he struggled to dress. The girl was clutching a sheet around herself, blinking vacantly at the performance. Rolland pushed his feet into expensive Italian shoes and pulled a leisure shirt over his flabby paunch. Still worried about the girl, Greg pried open the pretty little thing's eyelids to look into dilated pupils. She was coffee brown, confused and terrified. It was a shame such a lovely mouth had to be wasted on the likes of Rolland.

The American was pale and sweating. His eyes never strayed from the revolver. Greg left the girl, the butcher knife held loosely in his right hand. Lamplight shone on the blade. It achieved what the gun had failed to do, winkling words out of Rolland's mouth.

"For Christ's sake, you're insane if you think you can get away with this. There's no way out of here."

I gave him a push into a high-backed chair. "Just say what

you're supposed to say and you'll stay in one piece. Got it?" I asked with acid sweetness. "Otherwise these two *faggots* are going to carve you into tiny little pieces and feed you to the fish. We want the dogtags, all the paperwork, and the diamond. Give them to us, and you keep both balls. You follow? - "

His brain was working again. Panic overcame whatever he had been smoking. "You're private investigators?" He wheezed. "Fuzz?"

"You already know who we are," Greg said sharply. "We work for a London news magazine." He produced a smile like a cobra. "We took a vote and decided to make you an assignment, since you've buggered the first decent holiday we've had in years. Now, my fingers are starting to itch on this knife and I don't give a toss what gets cut off around here. The stuff, Rolland. Right now."

Still, the American resisted. I watched the tip of the blade slice through the leisure shirt, baring his flabby chest. The point circled one tiny nipple. Greg would never have actually used the knife, but as a frightener it was magic.

In the first place we needed our gear, and if Rolland was bleeding all over us and screaming he would be useless. In the second, we required him in one piece as a hostage. Lastly, Oliver Rolland was the kind to squeal at the slightest twinge of pain, and he knew he had a force of his "rude boys" just downstairs. Cut the boss, and we could find ourselves killing them, which complicated everything with allegations of murder.

But Greg can and will bluff with shirt of your back at stud poker. There is no viciousness in him, but Rolland was not to know that. The bluff was a rich one and the American began to panic as the tip of the knife pressed into the nub of his left nipple. I waited to see some tiny trace of blood. Rolland surrendered with a moment's grace.

"Safe," he yelped. "They're in the safe. Jesus Christ, you can't!" His skin was bright with sweat as he gaped down at the knife that could, at a flick of the wrist, take that nipple off.

"Combination?" Greg demanded. The knife was ominously still.

The numbers rapped out so fast, we knew it had to be the truth. Lying takes longer and Rolland was too doped, too scared, to lie adeptly. Greg lifted away the knife and I held the Colt on him while he scrawled the combination on the note pad beside the replica antique telephone.

"Wired?" I asked as Greg began to rummage through the wardrobe. He found an assortment of gaudy ties. The man's taste was execrable. Several of the ties bound Rolland's wrists behind his back. One of them, looped over his gullet and tied to his hands, would keep him quiet. "Is it *wired*?" I hissed. "Alarms?"

"Yes." Rolland seemed paralysed as he was tied, his eyes still on the knife. As if he had watched Logan play cruel games and knew what could happen to him at a whim, if we were in the mood to be spiteful, nasty. I could not help remembering Malcolm Dennison. Anger shook me and my fingers dug into Rolland's arm.

Greg checked the girl as I hustled him to the door and held him by the loop across his throat. If he moved, he choked, so he didn't move. "She's zonked out of her bloody skull," Greg said disgustedly. "I don't think she's going to make it out of here."

"So she stays," I whispered, listening at the door. "It won't be for long if we can get off the estate with the stuff . . . Leave her, Greg. She'll sleep it off."

Then we were out, the door closed behind us, and going down the stairs a little clumsily with Rolland manhandled between us. I let him lead the way. The safe was in the library on the ground level, under a rug, in the polished parquet floor. And it was wired to an in-house alarm. Rolland pointed out the mechanism, a switch on a panel under the writing desk, and I turned it off. Greg lifted the rug to expose the hatch in the floor. The cover lifted off and we saw the sunken safe.

The tumblers spun left and right. I gave Rolland a bleak look. If it did not open, he would pay the price. But it opened with a soft *click*. We did not dare put on a lamp, and Greg opened the curtains to let in what moonlight we had. It struck across the floor and into the pit of the safe, just enough for us to make out the contents.

Rolls of American banknotes, a whole tray of chipped ice, emeralds, diamonds, rubies. The log book from the plane was in a plastic bag, old man Hamilton's RAF dogtags on top of it, and the Hamair paperwork alongside. And we had won a bonus. They kept their weapons in it too. We traded the Colt revolver for a pair of matching Uzi machine pistols and several spare clips for each. Our twelve gauge and boxes of ammunition were stored with these heavier firearms. For insurance we took these too.

Greg rummaged at random through the rest of the safe. I saw ledgers and smiled. Rolland's books, the set kept under lock and key. Little polythene bags of white powder. An address book. A shipping schedule. Records of activities that were probably enough to send Rolland away for life, if not actually hang a noose around his neck.

His face was drawn taut as he watched us appropriate his paperwork. We took it all, closed the safe down and replaced the rug. Rolland whimpered. With luck, the minders, whom Shirley Hamilton had referred to as merely "gorillas", would not have access to the combination. In that case, they would never know what had been taken, if anything. If the girl who had been servicing Rolland had wits enough to keep her mouth shut, it was just possible the bodyguards might assume Rolland had simply gone out for the night, rather than being removed forcibly from the estate.

I had begun to think optimistic thoughts as Greg bundled up the gear and I manhandled Rolland toward the library's french windows. Beyond them I saw a shrubbery, and beyond that, the river. We could be seen on the way down to the landing, but it would be blind fate if we were.

I had my hand on the polished brass handle, the french windows open a crack, when Rolland made his move. He lurched sideways, crashed into the heavy, oak writing desk. It did not move, but the lamp toppled and fell to the floor with a clatter that would have raised the dead. The loop across his gullet was cutting off his air but he managed a strangled cry before I could slap my hand over his mouth and put him down.

He flattened out on the floor behind the desk and Greg dove into the concealment of an enormous leather recliner. The windows onto the terrace stood open, a breeze stirring the flimsy curtains. I cursed beneath my breath as we heard the sounds of movement in the parlour.

"Don't shoot," I hissed at Greg. I had my knee in the curve of Rolland's back to pin him down. "They'll hear shooting for miles!"

"They're going to think we went through the windows," Greg muttered as heavy feet thundered outside the library door.

After years of working together we think alike. We ducked down out of sight as the library's door slammed open and the lights came on. A babble of livid swearing announced two of the men who had manhandled us in the boat. They dove for the open french windows. When they had gone by us, we moved without a sound.

There is a satisfying sensation about the impact of a solid object against the skull of an ape who has earned the blow. The Uzis landed almost together, dropped Rolland's men before they even knew we were there, and then Greg and I dragged them back into the library. Greg cut the silk cords from the curtains and we took time to truss them thoroughly.

They were going to scream blue murder as soon as they came to, but until Logan and the boys arrived home there was no one to hear. If the minders were out on the town they might not be back till morning. I stood, hauled Rolland to his feet. He whimpered very quietly, as if realising for the first time, it was for real. He struggled halfheartedly and I tightened my grip. The muzzle of the Uzi combed through his hair. "You want me to belt you across the skull and carry you? Just give me a reason to!" The threat stilled his threshing and we got moving. The only sounds from his lips were choking gasps as he fought to breathe.

The way out was simple. Greg bundled up the collection of oddments and I hustled Rolland out, through the shrubs and across the lawns to the riverbank. The moonlight was bright enough to have betrayed us, had anyone been watching. No one was.

The lugger had tied up nose to tail with the red cruiser. On the landing, I released the loop across Rolland's throat and gave him a push onto the boat. He fell heavily, relieved just to get an unobstructed breath. "What about him?" I whispered as we untied.

"Chain locker," Greg said quietly. "We can rope the hatch shut and forget about him. We've got to move this thing. Fast."

It was the one place on the lugger that was secure, small and fairly soundproof. It was also dark, cold, uncomfortable. I set down the Uzi and picked Rolland up, shoving him where we wanted him. "Your cabin, Rolland . . . You can yell to your heart's content," I told him as I loosened his hands. The confinement was less than he deserved.

The hatch slammed on him and I tied it down with the bonds I had just taken from his wrists. He screamed a torrent of invective as I hopped back on deck. There, only the faintest murmur was audible from the locker. The lugger was loose and I punted her bow out into the river, away from the cruiser's stern, jumped back aboard as Greg rigged one sheet.

If one moment was especially dangerous, that was it. All it would take to finish us off was for Leroy Logan to be on his way back to base, and see us. We were just out of reach of the powerboats, with one small sail up on a sailing craft that was as antique as she was beautiful. We had the Uzis, and we had bound the house guards, but Logan would see where we were headed, and a river was not the place to pit big Evinrude outboards against sail, especially with wind and current dead in opposition.

My heart hammered at my ribs as Greg took the wheel and I set about hoisting the rest of the canvas. The booms swung over as far as they would go. We were sailing within only a few degrees of the wind – a peculiar feeling, making way with the wind in our faces.

And that wind was on the rise. I considered trying to start up the old Gleniffer as I joined Greg. The sky was inky black. A pall of cloud slid over the moon as we watched. In the east, a weather front marched over the horizon like a range of mountains.

"Better listen to the radio," I said. I went below for the transistor. "You see that?" I nodded into the east. "That's not Rita, but she's coming, and she's not far away."

A current affairs programme was on. We waited through the show for a weather bulletin. There must be one, with the hurricane hovering somewhere off the island's east coast. Kingston would be battening down, expecting the wholesale destruction that can happen any season, and often does.

She was out there like a monster, getting bigger by the hour, but Rita was still hours out in the Caribbean. There was huge damage on Haiti, Barbados, Martinique and the Windward and Leeward Islands. Kingston was on alert. Ships and large pleasure craft were pulling out of the harbour, lest they be smashed together at their moorings, or tossed up onto the quay.

Visions of Cyclone Tracy haunted me. Rita had been tagged "the storm of the decade". Scientists said Tracy struck Darwin with the collective energy of an atomic bomb. And we were sailing straight into Rita under sails, in a boat older than we were.

"Great," Greg muttered as I spooned myself against his back, both arms about him to make him lean back against me as he piloted the lugger. He held her in the deepwater barge channel. I pulled him closer, and he rested back against me, warm, familiar. I began to relax for the first time in hours. "This all we need. The damned hurricane as well."

"It could work with us," I said thoughtfully.

"Could swamp us," he retorted.

"True, but a hurricane equals pure chaos, and in the mess we can do what the hell we like. How's the saying go? In confusion there is profit. For a while they're not going to know who's dead or alive. It could be just what we need."

"If we don't sink," he added cheerfully.

"If we don't sink." I tightened my arms about him. "Christ, I love you."

"There's no need to sound so shocked about it," he reproved. "Only just realised, have you?"

"No. Maybe I just feel it more tonight than I have in years." I kissed the side of his neck, licked along his jaw, with its sandpaper stubble.

"The feeling's mutual," he told me in that growly, intense way he has of making confessions only I'm intended to hear. He twisted around to kiss me, just a quick peck, as he was trying to keep the lugger in the deep channel.

It was not too difficult. The markers outlining the way for the barges were like catseyes, reflecting even a glimmer of light. We had every rag up, trying to use a wind that gusted strongly, just off the bow. I stood back to let Greg handle it and admitted how lucky we were that his first lover's heart had been in sail rather than some other rich man's amusement. Sports cars or French antiques.

The river cuts almost due east and the current was dead against us. We were going to make slow time, and we knew it. We tacked to and fro in the channel, zigzagging to employ every breath of air. It was exhausting, but as minutes became half an hour and the Rolland estate disappeared off the stern we knew we were out and clear.

By midnight we had put five miles between us and the minders. It was possible Logan would be home by now, but I was sure he would make that knee-jerk assumption, and head seaward in one of the powerboats. He did not have the brains to handle logic. The wind was strong and fresh, carrying all sound away. If he was on the water already we would not hear his engine noise.

We must have been six miles upriver when Greg pointed off to starboard. "What is that, a tributary? Big enough for us, you think?"

Banks of reeds girdled the mud flats. A few hundred yards

143

from the river, we would be invisible. The tributary stream looked wide enough, even though manoeuvring might be difficult. "We don't draw much water," I said over the wind. "Give it a go."

The booms swung over as we turned into the stream. The canvas flapped, spilled the wind, and I trimmed, reefed back one sheet as the lugger heeled hard over to put the deck on a cruel angle. Greg peered ahead into the inky gloom, his face set into taut lines of concentration.

"I'm going to run us aground," he muttered. "What time's low tide?"

"About now," I guessed, recalling the fishermen's charts to mind.

"So even if I do ground us we'll float off." He put the wheel hard over and swore. "That was close."

I felt the drag on the starboard bow as she slid by the mudbanks. "Look, we'll be safer if we do run her nose in and wait to float off," I speculated. "The wind's getting up and this bucket is going to bob like a cork in a bathtub."

"Right." He put the wheel over again. "But I want to choose where and how she grounds, not just let it happen! Reef another sheet, Alex, let's take some of the sting out of it before it happens."

Only minutes later he called sharply, "Grab something!" And I closed both hands around the nearest boom, expecting the shocking jolt as the bow bit deeply into the reeds and mud. It would suck her in, hold her safely, and Greg seemed satisfied by the angle at which she had hit. The tide would float us off in the morning, and we had a bulwark against the wind for the night.

And we were confident we were well hidden. Greg tied down the wheel, helped me reef her canvas. Then we stood in the bow and looked at the sky. The moon and stars were gone. The weather front was almost on top of us now.

The tributary was wide enough to turn the boat around – just. If the hurricane came up quickly we would be in deep trouble, manoeuvring broadside to the wind. Greg put the transistor on as I made tea and hunted up a makeshift supper.

They gave a bulletin every half hour as Rita came closer, but the forecasters swore it was twelve hours out. We had the whole morning and early afternoon to find a safe haven for the boat and ourselves.

Tired and overwrought, we ate bread and cherry jam,

bought in Lucea just that morning. It seemed a century ago. We ate mechanically and in silence. The twin Uzis lay on the galley's work bench, squat, black shapes that did little to reassure. They would go to the Kingston police as part of the evidence. Although there are automatic weapons galore in the ghettoes, arming the gangs that rule there, they are not legal. I wondered how many of them were imported by Rolland, smuggled under the Goldmark banner, listed as machine parts or refrigerators on some manifest. Another lucrative arm of the illicit enterprise.

"I'll look in on Rolland," I offered as Greg threw rugs onto the narrow little bed.

"He won't have escaped," he said tiredly. "Forget him."

Still, I unroped the chain locker's hatch and angled the kerosene lamp into the darkness. The man was cramped between the anchor chain and the bulkhead, hugging himself and whimpering as the effects of his dope wore off, leaving him cold and angry.

"Connor, is it?" He peered past the lamp. "I'm going to take a delight in watching Logan bust you."

"What, and spoil the merchandise?" I asked acidly.

"No sale for you," he snarled. "I want you for myself."

"Lust, Ollie?" I mocked. "You Septic Tanks never cease to amaze me. I thought business came before pleasure."

"Business?" He made a lunge forward and I slammed the hatch on him. His voice carried through it with threats and promises. "I'm making you my business!" he shouted. "You hear me, Connor?"

"I hear you." I secured the hatch again. "Save your breath."

"I'm going to feed your balls to you!" he screamed.

There was more, all of it disgusting and chilling, but I stopped listening. I had no doubt that he would fulfil every promise if he got half a chance. Logan would be delighted to do everything in the book to us, and then improvise. If we survived that long. I doubted we would. I collected one of the Uzis, which Greg had left on the galley's workbench, and took it to bed. Rolland was shouting as much for his own benefit as to put the frighteners on us. He must be terrified for the first time in his life, I realised, and fluffing his feathers defensively. Like a monkey flashing his balls at an enemy. Just so much empty show.

Greg was already sound asleep when I returned to the cabin. I turned the lamp down low and stood looking at him for some time, savouring the sight of all that was mine. All I had come so close to losing. He had sprawled on his belly, the rugs loose around his hips. Anger shook me as I remembered the abuse he had already taken, out on the bay. Logan was going to answer for that, one way or another.

"Shove over, honey," I whispered as I slid in under the rugs. He came to for a moment, murmured in protest, then wriggled over and reached for me to pull me down. He was asleep again in the same second, surrendering to fatigue. We had a night's grace and animal survival instinct urged us to make the most of it.

Our situation was fair. We had the evidence, the culprit and our liberty. I put my head down and felt sleep tug at my mind at once. Now, we must keep that liberty, get to Kingston – and stay away from a hurricane called Rita.

9

A CRACK of daylight woke me. For a blind instant I did not know where I was, only that something was wrong, that I had to get up and move, the old reflex, fight or flight. It was very early, dawn still half an hour away. Memory returned with an uncomfortable jolt. We were in trouble. Again. I groaned.

Greg had been awake for a long time. He was bright-eyed, smiling at me, his whiskery chin propped in his palm as he studied me with a quizzical, amused, affectionate expression. He didn't say a word as I woke, just leaned over and kissed my forehead. His stubble raked me there but even that was so familiar as to be a welcome caress.

"Greg?" I spoke softly, tried to tune in to him. All I had to do was open up to him and feel it.

"Been watching you sleep," he said. No, he purred. Husky, sexy, his voice thick with emotion. "Just been thinking to myself."

"Thinking what?" I rubbed my palms up and down his arms to feel the whipcord of his sinews, muscle like spring steel under brown velvet skin. Male, beautiful, like the scent rising from his body, some heady concoction of musk, sweat, him.

"Just thinking how much I need you," he said with painful candour. "How bloody lucky I am to have you. How beautiful you are. How much I want you."

It was a litany I had least expected. There is a nice, old-world saying: Greg is my heart. I seemed to spend the first twenty-eight years of my life searching for him. I ran with the pack, bedded with so many lovers I can't even remember their faces, resigned myself to a lifetime of friendly sex devoid of love. And then I saw Greg, leaning on the wall of the Upland Goose Hotel in Port Stanley, and I was home.

I tugged him into my arms and held on. I can fall in love with him all over again any Tuesday. "My honey," I said into his hair, hardly trusting myself to speak.

"D'you want me?" he asked quietly against my throat. I felt his tongue there. "Want to fuck me, while there's time?"

"Is there time?" I was half teasing, half hopeful. My body turned on with a will of its own.

"It isn't even dawn yet." He sucked on my adam's apple, which bobbed as I swallowed. "Want to?"

"Yes." I smiled against his hair. "I had you last time."

"Doesn't matter. I don't keep a list." He lifted his head, rubbed our chins together, whiskers scratching on whiskers. "What d'you want, lover?"

"What do I want?" I lifted him on top of me. The weight of his body pressed me into the foam rubber mattress. The feel of his skin, the sound of that husky, sensual voice, had me achingly aroused already. My cock slid along his, as hot as his, as hard. He had been turned on for some time. "You know damned well what I want. I don't think there's time."

He wrinkled his nose at me. "Told you, the sun's not even up yet. The sky's dim but the big wind hasn't started, the storm won't get here till noon, so the radio said. And by that time we'll be far, far away." He licked my mouth, nibbled my lower lip.

"Got a lot of work to do today," I warned. "Don't want to make you sore, have you hopping around later."

He wriggled against me to rub his cock against my hip. "You trying to tell me you don't want to fuck me all of a sudden? I just don't believe it!"

I slapped his backside, decided the impact of palm and voluptuous cheek felt wonderful, and slapped him again. "I'm not telling you anything of the sort. Just hop it and get whatever it was you were frying eggs in."

He winked at me and slid out of bed. I did not move a muscle as he padded away to bring back a bottle of safflower oil. He set it aside and took the rugs off me. His cock was a beautiful, eight inch weapon nested in chestnut curls, brighter than the hair on his head. I leaned over to kiss it, sucked it into my mouth.

He poured a little oil into his palm and stroked the viscous fluid the length of my own cock. I'm no longer than Greg but I'm thicker. I arched back, watched him work as my body came to life, my breathing erratic. He oiled himself, opening and relaxing his muscles, clever fingers busy where I couldn't see them. I kicked the rugs over the side of the bed.

As he straddled me I gave a wounded moan. He held my cock in one hand and moved it where he wanted it, lowered his weight onto it, bringing the kind of pleasure that is so intense it almost hurts. He took me slowly, stroked his own cock as he went. It was a minute before I felt the softness of his buttocks on my thighs and he took a deep breath.

"That's got you." He sounded breathlessly smug. "I've got it all."

Lush with delight, saturated by it, I was paralysed. He leaned forward, hands on my chest, pinched my nipples as he rocked his hips. He moaned deeply, head tipped back. Tousled head and blue jaw made him look like an urchin whore as he rode me. I gave him my hands, fondling his genitals. He throbbed in my palms and caught his breath.

Grey eyes looked down at me, almost blind. He clenched about me, it felt as if he were massaging me with his insides. My nose filled with his musk and I tossed my head on the pillow in abject surrender to whatever he wanted to do with me. My hands slid up to play with his chest. He rocked on me until neither of us could bear much more.

Time was a meaningless concept. My heart was trying to jump out of my chest when he took my hands to his groin and put them where he had to have them. As I began to stroke and pull he fell forward to savage my mouth. I slipped my hand around, fingers searching for his beseiged anus. I shivered as I felt the slide of my cock, through my hand and into him, and out again as he worked. It was too much for me. I came with a cry into his mouth, felt him stiffen and roll his muscles around me as if to suck me dry. Then he came with a breathy curse. Wet heat splashed between us.

He lay limply on my chest. I lifted his head to look at him and kissed around his mouth while he was still panting. He yawned in my face. "Jesus, I needed that," he admitted, self-mockingly. "Was I selfish?"

"Stupid question," I chided. My fingers were still exploring where we were joined. My softened cock rested comfortably in hot, oily muscle. "Even if you were – which you weren't – you're going to fuck me senseless later, so what about it?"

"I'll hold you to that," he warned, eyes dancing.

"Nah." I palmed his cock. "Hold me to this."

He smothered me with a kiss for a moment and slid away. "What about a dip over the side to wash off? It's going to be a scorcher – listen to the wind. It's starting to get up now."

He was right, it was getting wild. The lugger heaved gently as the water began to chop. I dragged myself out of bed, dived the stern with him for a few seconds, to bathe, not to swim. We got out again quickly, before the leeches discovered us. We had too much to do, too far to go, to waste time playing. We also had a prisoner, and he had been in the chain locker for many hours. Time to let him out.

Past time. The locker smelt of urine and Oliver Rolland was spitting blood. Sometime during the night he had reined back on his panic and in the cold blue light of day he was out to make trouble. A glance at his stubbled, pudgy, ferret face and I knew what he would say.

The cabin smelt of sex as I took him up on deck. He curled his lip at me in scorn but the jibes and insults were not forthcoming. Perhaps he assumed provocation would earn him a beating. Perhaps he was right. My temper was short after the threats and promises made to me last night.

Greg was on deck, shaving while he waited for a weather bulletin on the transistor. He looked like a water sprite and I was in no mood to let Rolland verbally abuse him and get away with it. I had a Uzi in my hands, and Rolland gave it the respect it deserved.

In fact, he was talking business when he did find words. His tone was surly, forcedly civil. "You're making a big mistake. Ask Farris. Even if you haven't got enough brains to give yourself a headache, maybe he has."

I gave him a push toward the stern. "Shut it, mate. I don't want to hear."

"Big mistake," he went on as if he had not heard a word. "You could turn this to your advantage. Where's your business sense?"

"I said shut it!" I prodded his shoulder with the snub,

squat muzzle of the machine pistol.

"You mean you don't want to get rich in a hurry?" Rolland unzipped his pants, turned his back on me and emptied his bladder over the stern. I took a look at the equipment. "Adequate" was a word that leapt to mind. "Ransom, shithead. A hundred thousand," Rolland offered as he zipped up. "If you take me to the nearest phone, right now."

"Not interested." I sounded quite indifferent. It was not entirely the truth. If the hundred thousand was in pounds, sterling, it was very attractive. Greg and I could live happily on that. If Rolland let us get out of Jamaica to live at all.

"Not enough?" His face screwed up against the brightening sky. He had the look of a man a good deal older, and not healthy. "I'll double it."

"If you'll double it, you'll triple it," I said drily. "What's money, when the alternative is life or a rope?"

The lines about his eyes, the smoker's blight, deepened as he glared at me. He seemed to be doing mental arithmetic, and at last he nodded. "All right, triple. Three hundred grand, if you take me to a phone right now."

"Pounds," I stipulated. "Yank funny money won't do."

"Bastard," he hissed. "All right. Pounds."

I stood aside, gestured with the Uzi for him to move forward. Greg had finished his shave and the weather report was on the transistor. Rita was coming in, just short of the Jamaican coastline now. And Jamaica is a pocket-sized nation. "Guarantees?" I asked, playing out the word game with him. Greg heard the query and looked up, wondered what I was talking about. I winked at him and his eyebrows rose speculatively.

"Get me to a phone," Rolland muttered, "and you can keep some of the ice you lifted out of my safe. There's a million in cut gems there."

"You must take us for the biggest nongs in captivity." I shoved him roughly onto the deck. He sat against the side planking as I perched beside Greg and draped my left arm about my lover's shoulders. "Hear that, Greg? You hear what this creature's offering us? Cut gems that were lost in an aircrash last year. Christ, if we tried to fence even one out of the cache —"

"We'd be inside ourselves," Greg finished. He gave Rolland a hard look. "They're the same gems Hamair was carrying, aren't they?" The man made no attempt to deny it. "Even you can't get rid of them. You've had to wait till the

150

heat cools off. It'll be another year, maybe two, before you can break the collection up and market individuals, and you might have to recut the big stones to do it."

Rolland's mouth twisted. Greg handed me a mug of sweet black coffee. "Cash, then," Rolland offered. "I can't raise that kind of bread overnight but there's fifty grand in the safe. You probably saw it."

"We probably took it," Greg said acidly. The strategic lie. The money was still there, but Rolland did not know that. He had been flat on the floor when we rifled the safe.

He paled, his skin assumed the colour of candlewax. "I have sources," he muttered. "I can get more, but not till tomorrow. It has to come from Miami and there's a big wind coming, nothing's going to be flying."

"A likely story." I sipped my coffee. "A phonecall from you, and the only thing getting off that plane would be an army of minders. Just how stupid do you think we are?" He opened his mouth to protest but I turned my back on him. "Save your breath, Ollie, it's not our style even if I did think there was the slightest chance of getting away with it."

Greg seemed to deliberate over the proposition. "I could get used to being a creature of leisure." Then he shook his head. "Too many sins you have to atone for, old son," he told Rolland. "Hamilton was too good to end that way, with his skull stoved in and his reputation in shreds. And Jeff Mathers. Yeah, we knew about him. Then there's Peter Cole, Sandra Hamilton's cousin. You remember. The little black boy with the missing balls. You want to tell us about him?"

"He was snooping," Rolland said defensively. "I caught him stealing and boxed his ears. He pulled a knife. I was angry. I sent him for a whipping. The little shit was due it. I don't know anything else about him."

"You sent him to Logan?" I asked quietly. Rolland looked away. "You sent him to that animal?"

"To be punished!"

"And Logan had him for eight weeks," Greg said softly. "Shot up, gelded, screaming his little lungs out in your house, and you didn't know a thing about it? I just don't believe it."

"Believe what you like," he snarled.

Angry, I stood over him, watched his face draw into a mask. "Oh, I will. I remember everything you threatened for us last night. I imagine it's pretty much what Peter suffered." I shaved quickly and patted dry. "Keep an eye on him, Greg.

I'm going to shoot a few frames. You're getting all of this, I hope."

Greg tapped his head. "As good as black and white. The copy only needs typing up."

The wind was howling in the lugger's lines as I cocked the nasty little camera and framed Rolland through the lens. He tried to turn his face away. "Keep on the way you're going," I said unpleasantly, "and I'm going to tie you hand and foot and get my shots anyway." He glared up at the camera and I took a series of frames. With luck they would head Greg's copy. The story was a beauty, rich enough to buy us another holiday, since this one was thoroughly down the drain. Paris, Amsterdam, Athens, San Francisco. They may be a little short on yellow beaches, but they have various qualities to recommend them.

As I put away the camera Greg unfolded the road map and turned it to match the compass bearings. I joined him, just forward of the wheel, and dropped a kiss on the back of his neck. I no longer cared if Rolland saw. "Tell me if I'm reading this right," he mused, and traced a line with one finger, away from our position and cross country.

"Being a clever lad?" I looked over his shoulder, dividing my attention between his calculations and Rolland. The American glared up at the Uzi in my hand but was still and silent.

"Trying to be," Greg admitted. "Look at this. We're in this tributary, there's that hill. Look at the compass. Know what's about five miles on the other side of the hill? Falmouth."

"Falmouth, and our car." I whistled. "It's a ten mile hike, up and down, by the looks of it, through the forest. We might manage it by noon if we get moving, maybe stay over in Falmouth when Rita hits, go on to Kingston when the storm's gone through. How much money have we got?" We were getting low.

"Enough," he judged. "Be safer in a highrise hotel than on the road. We've got to find somewhere safe for the boat, too. Some place where she can ride out the wind and not smash herself to driftwood."

I frowned down at the American. "What about Rolland? You reckon he's fit for a five mile hike up hill in this heat?"

"Search me," Greg said quite maliciously. "I can think of nothing more amusing than watching him have a heart attack. We could tie him to a tree, come back for him later."

"His choice," I suggested. "What about it, Ollie? You game

to walk, or do we leave you?"

"I'll walk." He was pale, furious, but keeping a civil tongue.

"All right, get on your feet. You go back in the locker till we've found a place to run the boat aground. Move it!"

He tried one final time. "I've got a few kilos of grass, nothing but the best, and a Colombian emerald that wasn't on Hamilton's plane. They're yours. A phone. Take me to a phone. For Chrissakes be reasonable!"

Greg actually laughed. "He's begging to be gagged, isn't he?" And then his grey eyes turned literally to silver with fury as he looked at Rolland. "You think we'd touch your stinking money?"

Belatedly, Rolland seemed to wake up to the truth, that he was not going to bribe his way out. The civility was gone and he snarled at us. We would go to Logan, and what Logan would do to us would make an S&M party look like play-school. I did not doubt that Rolland could make it all happen. I slammed the hatch on him and went back on deck. Greg had heard every word and looked soberly at me.

"So we don't get caught," I said darkly. "We can't afford to. We knew that before we got into this, didn't we?"

He nodded mutely and handed me one of the punts to help shove the boat out of the reeds. The morning tide had almost floated us off already and she was easy to move. The wind was high, stinging our eyes, and the sky was completely overcast. It was humid, oppressive, as we made sail. It would not be easy to find a place for the boat, and we were running out of time.

The tributary began to narrow as we made distance from the river that cut down out of the hill to Montego Bay. We had almost given up the hunt and decided to turn the lugger around while there was still space to manoeuvre, when I saw a mud bank with a stand of vast trees on the eastern side. The trees would act as a windbreak and we could ram her bow into the mud until it sucked like quicksand.

I drew Greg's attention to it and he agreed. Jammed into the mud, she could not capsize in the wind. She would probably have to be towed off by a contractor or stay there till the next king tide washed up the river and floated her off, but it was a small price to pay for coming through the hurricane intact. I doubted her pot-headed owner would even notice she had not been returned. He would assume she sank during the violence of the hurricane. A lot of boats were going to be wrecked.

Greg put the wheel over and the wind was just enough. She picked up a startling crack of speed, canvas billowing full, hit the mud with a jolting impact, and bit deeply into it. The deck felt suddenly solid beneath our feet, no pitching and yawning with the movement of the water.

"Good enough," Greg decided. He tied the wheel before he left it.

We made every patch of sailcloth secure, battened everything down tight and packed most of our things away, to be collected when we could make it back. I put a few personal items in the bag along with the contents of Rolland's safe and my camera. The stock of the twelve gauge, anonymous in its sacking, protruded a little, and the bag was a dead weight.

The American limped out of the dark little cavern, blinked owlishly in the daylight. I pointed him at the hill. It rose quite steeply before us, thickly wooded, the trees lashing before the wind. "You're going walkies," I told Rolland indifferently. "Over the side."

The mud stuck to our legs, slick, fetid, disgusting. It dried out and flaked off again in the first mile of the forest, leaving the legs of my slacks and Greg's jeans stained pale brown. Rolland was in poor health for a man of his age. He was just forty, a matter of six years older than me, but he might have been twice my age. His arteries and lungs had been systematically abused for a quarter of a century.

High flyers, running in the fast lane, pay the price in the end. Greg and I smoked as kids, but Greg packed it in when he was twenty, one of the conditions imposed on him by his first lover, the rich admirer with the schooner. No booze, no cigarettes, were the house rules. The man refused to breathe anyone's second-hand smoke, and soon Greg was surprised by the pick-up in his lung capacity after he quit. I gave it up when my father died of lung cancer. Like the owner of that schooner, I would rather hold my breath than inhale second-hand smog. One day we shall see first wrinkles appearing and swear off alcohol as well. As we watched Rolland labour up the incline we were so disgusted, we would have undertaken any regimen to avoid such atrophy.

Slow and winded, he held us up with frequent rests that consumed too much time and left us cuttingly scornful. "Too much of the good life, not enough hard work," Greg told him as we stopped yet again to let him get his breath. We had found a stream. I drank and Greg scanned the wooded hills, making sure of our bearings.

I had the bag of valuables over my shoulder and held the Uzi loosely on Rolland while I cursed the man. But for him we could have been half way to Falmouth. We were angry and frustrated.

It was a few minutes after noon when we reached the crest of the hill that had taunted us since we left the boat. We stopped for a moment to check our position. From that vantage point we had a view out as far as the sea. The wind had risen sharply, the air was filled with dust, the sky leaden grey over the green of the roaring forest.

Greg had taken Rolland's watch from his wrist, since ours had been confiscated. He tapped its midnight blue face. "If the radio's right, the storm should be just about on top of us. We're running out of time, Alex. Going to get caught in it if we wait for this geriatric."

Oliver Rolland wore a hunted, feral expression. For minutes at a stretch I did not dare take my eyes off him. He fidgeted constantly, restless and making me restless, his eyes always moving, as if he was searching for something.

"Look at him," I said quietly. "This is his backyard. He knows where he is. This whole country's about the size of a pocket handkerchief. Anybody who's lived here long would learn the landmarks by heart."

The heat was scorching and the wind made it seem hotter yet. I was sweating heavily and smelling strong. Greg's clothes stuck wetly to him as if I had thrown a bucket of water over him. It would be easier on the legs on the downward slopes, I hoped, but the forest had begun to thicken, making detours more frequent.

A prod with the Uzi brought Rolland to his feet and we moved off again, skirting an impassable thicket. Underfoot, the topsoil had been sluiced away by runoff in the last storm, leaving mostly shale behind. The going was treacherous. Greg put a foot wrong and fell, hard. He slithered downward before I could catch hold of him. I dived after him, heart in my mouth, knowing he could sandpaper the flesh from his bones, but he found a handhold in the root mass of a young tree and pulled himself up.

And Rolland was gone. We had taken our eyes off him for no more than ten seconds, and when we looked back he had bolted. "He's played us for fools," Greg said tersely, inspecting his sore elbows and nursing a wrist that had been wrenched. "All that bull about needing to rest every ten minutes – all he was trying to do was slow us down until he could run. Jesus!" He was furious, not least with himself.

We had the bag of valuables, we were armed and he was not. We had all the trumps, but Rolland was loose in his own territory. "If he knows a shortcut to a handy phone we could be in deep trouble," I said over the roar of the wind. "These hills are peppered with farms and shantytowns, half of them don't even get on the map. If just one of them has a shortwave, CB on a truck, we could have Logan and the rest of those goons all over us in half an hour."

"Then we'd better find him." Silver-grey eyes looked at me, cat-like, glittering, angry. "And we'd better do it fast. See that? That's darling Rita."

I turned to look over my shoulder and felt my heart in my throat. The sky was like night. Rita was very big and very black, like a funeral shroud looming out on the horizon, and she was coming closer literally as we watched. For a moment I was back in Darwin, Christmas of 1974, roped to a lamp post with a bulk-loaded Nikon in both hands, fighting to breathe as the storm came in like the shockwave after a nuclear airburst.

The temperature dropped off steeply but there was no rain yet. The hurricane was over the eastern end of the island, battering at Kingston. Her daughter winds ran before her, preparing the way for the violence, the full fury of the storm itself.

And we were in the middle of nowhere. We did not dare split up, or we would never find each other again. Greg made for high ground, back the way we had come. He climbed a sturdy tree to cast about in all directions. Rolland must have been headed somewhere specific. Greg was trying to recognize some landmark.

We should have known. He looked down at me, pointed away to the north. "There's a hollow between the hills. Get up here." I used his handholds and squeezed in beside him, jammed against the trunk. "See that? Cleared area, nice, straight lines of tall weeds. Is that a ganja plantation or have I started seeing mirages?"

Rolland's home turf. I bit my lip. "He could have a radio there."

"He gets to it first, and we're dead." Greg gave me a shove. "Move. I don't know that I fancy playing Logan's games."

Running over the rough forest surface was less foolishness

than insanity. We took it as carefully as we were able, heading for the plantation on instinct. We were fast. We were desperate. The underbrush was often impassable, chest-high and as dry as tinder in the scorching wind. Detours cost us precious time.

It could not have been more than fifteen minutes after we had sighted the plantation when we halted in the last fringe of scrub and saw orderly ranks of tall, spindly plants, battered by the wind. There seemed no sign of life and we pulled up short to catch our breath.

"We might have beaten him," Greg gasped. "We took the shortest route and he's a physical wreck." Then he dragged both hands across his sweating face. "I feel like a wreck myself just now."

I scanned the plantation, counting its shoot holes as I wondered if there might be firearms kept there. The only structure was a shed at the end of the field, an open lean-to with a thatched roof, wicker and palm fronds, like natural camouflage, literally invisible from the air.

"If there's a shortwave set here, it'll be under cover," I panted as I got my breath back in gusts of the stinging, dusty air.

I watched Greg check the Uzi, charge it and knock the safety off. He was nervy, tight-mouthed. His bravado was thin. Macho, gung-ho camp. "Cover me?"

I refused the attempt at levity. "Oh, yes, I'll cover you," I told him. "With a quilt full of eiderdown, in a hotel in Falmouth after you've screwed my arse through the bed. So you be bloody careful."

For just a moment the steel in his eyes softened, it was my lover looking at me. Then the flint was back and we got moving. We scuttled down the fringe of the forest, doubled up and hoped the marijuana crop would conceal us from anyone in the shed. It was prime stuff, almost ripe for picking, tall and lush. I wondered at its street value. It must be destined for the rich American markets.

That we knew where it was, and who it belonged to, was enough to sign our death warrants. Rolland was fighting for his life, and trapped animals are dangerous. We did not underestimate the danger. Complacency gets you killed. I covered Greg as he sidled up to the door of the thatched shack and peered inside. Some part of my mind tried to recall the last time we had skulked around corners, under the gun. Beirut, 1984. Unwelcome foreigners "spying" on the Christian Militia.

A pace before me, Greg relaxed and beckoned me closer. In the dim cavern of the shack was an old woman, most likely left in charge of the watering system. She had a face like old, old leather, punished by the sun and the years, and she was terrified. There was a radio, a small CB set, portable and not especially powerful, but nowhere in Jamaica is very far from anywhere else. It was powerful enough to reach Montego Bay.

The woman peered at us in Rita's gathering gloom, frightened as she saw the guns. I stepped forward, told her we were not there to hurt her, and not from the police, but she did not seem to hear a word. Could she even follow an accent as alien as mine?

At the shack's entrance, Greg knelt in concealment to look out at thrashing plantation. "Calm her down," he hissed at me. "If everything looks normal when the boss gets here, he might blunder straight in and we can grab him again."

Some animal nerve, down inside, warned me it was sheer optimism. I spoke soothingly to the old woman and although she said nothing the hysterics quietened. We waited, crouched in the stifling dimness of the hut. Outside, early afternoon was no brighter than twilight.

We waited too long. At last Greg swore, raked his fingers through his tangled hair. "Rolland's been here. He's probably got us under surveillance right now." The wind whipped away the words. "If he hasn't just bolted. Christ, Alex, the heavy boys could be half way here." He gave the Uzi in his right hand a jaundiced look. "We're sitting ducks."

I looked into the old woman's leathery face, realising how nearly blind she was. The eyes were dull with cataracts. She could see, but not well. "Want to tell me, mama?" I asked. "Did Rolland use the radio before we got here?" Did she understand? Did she even hear? I bit my lip. There is no way you can force coherence out of terrified old people. I've seen journalists try, inflicting needless cruelty.

I shuffled over and crouched against the shack's flimsy wall beside Greg. Every bone in his body was taut. "Now what?" He lifted a brow at me.

"You're asking me?" I demanded. "We're ahead, we just don't dare wait around for the minders to come after us. He's got to be around here somewhere. I vote we go hunting." I hoisted the precious bag over my shoulder. "The aces are all in there, mate. All four of them."

"Out," Greg agreed, peering into Rita's twilight gloom.

He had taken a step out of the stifling interior of the shack before a shot thumped into the dirt at our feet. A second punched through the wall. In the gale we were almost unaware of them, but a third passed so close by my cheek that I felt it go by. I dragged Greg back into the shack and flattened out on the ground beside him. "He's armed – keep your bloody head down!"

So there had been a gun of some kind here along with the CB. Greg swore lividly as another round skimmed our heads. "He's that way, in the trees." He looked out across the valley hollow, and before I could stop him, bobbed up and ripped off a dozen rounds from the magazine. Uzis cycle at a ludicrously fast rate. You can expend a magazine in a matter of seconds. We had several spares, but not enough to engage in any kind of protracted exchange.

Rolland was on single shot. In a lull in the wind I heard the cough of a light assault rifle, probably the AR-15. Once heard, when it is firing at you in anger, never forgotten. It took me back to Belfast, years ago.

Rolland was in the treeline, I caught a glimpse of him as he bobbed up to return a few shots while Greg changed a spent magazine for a new one.

Rounds ricocheted off the stones close beside us, striking sparks. Rolland could keep us pinned down indefinitely. Doubtlessly he had a lot more ammunition than us, whatever had been stored along with the CB set. I hunted around for a way out as Greg squeezed off short bursts into the trees.

"Hold him there," I said over the roar of the wind. "I'm going to try to kick out the back wall."

The forest was lashing, a forewarning of the violence to come when the hurricane hit. The air was soupy with dust, so thick it was suffocating. At first we failed to notice the acrid tang of smoke. Greg kept Rolland's head down with shots a few seconds apart, just enough to buy me time to try the shack's back wall.

We noticed the smell of burning at the same moment and Greg called me back to the open frontage. "Alex. Alex!"

There is an unmistakable smell about burning pot. The crop was alight, perhaps touched off by sparks kicked up by stray rounds. The underbrush, and the ganja itself, had been dried to tinder by the hot wind, it would not take much to set it off. In Australia's dry country sometimes even the trains must stop running, because the sparks they strike off the rails leave a trail of spot fires behind them.

Or had Rolland set alight to the crop to get rid of the evidence, covering his arse in the event we made it out of there? We would never know. We saw the first orange-red lick of flames as I joined Greg at the front of the shack, and the smoke hit my lungs hard, buzzed my head. I had not touched grass or any other drug for years, and I coughed on it. The torpor would be the death of us.

"Out!" I yelled at Greg. The shack had already filled with the pungent smoke and I was dizzy. "This way!" I had the shack's back wall kicked halfway out and with his help the flimsy timberwork broke away and tumbled haphazardly.

I was too strung out to wonder whether the fire was Rolland's doing or just some act of God. Burning debris was caught up in the wind, held aloft like blazing kites, liquid orange, tossed away into the forest.

"Christ," Greg panted, "if the woods catch –"

There was no need to spell it out. In '83 we were in Australia to cover the Ash Wednesday fires that burned across an entire corner of the continent. A forest fire is a wild animal, untamable, terrifyingly unstoppable. If the forest caught, we were finished.

I remembered standing with the crew of a Country Fire Service tanker, my face blistering in the dragon's breath of the inferno as I fought for a few priceless frames. Greg had worked with the St. John's men, trawling for ghoulish copy. Both of us were jetlagged, tired and scared. Not an hour before the fire had gone through a town. Men working with a bulldozer to cut back a firebreak had been burned alive.

The old woman who minded the ganja went past us like a startled rabbit, disappeared into the woods, and I wished her luck. If she made it out, we would never know about it. Fragments of survival sense I had picked up as a kid flittered back, making me grab Greg's arm as he made to run for high ground.

"Not that way – fire loves to run uphill!"

"Which way, then?" he bellowed over the roar of the wind. "Down? There's a stream down there, runoff from the hillside."

It was the only option we had, and we ran.

The dried tinder of the underbrush, seasons dead, already smouldered brightly, set alight by fragments blasted about by the wind. The air was heavy with them, black and cherry red, whirling debris. We ducked them with the animal's fear of burning as we slid down the hill. Shale scattered away underfoot. We could have broken our necks at one wrong step.

At the bottom was a washaway, but the creek in the bed was shallow, pitifully small and inadequate. And there are stories of people trying to shelter from bushfires in more adequate pools. Burning debris, falling in from the banks, boils the water and anything in it.

Terror, real, live fear, began to rake over me like steel talons. I saw that wild look about Greg. He was filthy, coughing, showing the whites of his eyes like a horse about to bolt. I hooked one arm about him as I dredged my memory for survival techniques only ever learned in theory. I was never a bushman.

"We're going to have to dig in," I shouted. "If the bush is going to burn, the fire'll go through fast in this wind. If we dig in it'll go straight over the top."

That was the theory. Wombats, snakes, small animals that cannot run from fires, go to ground. Sometimes they emerge into a devastated landscape, bewildered but alive. Sometimes they don't.

"Dig into what?" He coughed hoarsely, smoke blind, as I was.

I had already seen the hollowed-out slope in the side of the washaway. Drifts of shale lay heaped about it. It would not be impossible for us to make ourselves a den, a nest. Literally bury ourselves alive and let the heat go by. The roasting draught from so many isolated fires made the air shimmer now. It danced, distorted as if we were caught in an open hearth. Fear was like spurs in my sides.

Down on all fours, I scrabbled into the shale. He took my lead, skinning his hands, digging until he was as bloody as me. The brush was alight, burning fiercely. Sheer terror kept us working. It was either dig, or get up and start moving, and keep moving. That is a mistake. You can never run fast enough, nor far enough – there is nowhere to run to. The flight instinct plays you for a fool.

We had almost finished the trench when Greg caught hold of my arm, fingers bruising. Pointed away up the slope at a horrifying sight. It could only be Rolland. His clothes were alight, even his hair seemed to be burning, and he was running. Running and running. It was the last we ever saw of him. We were too busy trying to bury ourselves in gravel in our hollow.

We pressed tight together. The bag of valuables and my camera dug into my belly as I lay face down, fought to breathe. The heat came up fast. It hurt the sinuses to inhale and I knew the brush right over the slope of the washaway must be burning. My back seared under the thin layer of gravel.

The bushmen swear that underbrush burns through fast, driven before the wind. All fires generate their own gales, swirling storms of convection. When the brush is gone and there is nothing else to burn, it's over, leaving the ground dwellers alive. Time to prove it out, I thought. I saw the absurdity of it as I lay there, clutching Greg as if my life depended on it and praying to a God I never really believed in.

If it was to be the end of us, now one would ever know what became of us. Farris and Connor went on holiday to Jamaica and vanished off the face of the earth. It would have been poetic. Tragic. But we have always had the luck of the devil, or perhaps the Irish.

The wind was a live thing, screaming in the trees like a banshee until we were deafened. Heaped with hot shale as we were, it was some time before we realised what we heard. Sizzling sounds, almost like bacon spattering in a frying pan, and then a drumming noise.

It was raining, first drops and then a deluge that turned the gravel to muddy pebbles and the slope above the washaway into a cascade. The temperature dropped like a brick. Suddenly we could breathe. I lay still, let the rain cool my searing back, wondered if I was burned or just singed.

Beside me, Greg stirred, struggled up to his knees. Filthy, drenched, blind and deaf but unhurt, we huddled against each other before the fury of the storm. Rita had arrived. She slammed into the forest with the explosive force of a warhead, and the fire was out.

Fear was gone with a tide of euphoria. We laughed like lunatics in those first few moments. Greg turned his face to the downpour, mud sluicing from him, and then he flung himself at me, caught, held, kissed. We punished each other in a savage celebration of survival. I left bruises on his shoulders that were visible a week later, and tasted blood in my mouth when he had done with me. Relief was a kind of insanity.

Then the storm hit us and the euphoria was replaced by healthy fear. It went through like an express train, terrifying, awe inspiring. We could find nowhere to shelter. We pressed together on the leeward side of a tree that seemed sound, tucked into the bole of it, with the vast body of it between us and the wind. It whipped like a sapling, groaned as if its roots would rip out of the ground. But it held and, two hours later, it was over.

The storm front left wan blue sky behind it. The hills streamed with water and the forest smelt earthy. All trace of the fire was gone in the mudslides as a dozen washaways filled to the brim. Cold and dirty, exhausted, we stood in the mud to watch Rita's angry departure. She was like a funeral shroud tossed into the sky, black and forbidding.

The storm front swung out to sea, to ravage points west. I got my breath back, stiff, cramped and sore. But I had Greg in my arms. Nothing else mattered to me. Bedraggled and forlorn, he was an urchin again, with that little boy lost look I could never resist.

"Come to daddy," I told him, and ran my fingers through his wet hair. His eyes were smoke-red and I had bitten his mouth. I touched his swollen lower lip. "Did I do that? I'm sorry."

"You're not," he said drily. "Daddy always did like biting his little boy. It's a good thing sonny doesn't mind."

"Okay, I'm not sorry," I admitted, and began to peel the sodden clothes off him. He stretched his arms over his head and let me strip him naked without offering to help. His back, buttocks and the backs of his thighs were scarlet. I guessed mine must be too. I fingered the skin and found him hot. "How bad is it?"

"Sore. Very. You?"

"The same. We were just lucky." I started to undress but he caught my hands and performed the service for me, kissing my chest and belly as he went. There was a kiss for my cock before he hung our clothes over the low branches of the tree beneath which we had sheltered. I frowned over his back. From nape to knees, it was as if someone had leathered him within an inch of his hide. I knew how damned lucky we had been.

The washaway was full now, the water running swiftly, and although it was none to clean it was cool and deep. I tugged him into it and we sat back to let the comparative chill take the fire out of our scorches. Relief made us drowsy but the coolness kept us awake.

In an hour it was not much worse than a little sunburn. It

would be tolerable by morning. Clean, cold, we perched on a rotting log to dry off as the early evening sun broke through the pall of the overcast. Tropical weather is capricious. Greg leaned heavily on me and yawned. We were tired and hungry. We were alive, and it felt wonderful.

Our clothes were stiff and uncomfortable, chaffing scorched skin as we dressed again. I had just begun to give some thought to getting out of the woods. Greg fixed me with a shrewd look.

"You do know where we are, don't you?"

"I rather hoped you would know," I confessed.

"I haven't the foggiest," he said serenely. "We're lost then."

"Sounds that way," I agreed cheerfully. Nothing mattered. I kept thinking, over and over, *we're alive, we're alive*. It was all I had the mentality to care about. I kissed the corner of his mouth. "Never fear. Your daddy was a boyscout once." For about a fortnight, when he was ten, before he was expelled for blacking another boy's eye in the pursuit of adolescent honour. In those days it irked me to be called a fairy. Only later did I learn to laugh.

"A boyscout?" Greg asked fatuously. "Prepared for anything?"

"Anything." I swatted his backside very gently, mindful of its tenderness just then. "We ought to make tracks before it gets dark."

"High ground, get our bearings?" He looped his arms about my neck, searched through my mouth with a loving tongue. "Daddy's going to find me a big supper and a soft bed, I hope. Or sonny won't have the energy to raise an argument tomorrow."

I watched him yawn and laughed. He meant it. "Two choices, honey, and I shall leave it up to you. We can push on, see if we can make Falmouth. See if there's anything left standing when we get there. Rita would have hit the place like a bomb, remember. Or we can go back the way we came and see if the boat's in one piece. If she's in good shape, great. If she's swamped, of course, we'll be arse-deep in stinking mud and ten miles from anywhere. Then again, if Falmouth's flattened, we won't be much better off! So?"

"All I really want is to lie down and sleep," he said honestly, "but the whole world is a mudbath . . ." He chewed his lip as he looked at the hills. "You know, Falmouth can't be more than three miles from here. Maybe not even that.

I've walked that far to get a newspaper before now."

"But which way?" I demanded, and looked up the muddy slope. "First thing is, we work out where the hell we are."

Many of the trees had been uprooted and many more were so weakened that they would soon fall. But the best, the strongest, remained sound. Greg pulled himself up into the branches of a survivor. Evening sunlight, slanting under the clouds, painted him in gold as he shaded his eyes and scanned the forest. He could see the hill we had come over, the ridge where we had lost Rolland, and was calculating his bearings.

"If I'm any judge, Falmouth's that way." He pointed away at right angles to the sun, almost due north. "And it can't be far after the chase Rolland gave us."

He dropped down out of the tree, into my arms. I could not let go of him, still so relieved to be alive that I was in love with life in general and him in particular. I gave him my hand, kissed his fingers when he took it, and noticed we were both a mass of cuts and scrapes from our excavations. His hands are fine and beautiful, like those of a musician. It was a pity to see them bloodied and raw, and I frowned over them.

"Hey." Those slender hands gripped mind with masculine strength. "We're alive, Alex. Isn't that enough?"

Hours before, when the fire was racing down off the hill and the air was a furnace blast, I would not even have noticed our scrapes. He was right, and I winked at him, following him into the tree-line as the evening became violet with a stormy sunset.

<hr />

10

WE came up on Falmouth's river just before daylight was spent and were shocked by the storm damage. Tangled masses of debris choked the swollen waterway. A car was floating in the shallows, and along the banks the crops had been flattened. The river ran high, fast and deep. It was still rising with the runoff from the hills.

Soon the hamlets inland of Falmouth would be under flood.

"Bodes ill for the town," Greg said bleakly as we made our way along the waterline. We hurried, as we were losing daylight.

Fortunately, nowhere in Jamaica is far away, even by British standards. By Australian understanding, the whole island would fit into the boundaries of one of the big, pastoral syndicate-owned sheepstations. We saw the lights of the town just as it got dark. It was difficult to judge the extent of the damage by moonlight, but we could see the roof was off the pub and some of the poor people's houses were nothing but a tangle of scrap iron and shingles.

One building escaping almost undamaged was the community hall, a red brick structure that had been turned over into an aid station and refuge for those in need. The locals queued up for food. The power was off. The lights we had seen were portafloods on batteries. The hotels, of which Falmouth has three, none of them anything special, catered for the homeless. Hungry and sore, we made for the nearest of the hotels. It was on its own in-house generators, I guessed. One light in four or five was on, making the building seem a mecca of welcome.

"We'll be lucky to get a room," I grumbled. The euphoria of simply having survived had worn off. Exhaustion and scorched skin made life less than pleasant. "There's going to be a lot of homeless in this town." I glanced back toward the soup lines at the aid station.

"You kidding?" Greg sounded cynical as he shared my backward glance. "You don't think they're going to let the riffraff into the tourist trap, do you? Hurricane or no. The Salvation Army's good enough for them."

I wish I could say he was wrong. He led the way into the hotel's lobby and fronted up to the reception desk. The woman behind it was white and looked down her delicate nose at us. We were dishevelled and dirty. Did she take us for vagabonds? I watched my lover become the urchin and turn on the pathos. He does it better than me.

She bought his story of a hard time and dire need, eating out of his hand. They had plenty of rooms. Many of the tourists who had booked the place out before Christmas had listened to the weather reports on the radio, as had we. They had flown out to Barbados and Antigua to get out of Rita's path of destruction. The hotel had plenty of accommodation while the homeless bunked down the road in the community hall. Greg collected the keys to a decent room and gave me a cynical look as he headed for the lifts.

The chart on the wall beside them said there was a first aid post on the second floor, where our room was. On the way back he knocked discreetly on the half open door, begged a lotion for terminal sunburn. The nurse was a little half-caste no taller than Greg's shoulder. She gave him a bottle of medicated oil, compliments of the hotel.

They had allocated us a room with twin beds, which made me grumble as he locked the door behind us. I was dying for a warm shower, and pulled him into the bathroom with me. The water ran tepid and I felt myself slowly reviving as Greg leaned on me, dopey with fatigue. Then we took turns to stretch out on one of the ridiculously narrow beds and be rubbed down with the lotion.

Our clothes were a mess, but there were extenuating circumstances and I shrugged off our dishevelment as we went down to the dining room. As they served the last sitting, we fell on the food. I didn't taste the first half of my steak. The last we had eaten was breakfast. It seemed a year ago. It would not have mattered what was on the menu, but in fact the food was excellent. The mushroom sauce was delicate and the peaches and ice cream following the steak made me think of home.

Greg wolfed his food and drank far too much wine before we switched to coffee. I watched him grow drowsy. I was just as tired, feeling less amorous than paternal. I jingled the key under his nose to stir him as we lingered over after dinner mints.

"Bed? Your boy scout found you your big supper, what about a mattress now? Or does that sound too mundane?"

The twin beds were a nuisance but I was physically spent, as useful as a eunuch that night. Greg flopped face down and in moments was asleep. I remember crawling into bed, chuckling as I remembered the king-sized in the room we had booked in Montego Bay. Then, blessed oblivion. I did not even dream. The feel of a mattress against my spine was heaven. I was comatose on half a bottle of wine.

The sound of the door clicking shut woke me, an eon later. I pried open my eyes to see that the other bed was empty. Greg's clothes were gone. The bathroom door was open, a billow of humid air issuing from it. He had been up for some time, and moved around quietly so as to let me sleep. I smiled after him, raked my fingernails through a day's growth of stubble. I shaved under the shower, luxuriated in self-indulgence, then rubbed in more of the medicated oil and stretched out on the bed.

The contents of Rolland's safe spread out across the quilt, and I opened the Goldmark account books with interest. They made peculiar reading. One page was given over to the trade in tomatoes and cucumbers, all perfectly legit. The next section dealt with the scheduled movements of boats carrying ganja. Some vessel called *Sunrunner* plied between Jamaica and Acapulco. There was a name, De Masio. That must mean something to the American authorities.

The records were followed by odds and ends about the trade in marine engines, the importation of motor vehicles, the export of sugarcane and bananas – again, legitimate business. The blind for what came next. I saw names and addresses, phone numbers in Paraguay, Ecuador, Colombia. Notes about deliveries made and accounts paid. A boy was worth twenty to thirty thousand in American dollars. A girl not quite so much, unless she was very young, very beautiful and virginal.

I wondered how much Greg and I would have fetched. We would not have gone to the same markets as the young boys, and the purchase price would have reflected different qualities. A man's strength and pride, sold to be systematically broken down for the sheer delight of pain.

I turned over several pages and came to the section detailing the trade in gemstones. There was the name of Geminex, in Haiti, and the dealers in Venezuela, Colombia and Peru who took the goods from Rolland to be recut, reset. The final shipment, which had cost John Hamilton his life, was bound for Cartajena to a dealer called Veejay Chaudry, an Indian exile, probably with obscure, rich and untapped markets.

Rolland had had a finger in everything, from drugs and prostitution on one end of the scale, to insurance fraud, murder and the trade in human bodies on the other. I held enough in my hands to have hung the man, and I was regretful that we had not managed to drag him out of the forest with us, so he could have been made to stand up in a court, in his own country, and answer the multiple charges.

Still, it was not over. Rolland's death meant only that someone else would take over the reins of this pocket-sized empire. He must have partners, family, a beneficiary who would inherit the mansion, the fleet of boats and cars, and the private army. There would be a hiccup in the administration but business would continue, and Leroy Logan would see to it that our names were right on top of the shit list.

It was still early and I knew we had to get moving. We had the drive to Kingston before us, supposing our car had come through the devastation unscathed. It was hidden high above the level of the river, but I could only trust to providence that it would not be flooded. It depended how much wild water had cascaded down from Cockpit country overnight.

The books went back into our bag and I was thinking about dressing when the click of the door announced Greg's presence. He was still deliciously damp, his hair not quite dry, and he had shaved. He was clad in muddied jeans, barefoot and bare chested, and carried a breakfast tray.

"You're awake," he observed, as he put the tray down on the bedside. "Room service isn't working so I'm the service this morning. Half of the staff has gone home to shantytown to dig their kids and dogs out of the mess." He stirred sugar into my cup. He drinks his own without.

"Service?" I surveyed his beautiful bare chest. "I'm all for this."

He leaned over to kiss me. "Anything for you, precious." One grey eye winked mockingly.

"Anything?" I looked at the tray. "As in, breakfast in bed?"

"Why not? Live dangerously." He spooned marmalade onto a slice of toast and held it to my lips.

I took a bite. "What have I done to deserve this?"

"You haven't done it yet," he told me in that sultry, husky voice.

"Oh?" I took another bite of toast. "And what is it I'm about to do?" I could guess. It did not take much working out.

"You're going to spread your beautiful legs and invite me in between them," he said, growly and intense. The tone suggested a deep, simmering hunger of lust. "Aren't you?"

"I could be persuaded," I admitted. My cock filled out before his eyes without him setting a finger on me. Familiar warmth coiled through my belly, exquisite tension. He can have me any time he wants me, he knows that. As I can have him. "I've been looking at Rolland's books," I said as we finished breakfast. I couldn't take my eyes from his chest. "There's more than enough to finish Goldmark. Ganja, fraud, murder, smuggling."

"And the slaving?" he asked pointedly.

"Names and places in Paraguay and Colombia and so on." Countries that are still full of Nazis. Members of the master race who made it away through the rat-lines, as often as not with allied help. We did a story on that particular scandal in '85. "Chances are, Interpol or the Americans can find the slave buyers."

"And maybe get the kids back," Greg added thoughtfully as he set the tray aside. "Those that survived." He looked at me with eyes that were dark and hot, smouldering. "If any did."

"Some would." I was guessing. "When you pay twenty or thirty grand for a toy you look after it, don't break it too soon. They come too expensive to ruin them too quickly."

"That stinks," he observed.

"Doesn't it?" I stretched out on the bed, one arm folded under my head. He was simmering. The creased denim at his groin drew my eyes. "Greg?"

He slipped his fingers into his back pocket, produced a half flattened tube. "Look what I got at the first aid station. My hands are smarting. I wanted something to put on them. There's a bright young nurse on duty. She gave me this. Don't think she knows where I'm going to put it, though. At least, I hope she doesn't."

It was a tube of medicated handcream. I took it from him. He had turned on without a touch but I needed his hands on me. Wanted him in me. I picked those hands up and turned them over to inspect their scratches and welts. His wrists had been cut by the wire bindings, and so had mine. We both had a lot of minor lacerations, testimony to our barehand digging in the shale. His nails were chipped and broken, and he had snipped them very short to get rid of the jagged edges. I would have to attend to mine.

I kissed his palm. "Jesus, we were lucky. And this was supposed to be a holiday away from strife."

"And it's not over yet," he added as he leaned in to kiss my chest. His teeth closed about my nipple and I held my breath. "I keep thinking about something Mrs. Mathers said," he mused moments later. "Leroy Logan is known in the ghettoes, even in Kingston, so she said. If Rolland used that shortwave at the plantation –"

"And you know he did. He'd been in the shack, he was armed!"

"Yes. Then whoever's got hold of Goldmark's reins will

have everybody from Logan down to the boot polisher out looking for us, as if their bloody lives depend on it. In fact," he added tartly, "their lives do!"

"So?" I threaded my fingers through his hair. "Kingston's a big place. Easier to get lost in the crowd there than here."

"Great minds think alike." He leaned over to take my mouth. "We'd better get on the road, as soon as we can." He moved away as he spoke.

For just an instant I was sure he was about to consign lust to the future, and I grabbed him by the shoulders. "Hey, where do you think you're going, mate?"

He laughed. "Idiot." He stroked my chest teasingly. I'm almost smooth. I always envied him the pelt of fine hair between his nipples. He's not a hearthrug, but had just enough hair to seduce your fingers. "So long as we're in Kingston some time this afternoon, that'll do. Phone Lansing when we're there, get him to clue in the police, otherwise we're likely to just get locked up. Let's face it –" he laughed, genuine sounds of amusement. "Would you believe two tatty looking characters who walk in off the street and say they're from *Perspective*? Might as well claim to be Batman and Robin."

"We've got a load of evidence," I argued with deep satisfaction. "And Rolland's dead. His operation will be on automatics right now. It'll take a few days at least for the command changeover, and that gives the police time to hit, and hit hard." I watched the deep rise and fall of his chest as he breathed. "Greg?" He arched a brow at me. Sultry. I swallowed. "Take your jeans off, honey." My hands were itching for his backside and denim would not do.

He laughed quietly and slid off the bed. He unzipped, turned his back on me and dropped them an inch at a time to his ankles, which left him bent and spread, tormentingly out of my reach. Then he kicked them off and turned back, let me look at all that belonged to me. I was as hard as I was ever going to get. He took it in his fist as if he owned it and opened his mouth. He looked up at me, licked his lips, teasing, making me wait. I held my breath, played his game. His hand tightened and his mouth slid over the blunt head at last, suckled delicately. I was in Paradise.

He made a thorough job of me, not neglecting an inch, inside or out. I had his bite brands on shoulders, both breasts, both buttocks, before he began to play with the cream. His palms left swathes of it across my chest and

171

between my legs. Concerned for the bedlinen, I rolled off the mattress and stretched out on the rug. He bent my knees into my chest and I felt my arse open, wanton, hungry for some part of him in me. I took his fingers first while I watched his face. A curious mix of calm and lust.

He fingered me for a long time, until the muscles there were soft with relaxation and I was about to scream with frustration. I needed it deeper and harder. I wanted to lie on my back but some instinct told me he wanted me to kneel. I was not about to deny him anything that morning. Perhaps I had been rudely reminded the day before of how close to death we humans live, how much life means. How much love means. It was special, a celebration of life. When he let me, I knelt up and kissed him hard, as I would not be able to kiss him when he was in me. He pulled my pillows off the bed to save my knees.

"Trying to spoil me?" I surveyed him from his tousled hair to the blind thrust of the cock that was going to fuck me. It glistened moistly in the filtered daylight from curtained windows. I shivered.

"I'm allowed," he said huskily. His voice betrayed his urgency while I felt languid and spoilt.

I knelt for him. He spread me but it was some time before he thrust in. I had not realised how close he was and took delight in it, in knowing how much he needed me. Then, a hot, solid shove, and he was there. I took every inch of him without a second's resistance. I felt completed, whole. As if, for a little while two people really can become one. He was gentle at first, vigorous later as he got close again, gave it to me the way I wanted it while his hands reached around under my belly and did everything.

I was dopey afterward. I lay like a corpse on the pillows on the floor while he went for a washcloth. It tickled between my buttocks, making me squirm. He flopped on the bed above me, just as lethargic. I needed a bath, and minutes later I went to run it as he rummaged through our bag for what remained of our cash. There was not much.

"I'm going to run a few errands," he called into the bathroom.

I stuck my head out. The room was humid, dewy. "Get us something to wear, will you? These clothes are just about fit for the bin." We only had what we stood up in, and if we were heading for Kingston we could hardly go looking like a couple of ragbags. Kingston's upmarket districts can be sophisticated and snobbish.

He turned on the radio before he left. "Listen for the news, lover. They might say which roads are closed after the storm."

The cricket was long finished, which was a major disappointment. The next Shell Shield match was to be played in Barbados, a long flight east. Jamaica had won this round, as the locals had predicted. Antigua would win the rematch. I took my bath, drowsed in the water, enjoying the phantom sensations of Greg moving inside me as I waited for the bulletin. The radio news was a catalogue of disaster.

Rita had wreaked havoc from one end of Jamaica to the other. Many boats were sunk, quite large vessels tossed ashore, people lost at sea, thousands homeless, dozens feared dead. The crops were destroyed, the rivers flooding. Only the tourists who had the balls to stay on after the storm warnings were sitting pretty in the hotels.

I pulled the plug on my bath, shaved while I waited for Greg. He was back as I began to grow bored and think about hunting for him. He had several plastic carrybags, and his feet were muddy.

"I went out to look at the car," he explained. He handed me one of the bags. "Jogged out to the hiding place. The trees held, but the whole road is a quagmire. It was ever such fun getting it out. The river is high – another day, and we'd be towing it out with a boat. It's filthy, but it's okay. Did you get anything on the radio about the roads?"

"No, they were too busy talking about the homeless and the fishing boats that are missing." I tipped out the bag's contents. Gaudy shirts, white slacks, sandals, underwear. Not my usual taste, although the quality was good. I made a face over the colours.

"Suffer," he said drily. "It's in a good cause."

"We are going to look like holiday wallies," I told him. I held a fruit salad shirt against him. "Like an explosion in a greenhouse."

"All that was left," he said. "Everything else went to the refugees. There's people out there who've lost the lot. The shops have been cleaned out – Rastafarians doing good deeds for their fellow man."

"Good people, Rastafarians," I agreed, thinking of Isaac and the shantytown that had given us a night's protection. I pulled on a gaudy shirt over the white slacks. I bundled my laundry into the bag and caught sight of myself in the wardrobe's long mirror. "Holiday wallies. Look at us."

Greg laughed again, swatted my backside and bestowed a caress for the lingering tenderness between its cheeks, which made me shiver. "We'll live. The car's in good nick, right outside. We might make Kingston in time for dinner tonight if the roads are half way decent. The coast road might be okay. The mountain roads are more direct but I don't know that I'd trust them. A lot of trees fell. The scenic ocean drive?"

"The coast road it is," I agreed, and led the way from the room.

We soon discovered, nowhere was especially scenic after Rita. By daylight Falmouth was a shambles. It looked bombed. It would take a month to clear the debris and pretty the town up again. The roads through the Cockpit country would be a mass of mud slides, overflowing washaways, fallen trees, and the coastal road accommodated most of the island's traffic.

The emergency services were out, struggling to cope, but many roads were still largely impassable. A young constable at one junction gave us fair warning: get into trouble and no one will come to pull you out. They were stretched too thinly to run about after people making fools of themselves. Many of the roads are unmetalled, and they would be closed until they had dried out and been regraded.

The car was caked with mud, but this did not matter since no vehicle was much cleaner. Greg elected to drive the first leg and we ran out of Falmouth, heading east, at eleven. We planned to lunch in Ocho Rios, which is a tourist trap. It was oddly devoid of foreigners.

The hurricane had pounded everything like a vengeful lover. We picked our way through the wreckage of rolled vehicles and spilled goods, making decent speed when we could keep the car moving. Ocho Rios was in fair condition, as most of the big structures are of the highrise type, like those in Montego Bay, built by international combines to attract foreign money. When they install a five-hundred-room hotel they don't want it destroyed by the next big wind.

Since the majority of the tourists had fled, we had a beautiful restaurant almost to ourselves. We ate steak and garden salad, and tossed for who would drive the second leg. Greg lost, and drank fruit juice while I indulged in a glass of wine.

The further we drove, the worse the damage became. The

railway towns in the east were very battered. The sea was still rough, the wind fresh and cool, raising whitecaps out to the horizon. As Greg handled the car I took down a longhand draft of the copy that would end in Lansing's hands. It was sizzling. Lansing was going to love it, and there would be a bonus in it for us. With the copy complete I turned to the short version, the report we would give to the Kingston police.

I noted the details, tried to keep it short. It filled several pages, despite the attempt at brevity. I made a second copy, and an inventory of the goods we were delivering to the authorities, as if some raw nerve, deep inside, was unwilling or unable to trust anyone. Rolland would have hanged on the strength of what we had, and in a way it was regrettable he would never answer the charges. But John Hamilton's name would be cleared and the insurance case would finalise, putting Shirley back into business.

Then there was Leroy Logan, and he would be going away for a long, long time on our evidence. I would never forgive him for the way he had handled Greg. I could imagine how Shirley felt for her cousin.

The sky was like red Russian gold with sunset when we drove into Kingston. It was battered but still beautiful, still looking like a postcard as we tailgated slow traffic into the suburbs and began to look out for a hotel. The brochures will tell you that over a thousand rooms are available in that city, but most of them had been occupied by people whose houses were damaged. Although few tourists had remained on the island there seemed to be just one room for rent.

It was a tiny shoebox with noisy plumbing and no view. But it had the two indispensibles: a double bed and a telephone. The phone was of primary importance. Greg's eyes lit up as he saw it, and he pounced as I pushed our baggage into the wardrobe and peered out into the street. The power was on, one street light in three working.

"Soon as Lansing tells the police to expect us," I speculated, "we can hand them the whole package and ask for protection . . . I don't feel safe here." I was watching the roving gang of youths across the street. They looked like trouble on the hoof. Greg came to look over my shoulder and his mouth tightened.

"What time is it in London?"

"What, late tonight, is it?" I watched the gang pass on, lost in the late twilight, and turned back toward the bed. Greg was already punching up an IDD number. I recognized the code of Lansing's private line. He sprawled on the pillows, eyes closed.

"It's ringing." He waited impatiently for the boss to answer.

I felt the same impatience as I shuffled over the bed beside him. I lifted him up to lie on me and pressed my ear to the phone with his. I heard the *brr brr* of a phone in London, thousands of miles away. Lansing might not be at home.

"Come on, answer the bloody thing." Greg muttered as I played with his hair for the pleasure of it. "Come on – oh, evening, sir, it's Farris. Yes, sir, long distance. We're in Kingston. There's been some trouble."

It was the understatement of the decade. Lansing shut up and listened. Greg outlined the whole story in verbal shorthand as I toyed with him, revelling in the freedom to. He slapped my hands away as Lansing's voice became intense, answered the terse questions as they came up. Then he resettled the phone in its cradle and turned over into my arms. The call would have cost a small fortune.

"He's getting on the blower to Kingston right now," Greg said thoughtfully. "Give it a few hours for them to make sense of the message, he said, and then just dump the whole thing into their hands." A yawn, a stretch, and he sat up. "I'm hungry. And we haven't got anything to wear that would get us into a decent restaurant in this town."

"And if we eat in blacktown someone somewhere is going to know our faces," I added. I tapped my nose and winked. "Ways and means, my son." His arms crushed my ribs. I often wonder if Greg knows how strong he is.

Above the beach, away from the upmarket face of Kingston, we found stalls selling a haphazard assortment of food. We played it as safe as we knew how. We kept the battered looking Ford in the shadows by the stalls, and Greg had one of the Uzis in his hand, under cover of the dash, while I bought a flotsam of rice, seafood, fruit, beer. The car pulled on, away from the lights and into anonymity.

The night was warm with Rita long gone. We sat on the beach to eat. No one noticed two lovers being close in the dark. Rash, impulsive, I put my arm around him. The tide was turning, music and laughter shouted out of the waterfront bars, the soft rush of the sea lulled me.

We loafed around, savouring the breeze before turning back to business. We had the bag of valuables in the car, but no idea where the police station was. Greg parked beside a phonebox and I glanced quickly about the half-lit street before sliding out. We were unobserved. A phonecall to the desk, anonymous and brief, and we were moving again. Ten minutes later we stood in the station's foyer, waiting while the desk sergeant sent for a senior officer. They were expecting us.

He was Detective Sergeant Rodney Patterson, one of the nicest men I have ever met. Courteous and affable, and good looking. His skin was the palest of coffee brown, not much darker than Greg tans after a long, hot summer. I remembered the foolish, cruel "caste system" that still exists in these islands. The arrangement is that darker-skinned West Indians are frowned on and often ostracized, barred from the clubs and from marrying lighter skinned islanders, on whom society smiles.

I wondered how it must be to be very dark, very poor, very gay. Life must be difficult for the thrice damned. The system looks absurd to outsiders, but it is a tradition, bred into them. It will take a miracle to change it now.

Patterson had taken the call from Matt Lansing. It was on tape, and he played it back as a clerk went to pull various files. I sat looking at the portrait of the Queen that hung over the desk, and Patterson poured Earl Grey tea. I held the bag in my lap. The Uzis were still in it. The detective frowned deeply as Lansing's voice issued from the recorder. He sang our praises. Greg actually found a chuckle.

"So," Patterson said, turning off the recorder. "You have something for us, so says Mr. Lansing."

I gave Greg a sidelong glance and unzipped the bag. "We took these from Oliver Rolland's safe." I put the machine pistols on the desk. "Under your gun laws, he would be in trouble for possessing these, I believe." Patterson merely nodded. He did not look surprised. You find M-16s on the street in Kingston. They are not legal, but they are all too plentiful. I went back to the bag, and set the gems before him. "He murdered a pilot called Hamilton to claim the insurance for these. The paperwork." I had shuffled everything into order on the drive from Falmouth.

Patterson's eyes widened a fraction. I set out the whole collection, piece by piece, finishing with the account books, with their notes and records as to the trade in human bodies. Greg spoke briefly about Peter Cole, Malcolm Dennison, and our own abduction. The threats and promises made to us. He mentioned Logan's physical abuse of us in passing, enough to make Patterson's wide mouth tug in disgust. Finally, I gave him the logbook, dogtags, the Hamair charter journal and manifests, the documents from the underwriter in Texas.

At last Patterson puffed out his cheeks and sat back, an expression almost of amusement of his face. "Are you gentlemen trying to do our job for us?"

"Trying to stay alive," Greg corrected. "You do know the name of Leroy Logan?"

"Of course we know it! The man is notorious. There has been nothing we could prove, and Rolland's lawyers are too high power to make the circus worth its straw," Patterson said acidly. "With this, however . . ." He nodded at the Uzis, the gems, the paperwork. "This time, we have them."

A knock at the door, and a clerk's face appeared. Files were spread on the desk and Patterson began to take notes. Greg read off the longhand report I had drafted on the way over, and he took it down word for word. "You realise you must remain on the island, now," he told us as he finished writing. "There will be questions to be answered."

"Ramifications – for us?" I asked. "We were up to our armpits in this shit!"

"Oh, technicalities," he said amusedly. "Tourists with unlicensed automatic weapons –"

"Used in self-defence," Greg snapped. "The Jamaican government and police department approve of and support the abduction of and dealing in the aforementioned white tourists, bodies for the South American markets, do they? No?"

"My small joke," Patterson admitted. "Naturally, nothing will be made of your use of the weapons. You brought them directly to us."

And they had been taken from us. We still had the shotgun, under the seat in the car, but after having an Uzi in my hand the shotgun did not inspire much confidence. I inhaled the aroma of Earl Grey tea as Patterson spread out a map and handed Greg a marker. He wanted the locations of the plane offshore and the ganja crop that had been burned. Greg marked them up and sat back.

"We're going to need police protection," he said quietly. Patterson looked up at him over the map. "It's not going to take Logan long to work out that we've come to the police. By now, they'll know this little cache is missing from the house, and even though Rolland is dead –"

"The machine goes on." Patterson folded the map. "Yes, of course. Have you been assaulted here in Kingston?"

"Not yet," I said carefully. "But if Logan is a big noise here – and Jeff Mathers' widow told us he is – there'll be people looking for us."

"Where are you staying?" Patterson picked up the phone.

"At the Hotel Croydon. The only place we could get a room."

"I'll give you an escort back there, and a plain clothes officer on your floor," Patterson offered. "It won't take long, Mr. Connor. We can't afford to waste time – Rolland's operation could be in the process of scattering to the four winds even now. If we're to take them, we must do it before they vanish back into the woodwork."

Greg leaned forward. "Tonight? You'll move tonight?"

"We'll certainly try to," Patterson said. "I'll have a squad fly over from Kingston by midnight." He had been disgusted and angry as he heard of the corruption of his colleagues in Montego Bay, but not surprised. The rot is very widespread. "We'll need further details from you, and you can formally identify the men who abducted and abused you. We'll need to find the woman, Shirley Hamilton and the boy, Dennison. They are currently under the protection of a Rastafarian community, so you said?"

"Yes." Tired and restless, I ran my hands through my hair. He made the call, arranged an escort back to the Croydon. The knowledge that Leroy Logan would be in custody by morning – or dead, if he shot it out with the police, which was likely – was sweet. I kept seeing the man's big hands working between my lover's legs. I kept thinking about Shirley's cousin. My heart bled for the kid. A bullet was too good for Logan.

"We can go?" Greg stood, hooking his thumbs into his back pockets.

"So long as you stay in Kingston until further notice." Patterson showed us to the door, and we were free.

A car waited outside. It shadowed us, right on our tail, until Greg had parked and locked the Avis car. The shotgun was still under my seat – no way to get it out under the constable's nose. A young plain clothes man with the telltale bulge of a pistol under his jacket got out of the policecar and followed us up. We left him by the lift, along from our door, and smiled goodnight.

I was weary and yet unable to rest. Greg prowled like a caged cat. "I need a typewriter," he said, looking at the time. It was ten. "This lot has to go back by fax in the morning. Damn." He searched our belongings for the black ballpoint, and settled for bold, clear longhand. The phone book listed a local stationery supplier as a fax service, and the copy would roll out of Lansing's own machine.

The film was more difficult. I unloaded my camera and packaged up the unprocessed stock, consulted the phone book again for an international courier that would get it into Lansing's hands a day after he received the faxed copy. I would not see the pictures until we were home.

It was after midnight when we crawled into bed. Greg cuddled up, his body still tense, strung out. "It'll be happening about now," he said quietly, moistly, into my neck. "It's only a short hop over by plane. They should have hit the mansion from the river."

"Leave that to them," I told him. "I only wish I could have been there to get the pictures."

He dug me in the ribs with one sharp elbow. "We've pushed our luck far enough for one affair. Go to sleep."

I closed my eyes, but sleep was a long time coming.

He was still sound when I woke. I showered, phoned for the courier to pick up my film, and sent for a little breakfast. The raid on Rolland's mansion would be history, so I hoped. I was as eager to have the news as Greg. We went down to the Croydon's lobby to hand my film to the courier. I was filling in the dispatch form when I heard a voice I knew. Greg was buying postcards and Patterson's voice surprised us from the door. Our plain clothes officer looked hung over and fatigued, but he stood vigil by the hooded phones.

"You're looking for us?" I asked, signing my name on the form and collecting the pink slip. The dispatch pouch would be paid for upon receipt and the boy just gave me a smile and left with it. "What have we done wrong – or right?"

"Not a thing," Patterson said quietly. Too quietly. I shot a glance at Greg as he pocketed his postcards. The detective looked tense. "In fact I came to ask a service of you. We need you at the lock-up this morning to identify the men we took into custody in the early hours."

"Identifying Logan will be a pleasure," Greg said tartly.

But Patterson's teeth worried at his lip. "Logan was not one of the arrestees. We took several of the men, and enough evidence to convict a regiment on fifty counts. There was shooting along the river." Greg and I waited. "Logan made it away on one of the motorbikes. We found the bike not far away, dumped, but Logan has gone. It could take some time to find him, and I don't think we can give you adequate protection without locking you into the cells."

"Logan." Greg leaned against the wall's cream paintwork and gave me a grim look. "He'll come straight for us. You realise that."

"And he'll have a good idea where to come," I added, "since he'll know from the where the blade fell. He'll have his little mates here in Kingston gunning for us, won't he, Sergeant?" My blood was like icewater. There are guns without number in the ghetto, and we did not even have the Uzis now. A shotgun did not seem much protection against M-16s, and in fact we had that illegally. If Patterson had known about it, it would have been swiftly confiscated in accordance with Jamaica's ineffective but explicit firearms legislation.

"I can offer you police protection," Patterson said regretfully.

"A holiday in the cells?" Greg said scornfully. "It's the only place we'd be safe! We're not secure in Jamaica or anywhere else, till you churn the mud up and find Logan and the rest . . . Who was holding the Goldmark reins, with Rolland dead?"

Patterson stirred, spoke reluctantly, as if he should not be telling trade secrets. "His brother, Lionel. We are in contact with the United States authorities. Their FBI has dropped on the mainland operation – from a great height. There is only Logan at large." He paused and looked away. "I would not like to see you pay the price for this. We must locate Logan at once. I'll pull strings, get you a flight out."

"Barbados?" Greg asked, looking at me.

"Holiday season," I said doubtfully. "And Rita did a lot of damage, remember. How's London sound? Lansing owes us, wages and bonuses! If we take a flight home we can start again – we're due a holiday. This has been an assignment. It could take a week to track Logan down. Or longer."

Greg stirred, angry and resentful. "Why not? We've had just about enough of this." He gave Patterson a grey-eyed glare. "Thanks for the warning. You've got some trash you want identified? If you can give us a bodyguard we'll just shuttle over to Montego Bay for our gear and get off the island by tonight. We'll blow through so fast Logan won't know we were ever there."

"Very wise," Patterson agreed. "I want to apologise on behalf of my department. And on behalf of Jamaica, if it comes to that. You've seen the ugly face of this country. It's not a very good advertisement for our charms."

I shrugged pragmatically. "On the contrary. No place is much different, and a little integrity goes a long way. We ought to be thanking you, Sergeant."

He drove up over to the lock-up, and we peered into a cell where a dozen rude boys had lined up against the wall. Picking Rolland's men was easy. I don't think I shall ever forget those faces. They were marched out and we were free to go. "Free" was not quite the right word.

"Will you lunch with me?" Patterson asked as we left the lock-up. He held open the rear door of his car. Greg gave me a wary look as he slid inside. Was Patterson just trying to be sociable, or were we in some kind of trouble? "I know a wonderful little cafe not far from your hotel," the detective added pleasantly.

"Why not?" I followed Greg into the car.

Patterson pulled out of the asphalt wasteland of the lock-up's rear carpark. I sat waiting for the storm to break but Patterson said nothing about Rolland's business, or Logan. We parked beside one of the tourist-trap restaurants, an establishment that looked like a native Jamaican cafe but was in fact a plastic replica. Patterson was still smiling as he ushered us inside. I smelt seafood and wine. Some local artist had painted porpoise and seahorses in a fresco around the walls. Overhead, fan blades turned languidly, stirring the humid air.

A beautiful youth brought the menu, and since Patterson was picking up the tab, I ordered the lobster. Greg took the wine list. "Are you on duty, Sergeant?"

"Yes, but by all means order for yourselves," Patterson said easily. "For me, mineral water."

I leaned back into the green basketwork chair and looked out through vast plate glass windows at the passers-by. "What's this about? It feels like we're being softened up for something. Charges?"

"Charges?" Patterson smiled faintly. "Why, what have you done to answer for in a Jamaican courtroom?"

I thought about the shotgun in our rented car. "In all the excitement, we seem to have forgotten about one of the firearms," I confessed. "Until we took the Uzis from Rolland's safe it was the best we could do – the shotgun we took from a pub called The Maroon, over in Montego Bay. As a matter of fact, Shirley Hamilton took it from the barman while Logan was trying to make fish food of us. Guts seem to run in the Hamilton family.

"I read Hamilton's file last night," Patterson said thoughtfully. "And Jeff Mathers'. Which reminds me, gentlemen, there will be a reward from the insurance company, of course."

"For the return of the stones?" Greg leaned across the table.

"Yes." Patterson paused as the boy brought his mineral water, and the waiter squeezed between the tables toward us. "Also, the Jamaican government offers a quite generous reward for information leading to the arrest of dealers in marijuana, and illegal firearms."

Greg sampled the crisp white wine and chuckled. "We cover the costs of one wasted holiday, then."

The policeman's expression darkened. "You leave us with a poor impression of Jamaica, and this concerns me. Your editor is a very influential man –"

"If you're thinking you can persuade us to omit the details about police corruption in the Montego Bay area," Greg said sharply, "forget it. If the police there had done their damned jobs, none of this would have happened. And you wouldn't be turning Paraguay and points south inside out looking for castrated merchandise!"

The plain talking produced a visible wince and then Patterson pasted on the diplomatic smile. "No, of course I won't ask you to do that. Your whole function is to report facts." He leaned toward us. "I am here on behalf of my superiors to ask you to do just that. To report facts. Not sensation and allegation."

I smiled at Greg. "You mean you don't trust us?"

Patterson puffed out his cheeks as he considered his lunch without seeing the plate. "Let me say, the gentlemen of the press have a reputation that leaves a lot to be desired."

"And *Perspective* has a reputation of its own to prop up," Greg added. "Relax, Sergeant. We live on fact. The truth is sensational enough without our rearranging it."

"And we'll put in a good word for your people," I offered. "If you can get the mess cleaned up."

"Logan." Patterson sipped his mineral water. "The problem with Jamaica, as with any island, is that the sea is a fugitive's ally. If he gets hold of a boat he can leave any cove around a coastline five hundred miles long. He may have left the island already."

But Greg shook his head slowly. "I'm just guessing, but I'm sure he'll want to settle accounts with us before he gets out."

"Yes. I have put this case to my superiors already." Patterson abandoned his meal for the moment and steepled his fingers on the edge of the table. "And I have a proposition to put to you. Turn it down if you wish. No one will blame you if you do. It is dangerous, I shall be the first to admit, although it was all my idea." We waited, frowning deeply at the man as Patterson seemed to wriggle in embarrassment. "We want Logan. While you gentlemen are on the island, we know where he will be – waiting for his chance to make mischief with you! As soon as you are gone, he has no reason to stay. We may never pick him up, and he will simply begin again in the same enterprises in Trinidad or Honduras."

A moment's silence reigned, and then Greg said, "You want to use us as bait?" Patterson nodded. "What do you want us to do? Walk around, show our smiling faces, let him see us. Let him make his move? And then?"

"And then my men will take him." Patterson made a swift neck-wringing gesture. "You will never be out of sight of my squad, on the street, and your room will be secure, I can assure you."

Butterflies churned in my stomach. I looked at Greg. He wore a sober expression, a mask for turbulent thoughts. Only his eyes betrayed the calculations going on behind that mask. Sharp as a hunting wolf, they looked piercingly at me. At last he said quietly, "I'm game. It'll make a hell of a sequel to the story we faxed Lansing earlier. And Logan isn't the only one wanting to see accounts settled."

His mouth tightened. I knew he was recalling Logan's hands on him, the threats and promises that had been made. The butterflies settled and I nodded. "All right, Patterson, you're on. You'll want to set this up at once, I suppose. And it's not going to work if we barricade ourselves into a hotel room like a fortress. How good are your people?"

"Good enough," Patterson promised us, as if a weight had been lifted off his shoulders. He smiled at us both. "They have a lot to prove, in the eyes of the international press. Their honour is at stake, if you will." He returned to his meal.

"Leave the details of the reward settlements to me. I'll hurry things along, since you're visitors to the island. For now, come back to the office with me and let me make arrangements."

We finished lunch in an uneasy silence, and Greg was still silent as we were shown into Patterson's office and a secretary brought coffee. "Second thoughts?" I asked, when we were alone.

"No," he said blandly. "I'm just trying to work out our luck. We keep blundering into the shit and somehow climb out smelling of roses." He gave me a conspiratorial wink, and then gave his attention to Patterson, as the policeman returned with an open file. The name on it read: Logan, Leroy.

11

IT was evening before Patterson's arrangements were complete. The shotgun had been picked up, the Avis car delivered to the Kingston agency, and a squad car drove us out to the airport. Were we observed even then? I could not forget what Mrs. Mathers had said. The Kingston ghetto knew Logan. If he made a phone call, his associates could be watching us. And Patterson knew that. I gave the man his due, he was shrewd, the consummate professional. The corruption of his colleagues in Montego Bay angered him, as did the trade in black bodies.

Three gaudy old cars followed the police vehicle. Their occupants looked liked touring Coruba salesmen, the worse for wear after quality-testing their product. In fact, they were the best men Patterson had, and heavily armed. Airport security officers waited for us. The metal detectors were off, and the whole party boarded a low-profile domestic shuttle without incident. Greg and I sat between four of Patterson's bodyguards, and still my nerves were like piano wires.

Coffee was served and as we began to relax Greg put his head back, closed his eyes. "New Zealand," he said cryptically, cynically.

"New Zealand?" I helped myself to the last shortbread.

"Far, far away," he reasoned, "from Logan and his box of toys."

"Cold feet?" I spoke softly, under the background buzz of the plane, a noisy, rattly old DC3. "You want to pull the plug and get out?"

"Give it a few days," he mused. "If Logan doesn't make his move by then we can assume he's not on the island. And I can live without the anxiety!"

I wished I could have touched him, if only to offer moral support. I envied the black couple sitting ahead of us, at liberty to kiss while they laughed over whispered secrets. "We haven't been to New Zealand," I said, hoping to divert him. We almost went there on assignment when the French secret service sank the *Rainbow Warrior*, but Lansing had us earmarked for more dangerous games.

"New Zealand, then." He gazed out at the cloudy twilight sky. The sun was just down, the plane seemed to be floating on pink cotton wool. "Of course, it'll be cold there. No outdoor sports."

"Indoor sports?" I winked at him. He laughed quietly. "We'd better send a message to Falmouth about that boat. Jesus, we don't even know if it's smashed or salvageable."

"Neither does the owner," Greg added. "For all he knows, we sank it and drowned. He won't be expecting to see us again, not after Rita."

The wind off the sea was cool as we left the plane. The bodyguards kept close, hustling us through the airport while appearing to simply get in our way. A young man in plain clothes waited for us at the car rental desk. I glimpsed a police badge and arched a brow at him in question. Patterson had been thorough. Only we knew the car I drove out of the airport was a police vehicle, with a policeman hunched down in the back of it. If Logan or one of his rude boys was watching, we must have looked like sitting ducks.

My nerves crawled as I parked beside The Marina, where our bags had been under lock and key. Two officers in plain clothes appeared out of the shadows, following us into the vestibule. They stepped into the lift with us, and a soft Jamaican voice said, "The room is quite safe. We checked it less than an hour ago, and it's been watched since."

A little reassured, we left the lift. I glanced back to see one of the two bodyguards take station beside an enormous floral arrangement. If one bothered to notice, his revolver was visible through his jacket. Greg dug through his pockets for the key to a room we had never used.

My first concern was for my cameras, but I need not have worried. Our bags were undisturbed, as we had left them. Rolland's men had rummaged through them once, the afternoon before we were jumped just above the beach. They must have been satisfied with the innocence of cameras, underwear and suntan lotion.

The room was small and plain by comparison with the one we had booked at The Grand. We had spent less than an hour in it, and I gave it a sour look as I repacked my cameras. I wondered if the staff at The Grand had entertained suspicions about two men, sharing a holiday, and a bed. Probably. The receptionists only giggled, but had we been Jamaican rather than tourists, we would have been vilified. So long as you are paying handsomely, you are due polite disregard.

Greg surveyed the room and its bed, made up with lilac-coloured linen, and turned his back on it. "Do you want to eat here of go out?"

"We'd better show our faces," I said drily. "No good being here and Logan not knowing." I opened the door a crack and beckoned the bodyguard closer. "We're going to go out for dinner. Give us half an hour to shower and change, and then for Christ's sake, don't be far away!"

As I closed the door I saw the man running up the aerial on a discreet little radio transmitter. Greg was already in the bathroom, preparing to shave. "If we give Logan a good look at us, he might crawl out of the woodwork tonight, and we're off the hook."

"Optimist," I accused, and kissed the back of his neck before I set the shower hot.

In fact, he was right. We had to be visible. I was not hungry, but when we left the room, a few minutes before eight, we turned down toward the waterfront where we knew several decent restaurants. I chanced a glance over my shoulder. Three big men shadowed us, keeping as close as they could without being obvious. I slowed my pace, holding Greg back to make their job a little easier.

We ate chicken and fried rice, chose the Budweiser rather than wine, in the interests of our wits, and lingered over the meal. The restaurant fronted onto the beach. Beyond a low wall, boys and girls played volleyball in the warm sand. Our bodyguards stood back, out of the lights and music – surely only we would know they were there.

After the pastries, Greg shook his head. "This is no good.

Logan won't have eyes and ears in this kind of place."

"Blacktown?" I was about to send for coffee, but hesitated as Greg scraped back his chair.

"Do you want to settle this, or string the agony out?" He beckoned the waitress and took the bill from her.

"Blacktown," I concluded as I threaded through the tables after him to the cashier's alcove. Our bodyguards moved with us like shadows.

We ambled slowly, as if we were hunting for some kind of nightlife. Action was scarce, but we stumbled on a round of amateur boxing competition. A couple of welter weights hammered at each other like fighting cocks, half killed each other for a little silver cup and a few dollars. I did not see much of the fight. My eyes were everywhere in the crowd. Paranoia painted Logan's face onto any man even vaguely similar.

After an hour in the heat, noise and overpowering aroma of crushed male bodies, Greg nudged my arm. We slipped out of the pall of cigarette smoke and into the cool of the street. It was dark, the streetlights sporadic this deep in the local quarter. My heart thumped at my ribs and I tried not to look for the bodyguards, which would only point them out to Logan's men, if we were already tailed.

We walked back toward the sea. The heavy, voodoo beat of a reggae band called us into a late-night club. A bevvy of island girls bounced around, topless and pneumatic. Dedicated boozers were snoring peacefully by the bar. The show was over when a voice we knew called my name.

"How wonderful to find you here!" Shirley Hamilton said as she pushed her way through toward our corner. Greg pulled up a spare chair and beckoned the waitress. "Isaac had the news from his cousins on the fishing boats. A big shootout on the river, and it's all over!" She smiled up at the waitress. "Pink gin, please." Then she turned back to us and laughed, effervescent with relief. She looked ten years younger than she had the day we met her at The Maroon. "I ought to be thanking you, but I don't know where to start."

"Don't," Greg said softly. "Not yet, love. You're not safe . . . Did Isaac get the news that Leroy Logan got out of Rolland's place?" The girls face stiffened, its good humour vanished. She shook her head. The fingers about the beaded handbag began to tremble. "The Kingston police suckered us into baiting a trap for Logan," Greg went on in an undertone. "We're just showing our faces. As soon as he makes his move, there's three .38s ready to stop him dead. And I do mean, *dead*. No, don't look!" She was peering over both shoulders, trying to pick the bodyguards.

"Logan won't be after me, will he?" she whispered as she took her drink from the waitress.

Greg and I looked at each other, and at last I shook my head. "We're his first priority. We must be, or you'd be dead already if he wanted you dead." She shivered visibly. "Look, go back where you came from and stay safe. If he makes a move to take us – and he will, if he's on the island, it's the only reason he'd have stayed on Jamaica! – it's all over." Famous last words? Greg gave me a sidelong look but said nothing.

"I came here to thank you," she said bitterly. "And I still do."

"For what?" Greg found a smile for her. "All we did was look after our interests. It was our backsides Rolland wanted to kick. Among other things." The last was said ruefully, and with a wink at me. We had our own scores to settle with the man.

She sipped nervously at the gin. "You've got police protection here? Then I'm as safe here as anywhere! I wanted to tell you, the insurance company sent a man to see me this afternoon. They're going to pay out since the cargo was recovered and Goldmark is being hauled over the coals in America. I'll get enough out of it to start again."

"Another aircraft?" I asked.

"Yes. A Beechcraft, something we can afford. Jeff Mathers' wife wants to come back, run the office while I do most of the flying. It'll work out. Nothing can bring back my dad and my cousin, but . . ." She shrugged. "Rolland is dead. They didn't hang him, but he wouldn't have been any deader if they had."

"He burned to death," Greg told her quietly. "In the bushfire. Hanging would have been kinder."

"Yes." She sobered and was silent for a time. "I just want to say thanks. I owe you a lot, but somehow I doubt it's a debt I could pay off." She was teasing us. She was not the type to tender favours if her knight errant expected them. An old-fashioned island girl with very proper morals. So she had noticed Greg and me. She was mocking, humour at our expense, but it was a gentle mockery that amused us too.

"You don't owe us anything," I told her honestly. "We were sitting targets without the key to the puzzle. You put us onto it." I have her my hand across the table. "Now, get out of here, go back where you came from. Logan won't worry about you until he's had a crack at us, and when he does take that crack the whole thing is over." She took my hand and leaned over to kiss Greg's cheek. "Be lucky," I told her as she left us. The last we saw of Shirley Hamilton was a swirl of yellow skirt as she made her way out past the boozers at the bar.

"Your faith in Patterson's men is touching," Greg said drily as he finished his beer and stood.

"And you don't trust them?" I upturned my empty glass on the coaster and followed him toward the door. Behind us, our three shadows stuck tight. "If you don't trust them, we ought to be out and running, right now."

"Maybe we should." He stopped for a moment in the doorway and looked back at the bar. "Did you see the tall, skinny-legged ferret, just before Shirley arrived? Saw us, dived at the nearest phone. Come on, Alex. We've done our bit for tonight."

"They've seen us," I concluded. My spine crawled as we turned out into the street, heading toward our hotel.

It would take Logan time to react, organize some action. With the door locked behind us, and our bodyguard on station down the passageway, I picked up the phone to punch Patterson's private line. He answered at once, as if he had been waiting for a call.

"We think we've been seen," I said tersely. "Let your men know. The perfect way to get rid of us would be to snatch us out of the room and lose the bodies overboard in the night. Everything a big mystery, no one to point the finger at!"

"Lock your door and leave everything to me." Patterson sounded as tense as I felt. "Stay in your room, no matter what you hear, do you understand? So long as we know where you are, we can control Logan's activities."

I hung up with a perfunctory acknowledgement. "Logan's activities," I mimicked. Greg gave me a glance over the bed, which he was turning down. "Stay in the room, he said. So long as he knows where we are, he can control Logan's *activities*. Christ!" I was thinking of that young boy, Shirley's cousin.

"Patterson's right, though. We stay put." Greg hung his jeans over the back of a chair, threw shirt and underwear into a bag for the laundry, and slid into the bed. The light doused moments later.

We were both tired out by tension and yet knew we would not sleep. We might have had a chance of at least resting, but as we met in the middle of the bed something cold and hard jabbed my leg and I threw back the quilt. Greg snapped on the light. "What the fuck is that?" He had felt it too, and scrabbled after the object.

It lay malevolently in his palm. "That," I said quietly as an uncomfortable chill shivered my gut, "is a hollow nosed .303 centerfire cartridge. Heavy calibre, for a long shot . . . They've been in here, before the police checked the room. Patterson's goons just made sure there was no one in here. They wouldn't have thought to look in the bed."

"Jesus." He rolled the rifle cartridge in his fingers and then handed it to me. "So Logan's on the island. This was to let us know, even if we weren't quick enough to see the informant at the bar." He closed his eyes. "We'd have been dead tonight. You realise that."

I took him against me and held him tight. Of a sudden he was cold. I pulled the quilt over our heads. "We just do as Patterson says, and stay right where we are. Greg?"

His mouth hunted for mine. His fingers dug into my shoulders, hurting a little. It was an hour before we settled, and sleep was impossible. I was still wide awake in the hour before dawn, and when Greg sat up I put on the light. He looked hung over. "Breakfast?" I suggested, already reaching for the phone.

The kitchens were not on yet, and we were sent toast and cereal, fresh coffee and cream. We ate in bed, both of us looking at the .303 cartridge. "Ought to tell Patterson about that," Greg said tartly. He dusted crumbs off his chest and poured the last of the coffee.

I hoped Patterson had news for us. If Logan had been in our room to leave the bullet, and if his informant had phoned home as soon as we were seen and recognized, it could be all over. I phoned Kingston while Greg messed about in the bathroom. It was barely daylight. Patterson sounded tired. He would have been on duty the whole night, while his set-up was running.

"There was a disturbance," he allowed, almost grudgingly.

"A disturbance? What the hell does that mean?" I demanded.

"An intruder on the ground floor. My men surprised him and he made off again. It was probably only a burglar," Patterson said carefully.

"Or it could have been Logan. If your men let him see their guns, and they're pretty bloody obvious, Patterson, of course Logan would get out again. The man's not an idiot."

"Yes." The line was quiet for a moment. "It might be safe to assume that he now knows you're guarded. He is aware of the trap set for him."

"So what happens now?" I sprawled on the bed, weary, eyes closed, listening half to Patterson and half to my lover's quiet movements about bedroom and bathroom. "Will he try again in the hotel?"

"Probably not," the policeman said shrewdly. "Too many nooks and crannies, too easily guarded, in a building that size. It puts the odds in our favour. Logan wouldn't buy that, not in his position. Running."

"So, if he wants to take a shot at us, it'll be in the open," I concluded. "A long shot. Jesus Christ." I told him about the bullet in quiet, bald phrases, and heard undertone swearing.

"I can't ask you to go on with this," Patterson said regretfully. "I don't think you need me to outline the dangers. If you want to get off the island, you're free to go. We'll do the best we can with Logan."

And if they missed him? If Logan made it out, to Barbados, Honduras, anywhere he had friends, business associates? How desperate was he to bury the pair of us? Greg appeared from the bathroom, one towel knotted loosely about his hips, the other hanging about his shoulders. He sank the mattress beside me and put his hand on my chest.

"If we tried to get off the island," I mused, "he would be perfectly capable of taking a shot at us at the airport. It comes down to the same game, Patterson. Skeet shooting, and we're the skeets! Look, let's set something up and get it finished. I've got a .303 hollow nosed in my hand that lets me know he wants us. Bet your pension that was him creating your little 'disturbance' last night. So if we're going to be targets for a rifle shot, let's give him plenty of room. The greater the distance, the better the chance he'll misjudge the wind or the drop of shot, and miss with the first round, yes?"

"You know your firearms, Mr. Connor," Patterson observed.

"A lot of Australians do," I said tiredly. "It was always a big, rural country. Why don't we set something up out of the town? I don't know that I like the idea of innocent bystanders in the crossfire."

He made noises of agreement. I could tell he was relieved,

that his scheme was not about to unravel. I wondered if he gave a shit for us, behind the diplomatic façade. "If we are going to arrange an incident, I would prefer to do it quickly. The more time Logan has at his disposal, the stronger he will become. At this moment, Rolland's organization is in complete disarray, but Logan will soon have access to manpower and weapons that will place you and Mr. Farris in much greater danger."

"Today, then," I said quietly, looking up at Greg. "Hold the line for a minute. I'll let Greg in on all this." I put the phone down, muffled by the bed to buy us a little privacy.

"I heard most of it," Greg told me. "Loud connection. You're talking about getting out of Montego Bay, and putting some distance between Logan and us. Gives us half a chance."

"If he fluffs the shot with the first round," I affirmed. "Either that, honey, or we try to get out. *Try*. He can drop us at the airport, and in that kind of scenario we haven't even got the option of shooting back." I reached up to kiss his mouth, and his tongue flicked mine. "I don't see that we've got much of a choice."

"We haven't." He raked his fingers through his hair, tousling it, and took the phone. "Sergeant Patterson, this is Farris. I've been thinking, while you were talking to Alex. What about the river country, upstream, away from the town? It gets marshy and wild. The best shot Logan could get at us would be from the bank, because you people could put a boat on the river right behind us, block him out. It gives us a chance and keeps the civilians out of the way. He's going to know he's being set up, but if this doesn't draw him, nothing will. Interested?"

"Very," Patterson said. The line was loud enough to carry quite clearly in the quiet room. "I have a young man called Hardey covering your room at this time. He and I will set the whole thing up. But until everything is organized, please stay in your room. You understand?"

Greg held the bullet up for closer inspection. "Oh, we understand. I think we know a location for this little shooting party that would be ideal. We told you how we ran the boat aground, before the hurricane. We ought to go back and see if it survived."

"Excellent," Patterson said readily. "Hardey will see to everything. I can't come over to Montego Bay until tomorrow, but I will be there as soon as I can tie up loose ends here.

Oh, incidentally, I have good news for you. The rewards for the return of the jewels, and for information leading to the closure of Rolland's enterprise will be paid shortly. And I understand that it amounts to a very sizeable sum . . . I'll be in touch, Mr. Farris. Sergeant Hardey will see to the details, with my authority. I can tell you, the squad backing you is quite competent to undertake this exercise."

" 'Exercise', he calls it," I echoed as Greg hung up the phone. He flopped belly-down beside me and I sat up, rubbing his back for the simple pleasure of touch. His brow creased in thought. "What are you thinking now?" He has a journalist's corkscrew cortex.

"Money." He stretched under my hands like a cat. "What would you say the pot-head would take for the boat? What's it worth?"

"Depends," I mused. "How desperate's the kid for money? I presume you're talking about the reward payout?"

"If it covers the asking price."

"If it doesn't all we've got left is our retirement fund, and I don't know how intelligent it would be to spend that."

The retirement fund is a pool of money in a high interest account, added to religiously, every week and especially if we find ourselves on bonuses, or if a pony gets its nose in front. It's there against the time one of us comes home incapacitated. It could happen any day. We don't delude ourselves. We have been beaten and shot often enough to be aware of our mortality. If one of us is missing a limb, or has split vision, or some injury, we need to know we can live in comfort. We have expensive tastes, and the pension will not cover them.

Dip into our retirement fund to buy a boat? I mulled the idea over but dismissed it. "No, it was just a thought." I stooped to kiss along his spine. "And in any case, you're counting your chickens. When we get out there we might find a heap of junk where a boat used to be."

He turned over and looked up at me out of enormous, storm-grey eyes. "Or we could end the day extremely dead. Patterson's taking liberties. If I thought we had half a chance of living happily ever after with Logan at large, I'd be out and running now."

He had pulled me down and I had his towel off when a knock from the door interrupted. He swore, and pulled on clean white denims as I dressed quickly and went to admit young Sergeant Hardey. Very big, very dark, very softly spoken, he smiled almost shyly at us. I realised belatedly that the bed told its own story. It was too late for deception, but Hardey did not seem to have taken umbrage. In fact, he kept studying us surreptitiously, and had he been white I'm sure he would have blushed scarlet.

Was he gay, and too scared to come out? The West Indies is not a good place to be gay. My heart warmed toward him, and I rang down for a second breakfast for three as Greg searched out his road map and weighted it with a vase of roses on one end of it and a heavy smoked glass ashtray on the other on the table under the window. They leaned over the map, and Greg's fingertip traced the course of the river.

"We took her upstream, turned into this tributary, and ran her aground right below a hill, about here. There's nothing for miles."

"Only mud and mangroves," I elaborated. "If you could put a boat on the water behind us, Logan would find it awkward to get a clear shot."

"Too awkward?" Greg wondered.

I straightened from the map. "You want to make it easy for him?"

"I didn't say that," Greg said sharply. "But if he doesn't take a shot, or if he does, and the police sharpshooters fluff it, he'll just try again tomorrow." He folded his arms on his chest, a defiant posture. "I'll be the tethered goat for once, Alex. Not twice. If this doesn't work, we're just begging for trouble if we try it again."

Hardey frowned deeply at us. "I could get you to the airport, onto a plane out." We looked speculatively at him and he seemed to squirm in an agony of embarrassment, so shy of us it was painful. "In a truck, right to the plane. He'd never get a clear shot."

"And once we were gone, he'd vanish," Greg said quietly. "Out of Jamaica, set up again in Trinidad or somewhere. Next thing we know, he's in London, looking for us, and we'll be just as dead there. That wasn't what was on my mind." He looked at me. "If this goes wrong on the river tomorrow, Logan's not the only one with friends. Well-armed friends."

"What, Isaac's Rastafarians?" My brows rose.

"I'm sick of being hunted," Greg said hoarsely. "Two can play at Logan's game. The bush country here is no different to the bush in Laos and Thailand, and we survived there. Time to go hunting, with the kind of guns the Rastas seem to have plenty of."

"If your sharpshooters blow it," I said to Hardey, "I'm with Greg. If it comes down to a matter of tethered goats and tigers, I'd rather be a tiger."

The young man puffed out his cheeks. "Patterson would never go for it."

"Patterson would have to find us," Greg retorted. "We dodged a Khmer platoon for a week to get a story. I think we could stay out of Patterson's way. We might hand you Leroy Logan alive, if slightly damaged."

"If you killed him," Hardey said hesitantly, "there would be complications. You'd be using illegal firearms. They could call it murder, unless it was self-defence at the end, and even if it was self-defence, there would be firearms charges. Patterson would probably try to straighten it out for you, but he isn't a magician."

Greg and I studied each other in silence. I arched one brow at him in silent question and he shrugged minutely. At last Greg sighed heavily and perched on the side of the table. "How good are these sharpshooters of yours?"

"Good enough," Hardey said without brashness. He rolled up the map and stepped back from the table. "I'll take this and arrange for the boats and the squad. Stay in the room today, please. I'll let you know the details as soon as Sergeant Patterson has authorized the exercise."

The word taunted me. I slammed the door after Hardey and resorted to a shot of whisky to settle my nerves. Greg still perched on the table but said nothing. What was there to say? It could turn ugly in any number of ways, and the ugliest picture to visualise was Greg and myself doing time in a Jamaican nick for insuring our own lives with the "murder" of Leroy Logan. Dead men cannot be prosecuted, no matter their crimes, and it is the survivors who must face the music. Unless we had witnesses, what else could it look like, but the deliberate killing of a man? Neither Greg nor I would pull a trigger even on Logan, unless there was no other option, but how would we prove that before a jury?

The day was a year long. We ate in the room, played cards, listened to the radio, made love halfheartedly in the afternoon. I could not keep my mind on our wrangling, and at last cursed Logan for spoiling even that. Greg sent for drinks and we shared the hot tub instead.

A knock at the door at six announced Hardey. He was all optimism as I let him inside. "Tomorrow, at eight, we begin." He thrust a boat hire slip at me, and I had to smile. The *Light Fantastic* was ours for the day. "I will have two men covering the boat ramp, two will cover you from the room here and out to Conway's. Take the boat well offshore. You will be safe until you enter the river, at which time Logan will almost certainly be on the water and after you. Cut speed in the river mouth and wait for the white launch with red trim. That is our boat. Very fast, I promise you. Two of the best marksmen I've ever worked with will be on it, and so will I. All we need is a clear sighting of Logan."

"And with us as bait, you should get that," I said tartly.

"All right. Eight in the morning. Good evening, Sergeant."

He hovered at the door, looking us over and glancing covertly at the bed. I felt a moment's genuine pity as I closed up and locked the door. "He's on his way to the funny farm," Greg said sadly.

"You've noticed." I slid the boat hire form into my wallet.

"I'm not blind." He snaked both arms about me from behind and rubbed my chest. "I'm sorry about this afternoon. I couldn't keep my mind on the job. I mucked everything up for you, didn't I?"

"I thought I mucked it up," I said honestly. I turned into his arms and nibbled along his prickly jaw. Whiskers rasped on whiskers, making him smile. "He's a good-looking kid," I added thoughtfully.

"You're not considering –?"

I swatted his arse, hard enough to produce a yelp. "I was just thinking how much he'd be in demand at one of two of the pubs at home. He's in the wrong place, wrong time."

"Pity, Alex?" He threaded his fingers through my hair, rubbing my scalp, which can be an astonishingly erotic sensation.

"It's a healthy emotion," I said drily. "It's going to be a long night."

He chuckled at my waggled eyebrow. "I dare say we'll think of something to do. Make up for that washout this afternoon." He turned away from me quickly, hoping to hide the sudden tension of his face, but I saw.

"Greg? What?"

"I feel like a condemned man offered a hearty breakfast," he said bitterly. "No, Alex, don't say it. Leave it alone." He fended off my attempts at cheer and smacked my mouth with a kiss that almost bit. "Phone for something to eat. Waiting makes me hungry."

"Nervy," I corrected blandly.

He shot me a glare that softened into a curious half-smile. "That too."

12

I WAS tired by the night's unpleasant anticipation when Hardey knocked at our door. It was just before eight. We were dressing to leave. I let the policeman in and was about to make some sharp remark about being trusted to be punctual. Then I saw the sport carryall he had brought, and merely waited. Unzipped, it disgorged two kevlar vests, the thin, seemingly flimsy kind that are designed to be worn under police uniforms, every working moment.

Deep brown eyes studied us one at a time, and Hardey said, "Wear these. Patterson's orders."

"How thoughtful." Greg slipped off his shirt. I saw the tip of Hardey's tongue moisten his lips, a little give-away gesture, as he looked over my lover's body. The velcro rasped into place and Greg adjusted the fit of the vest. "Going to sweat inside this today."

"Suffer," I retorted. I pulled my own shirt over my head and tried the kevlar for fit. It was not as heavy as I had imagined. "This isn't going to stop a .303 round at close range. You know that."

"I know." Greg pulled on his blue shirt and raked back his hair. "And if he shoots low –" he patted his flat belly "– we might as well not be wearing these sweatshirts at all."

"Cheerful." I gave the policeman a hard look. "Any problems?"

But he shook his head at once. "Everything is set, and Patterson is coming over this evening, if he can get away. He must report to officers from the American State Department first. They may detain him." Hardey hesitated at the door. "Stick to the plan. I'm sure you'll be safe."

I wished I was as complacent as I followed Greg out of the hotel and into the bright, fresh morning. The sea was green, the sky that deep, burnished, tropical blue. Little rivulets of sweat prickled my ribs inside the kevlar vest. Behind us, Hardey and two others shadowed us at a discreet distance. My eyes were everywhere as we walked toward Conway's ramp. I began to chastise myself for jumping at shadows. After the odds Greg and I had gambled on in the past, Patterson's game was decent enough.

"Fat Conway" was absent from the ramp. He would have been taken in with the rest of Rolland's support group when the rude boys began to volunteer information in the hopes of saving their own skins. In Conway's place was his wife, even stouter than the beached whale. She seemed delighted to be rid of her husband. I handed her the boat hire slip, and as Greg hopped aboard I started the outboards.

We breathed a little easier as we headed fast away from the ramp. With a quarter mile of water between us and the tourist hotels I turned east toward the river. The *Light Fantastic* was fast, but I deliberately kept the speed down. Logan must have time to get the call from his informants, and get a boat on the river, or the whole exercise was pointless. We were clearly visible from the shore, making slow headway against the current, and just short of the river mouth, where brown, silt-heavy water poured out into the sea, I shut back the outboards.

"Let's give the man a chance," I said bitterly. "Ten minutes?"

"But no longer," Greg guessed. "If he's managed to get his hands on a powerboat, those damn things get up and fly." He glanced at his watch, and sat on the side of the boat. "They ought to be able to see us from shore without binoculars."

"And a 'scoped rifle would make Logan's job easy," I added as my narrowed eyes swept along the coast. "Not from there, though. Tourist beaches."

Greg took the wheel when we moved off again, and the cruiser butted into the muddy river waters. If ever we were in jeopardy, it was as we cut speed to connect with the white police launch. I saw it first, disguised among smaller pleasure craft. A moment later Greg saw it too, and opened the throttles. The cruiser picked up speed, and I looked back to see the launch not far behind us.

At least our backs were safe. Greg slowed to navigate around barges and the residue of storm damage, and the launch matched pace with us as we made our way upstream. The waterways were choked with debris, the banks silted with mud. Dredges had cleared the midwater channel, but our tributary would be impassable for craft drawing much more water than the cruiser and launch. I wondered if the *Spirit of Jamaica* was too deep-draughted to make it out, even if she had survived the storm.

The launch rode our tail, a dozen boat lengths behind. We ambled by Rolland's mansion, with its private landing stage and rotting old boat house. The door we had chipped off its hinges lay in the shallows among rank waterweeds and rusting debris. The red cabin cruiser was still tied up at the landing, but the yellow dive boat was missing.

"You see what isn't there?" Greg said quietly. I answered with a grunt as I looked over the property. We had barely glimpsed it as we were hustled in, naked and hurting. It was decadently expensive, and it was embittering to know that the wealth behind it was derived from such human suffering. Nothing ever changes.

I looked back, beyond the police launch, searching the river for a daub of yellow. Where was that dive boat? Had Patterson's squad had it and lost it? Or had it never been in their custody? I felt the familiar churning in my stomach and touched Greg's shoulder. "Move it. So long as we're moving we're halfway safe. I'll keep a look out."

We powered on up the river, making good time where the lugger had battled against current and wind to make headway at all. The mouth of our tributary was choked with debris. Just sufficient space remained for the cruiser to squeeze through, but the water level was still high after the flooding.

As Greg throttled back to ease us through I saw movement on the far bank, something red, a flash of sunlight on glass. A windscreen? I put up a hand to shield my eyes as corneal after-images danced in my vision, and caught a glimpse of a big 4x4. "That could be trouble."

"Could be joyriders," Greg muttered. "Get down in the boat, Alex. Don't make it easy for him!"

I sat down casually, as if I had not even noticed the vehicle. Greg took the cruiser smoothly into the tributary and, behind us, the launch waddled through the reed banks. "We're running out of time," I said tersely as the outboards cut back to just above idling. "If he doesn't make his move soon he won't get a chance. Christ, is he even there? Or is all this just paranoia?"

"He's there." Greg shaded his eyes to scan the banks. "You

think he doesn't know that launch is setting him up? He'll have a good look before he commits himself . . . You see what I see?"

I bobbed up out of the well of the boat. The *Spirit of Jamaica* had almost floated off with the rising storm water as the river swelled with runoff from the washaways up in the Cockpit. She looked in perfect condition, just a little muddy. Greg brought the cruiser alongside, and hopped aboard to tie up. In the sudden quiet I heard the police launch cut speed, but its inboards continued to idle as it drifted in toward the mud banks. No way could its presence behind us be a coincidence. I swore lividly as I stepped over onto the lugger. What kind of fool would Logan be to show his hand now? Every rich opportunity, on the river, had gone by.

No one could have been on the lugger since we left her, which was pure luck. Looters had been busy in the ruins of the shantytowns, but we found our things just as we had left them. Even the cabin smelt clean, so she had been watertight. Inside, in comparative safety, we took a moment to get our breath. But Greg was restless, unable to be still for long.

"I'm going to go and look at the tackle and sails. The sharpshooters should have taken a good look around by now –"

"So will Logan," I snapped.

"Then the sooner he crawls out from under his rock, the sooner they can drop him!" Greg stooped to look out through the muddied glass at the launch, which was riding downstream to cover us. "The waiting's going to kill me, never mind Logan." He swung open the low cabin door. "Coming?"

Sweating heavily inside the kevlar, I followed him up on deck. We spent the longest half hour of my life checking her lines and canvas. Then Greg cracked a can of Coors and stood in the shade to drink. "He's not going to go for it, is he?" He handed me the can, and I took a draught of the tepid, bitter liquid. "He had a hundred chances on the river. What in Christ's name is he playing at?" He took back the can and drained it. "You reckon the diesel would pull her out? The bow isn't wedged in too deeply now. You know, the kid who owns her probably thinks she sank in the storm. Now, we'll take her back, hand her over so she can rot at anchor, or run ganja into American waters till the Florida Coast Guard sinks her!"

I crushed the flimsy aluminium can and tossed it into the

cabin. I whistled stridently over the growl of the launch's idling engines, and when Hardey's face appeared, gave him a wave. The launch wallowed up, rocking the lugger against the mud. "He's not going to bite," I called, and did not care if Leroy Logan was near enough to hear. "Maybe he doesn't fancy shooting it out with half the Kingston police! It was worth a try, but as soon as we turned off the river into the tributary, the game was over."

"Give him another hour," Hardey suggested. "It might take him that long to get out here."

"What about the yellow dive boat?" Greg asked sharply.

"Dive boat?" Hardey's face was blank.

"The one that was missing from Rolland's landing," he elaborated. Hardey merely shook his head. "Then if he got out with that, he's mobile. If Logan wanted to jump us on the river, he'd have done it. Shit."

"You want to go back?" I asked, speaking to Greg and ignoring Hardey. Years of experience have taught me to value Greg's instincts.

His teeth worried his lip for a moment. "Give him half an hour. Maybe he'll get cocky enough to push his luck. It's not as if this is a covert set-up. He knows bloody well, all we are is an engraved invitation to a shooting party." He turned back to Hardey. "Pull the launch out of the way, give him room to move . . . but don't go too far away, will you?"

"Last chance?" I asked as the launch shoved off. "And then what?"

"Tethered goats turn into tigers," Greg muttered. "Let's have a look at the diesel while we're here."

In fact, he could not be still. He needed something to occupy his hands, and he put up the hatch on the greasy old engine. The Gleniffer was thick with oil, there was little we could do with it but prime it and hope. It started with a belch of black smoke. I shunted the throttle open, felt the drag as the prop thrashed in reverse, struggling to pull her off the mudbank. As she began to shift, I shut down again.

"She's safest where she is," Greg agreed. "We can come back for her in a few days, when this mess is straightened out." He wiped his hands on a scrap of ragging and slammed the engine cover. "I've had enough of this, Alex. We're out, right now."

So the hunted became the hunters, I thought bleakly. It meant finding Isaac, the Rastafarian community that had kept Logan off our backs once before. This time, our chances were slimmer. We transferred our belongings from the lugger into the well of the *Light Fantastic*, and as Greg started the outboards I untied us. The cruiser turned about in shunts, its wash rocking the police launch as we drifted up alongside.

"We've had enough, Hardey," I called over the combined engine noise. "It was worth a try, but it isn't going to work. We're going in."

Anger twisted my insides as Greg took the cruiser back along the tributary. The water was feet lower now, with the run of the tide, and I heard the bottom scrape as we butted through the reedbanks. We had not realised so much mud had silted up after the storm flooding, and Greg swore as we broke out into the main river.

"We didn't bottom out hard enough to hurt, did we?" I asked, deferring to his greater knowledge of boats.

"No – but the launch draws more water than us," he said tersely.

His meaning hit me like a clenched fist. He closed the throttles and the *Light Fantastic* wallowed in the water. Behind us, the launch struck the submerged mud much harder than we had hit. Its inboard overworked, straining to force it over the obstruction, but it seemed to be almost stuck, only jerking forward a fraction at a time.

Over the revving of the launch's inboards, and the harsh idling of our own outboards, we did not hear the explosion of noise from the big yellow dive boat until it was almost on top of us. A shot smacked into the seat not a hand's breadth from Greg's shoulder. The back of the seat tore out in a wide chunk, characteristic of the effects of hollow-nosed rounds. I spun, saw the dive boat in the same moment as Greg put the wheel hard over and opened the throttles wide.

The cruiser stood on its tail, taking off toward the town and its tourist traps, and we ducked as the shots sang overhead. The inboards overran to tear the police launch out of the mud, and many of the rounds we ducked were from Hardey's marksmen. I peered back at the yellow powerboat, saw a heavy rifle aimed loosely at us. It kicked like a mule, but the bullet was so wide it did not even find our boat.

As Greg began to curse I tore my eyes away from the powerboat, and saw the tangle of pleasure craft up ahead. He cut speed to avoid a collision, weaving through a gap that afforded a foot to left and right. Behind us, the powerboat must also slow down or pile into something, but I heard the cracks of .303 shots and ducked into the well of the boat. Being unarmed was a helpless, crippled feeling.

With the pleasure craft behind us, Greg opened the throttles again, and as we began to accelerate I looked back. I saw a flash of white, far behind – the launch was free, and would make up distance since the dive boat was slow through the knot of pleasure craft. We were travelling much too fast for safety on the river, but distance was our only defence, and Greg wove the cruiser this way and that with a fraction to spare.

The hoarse bellow of the launch's loud hailers called after us, demanding that the dive boat stop at once, but instead I saw the sharpshooter up on the flying bridge turn his back on us to fire at the launch. The police boat swerved as shots impacted with the windscreen, but its pilot kept up his speed. Pleasure craft scrambled to get out of the way, and several swamped.

It was only a matter of time before we hit something. Greg swore as the side of the cruiser smacked into a little motor boat that seemed to have stalled in midwater. We went by with a scraped hull, but behind us the smaller boat upturned. I craned my neck to see its owner dive for his life and strike out for the bank. He had seen what I saw a fraction of a second later.

The dive boat hit the upturned motor dinghy and took off over it. Little damage was done in the collision, but she landed badly, meeting the water on her side. She wallowed like a pig in mud, and the inboards stalled out as a wave of river water crashed over her stern. I counted seconds as the pilot tried to restart the diesels. The exhausts belched, but she lay dead in the water, rocking with the backwash from the banks.

Greg shut back our outboards and we hung on the river current to watch silently as the police launch came up on Rolland's yellow powerboat. A spatter of shots was exchanged under the bellow of the loud hailers, and then, as suddenly as it began, it was over. The river behind us was a chaos. It would be no more than luck if no one had been killed.

As we saw one of the police marksmen swing over onto the dive boat, Greg turned the cruiser around and headed back up the midwater channel toward the launch. No one was shooting now. I saw nothing moving on the big yellow powerboat. As we drew near, and Greg cut the outboards, I cupped my hands to my mouth. "Sergeant Hardey? Sergeant!"

But one of the marksmen, a big, burly kid in faded Levis and a red teeshirt stretched taut over inflated muscles, called back to me. "De Segeant's dead. Took a bullet in de skull, man. You want to come over and tell us which one of these bodies is your man?"

Hardey was dead? Greg and I glanced at each other as we tied up alongside the launch. He lay crookedly in the well of it, and blood had flooded across half his face. "His worries are over," Greg said softly to me. I wondered if anyone else even knew what his "worries" were. I felt an acid pang of grief, and then blocked it as I climbed over onto the dive boat.

Four bodies lay on the baking deck. One of them still twitched, one was filthy with the outpouring of a gut wound. None was Leroy Logan. My mouth dried and I sat on the dipping side of the boat. The marksmen were waiting. I dragged both hands across my face and cleared my throat. "Logan's not one of them. You've bagged his muscle here."

"And we," Greg said quietly, "are in deep trouble." He touched my arm to draw my attention to the big CB radio set. A crackle of static and a jumble of dislocated signals issued from it. "Alex?"

I got my feet under me and forced my mind back into gear. I spoke to Greg, not to Hardey's young constables. "Best chance we've got is to get our gear out of the hotel, hire a car and vanish." I gave him a bleak look. "We've done it once."

"The Rastas?" he asked. I nodded. "Hardey swore we're begging for legal trouble. Then again, we've got to be alive to be charged!" He stirred. "All we've got working for us is time. Logan would have been listening in on that CB, but maybe he won't guess which way we'll jump." He gave the big shortwave a dirty look, and then turned back toward the constables. "Do you want to escort us back to the hotel, fast? I don't know how safe it is out here. Who's in charge now?"

The kid in the red tee shirt gestured with a neat pocket R/T. "We report back to Sergeant Calder, out of the Kingston office."

The launch pulled out five minutes later as a fleet of assorted local police craft arrived to sort out the chaos on the river. Greg and I sat in the stern, watching the highrises go by. Up on the bridge, Calder was on the radio. We heard bitter cursing as he took the report, and then the message that our bodyguard would be waiting for us on the beach below our hotel.

I felt naked and vulnerable as we walked back up. Hardey's death made me painfully aware of our mortality. But the bodyguards stuck tight, shadowing us through the vestibule and up in the lift. In the passageway outside our room, one of the burly young men took station. I saw the butt of his revolver as his jacket pulled open. His colleague paused to answer an R/T message, and as I heard my name I stopped with our key in my hand.

It was Calder: "Tell Mr. Connor and Mr. Farris to remain in their room for safety's sake. As soon as I can, I'll be over there. I need a report from them both."

"We heard," Greg said as the young man began to relay the message. "Tell him not to be long. We're not hanging around."

Eyebrows rose, but our guard told Calder exactly what Greg had said, and we did not wait to hear his reply. We had to pack and move. Greg was right, the only advantage we had was time and surprise. "Calder can have half an hour," I said as I locked the room up behind us. "We haven't done anything to be charged for."

"Yet," Greg added as I pulled out our bags and began to rummage for the bare essentials. He paced like a caged cat until he found the bottle of Black Douglas that had come up, compliments of the house. He poured us a couple and sat on the window ledge to watch me slamming oddments into a suitcase. I was angry but he seemed curiously calm. "Punch something," he suggested. "It helps."

"Don't tempt me," I growled.

He left the window ledge to shove my untouched glass into my hand. "So swallow that. If you're going to be blue, enjoy it."

I tossed down the rich spirit. He refilled my glass and poured a second for himself. We needed the Dutch courage. "Look on the bright side," I began, whisky-hoarse.

"There's a bright side? You surprise me."

"It'll make a great follow-up story. Lansing is going to love us."

He made a face. "Quite apart from the fact it's a principle of mine never to screw with my boss, I never fancied Lansing."

"You know what I mean," I remonstrated.

"I know what you mean." He regarded the Black Douglas

bottle and put the cap back on with a sigh. "I'd better pack. Calder can have ten more minutes, and then we're out, by the back exit." He put the bottle down on the rug by the bed and pulled the small suit case toward him.

I had packed a few odds and ends, the same basic gear as we took the first time we performed this vanishing act. As Greg threw his things into the case I draped one arm about him and took the lobe of his ear between my teeth. We were running for our lives, and the odds were poor. We knew what we were up against. Like me, he needed to be close for a moment, and as he finished packing, locked the case and set it on the floor, he turned into my arms to kiss.

Engrossed in him, I was slow to react, did not immediately recognize the sound of a key turning in our lock. Greg wrenched away from me, but even then it was that split-second too late. The door slammed back on its hinges, and a monster we knew filled the doorway.

Logan seemed bigger between walls. He was alone. The gun in his right fist was the same American police Colt we had taken from the guard on Rolland's boat shed. The noses of .38 calibre shells peeked from its chambers. Dangling from Logan's left fingers was a hotel maid's pass key. There was no time even to curse or register the shock ripping through me. I expected to see the gun discharge, and could only hold my breath.

Logan stepped into the room, kicked the door shut and leaned on it. The Colt looked like a toy in his massive hand. "You faggots goin' somewhere?" He had seen the suitcase.

"We're leaving." I levelled my voice with an effort. The phone was on my side of the bed. Could I make it that far? It was on Logan's side of the bed too.

The Colt levelled on Greg's belly. "Pull out the phone cable. Do it! Or pretty boy gets the first bullet!"

He meant it, and I complied at once. How the hell had he got past the guard outside? "You've got a mate in the hotel, have you?" I asked. "He just gave you the pass key, you came up by the servants' lift?"

"Clever." Logan's grip shifted on the gun. "Smart-mouthed white-arse. You's dead, de pair of you. Dead as that copper outside. I just wring his neck like a yard fowl, like I'll wring yours, after I's finished playin' with you. I's going to mess you up till dey wonder who de hell you ever were. Get on de floor. On your face. And you, pretty boy, get over here."

I knelt, watched Greg come around the bed. He looked like a child beside Logan. My heart was in my mouth, choking me. Greg is good, but Logan would snap him like a twig if he made a fight of it. As I went down on my belly the Jamaican ordered Greg to strip. I heard the rustle of cotton and denim, saw Greg's bare legs. Something light and coarse landed on my back.

Rope? Under the gun, Greg stripped me and tied my hands and ankles together, making a bent bow of my spine. He was white and silent but he tied me as loosely as he could manage. My spine is still whippy. I bent it painfully while he tied me and then could afford to relax when Logan assumed I was helpless and hurting. I was certainly helpless, but not in pain, merely scared shitless.

We were a rush job. Logan was on the run. His only toy was the revolver. He had Greg on his knees, the muzzle of it in his hair. A fat cock demanded sucking. Greg obliged. I heard him gagging as he worked, and tested the ropes. They gave a little but were still too tight. Logan was excited, fucking Greg's throat until he retched, dry heaves that must have hurt. A large hand wound into his hair, wrenched his head away and pushed him flat over the foot of the bed.

Logan knelt over him, pinning him down with his sheer weight. The Colt was thrust into the hip pocket of his patched denims. He had us right where he wanted us, and my heart hammered as I watched Greg's face twist with pain and anger. That thick cock rammed him hard, but it was slick with saliva and Greg is no novice. He took the pounding as Logan worked himself into a frenzy, growling obscenities. Blinded by lust, getting close, he buggered Greg until it was me who could have screamed. Greg was silent.

The ropes gave a fraction and my skin burned with the friction as I punished my muscles. Over the curve of the bed, I saw Logan's broad hips, pumping furiously, the butt of the revolver protruding from his pocket. I wanted that gun so much my fingers could literally feel it. I fought the ropes that seemed to have snagged and were too tight to move further.

In his frenzy, Logan was vulnerable. He did not see Greg reach over the side of the bed, but I did. Cold sweat broke from every pore. I had forgotten the whisky bottle was on the floor there. I could just see Greg's right hand close on it, white-knuckled. I held my breath. Greg waited. Waited, taking it.

And then Logan froze, starting to come, buried balls-deep

in the body I had thought of for so long as belonging to me. Greg was shaking, in fury and in pain, and I could only guess at, and glory in, the insensate strength as he swung the whisky bottle up and back. Logan caught it full in the face, over nose and eyes. Blood spattered Greg's back as the jerking cock wrenched out of him, and all I saw was a tangle of limbs, the bottle uplifted once more. Then the thud of a sickening impact before Logan could even begin to struggle for the gun. The first blow must have been a beauty, blinding him before he knew what was happening.

It was over. Greg gasped breathlessly as he rolled off the bed onto his knees beside me. His fingers were clumsy, useless, as he tried to untie me. The knots defied him. "Stop, get your breath, I'm okay," I panted. "Is he out? Out cold? Greg! Come on, baby. Is he out?" He sat on his knees, head tipped back. "You hurt? Bad? Turn round, let me look at your arse. Greg!" He took a deep breath and returned to the ropes. He managed the knots with an effort and as I unbent my spine I dragged him into my arms.

On the bed, Logan was quite still, and I turned my back on him. I wanted to look at Greg and would not brook his arguments. He let me check him without a word. There was only a little blood but I knew he must feel tainted. He was silent, trying to control the shakes. "Why don't you go and have a bath? I'll see to Logan."

He spoke at last, his voice low, monotone. "No need. I think I've killed him."

"You – what?" I got to my knees and looked at the man again. Greg had hit him only twice, and the second blow must have been somewhere behind the ear. His head was on a sickening angle. Death had come so fast as his neck broke like a fresh carrot, that his cock was still engorged. The police coroner would know exactly where it had been after a three-second exam. They would require a police doctor to look at Greg in verification, but I would have insisted on that in any case. Rape is not a game.

Logan's nose was smashed. After the first blow, he must have been blind and insensible. Still, he must have threshed, and in the struggle my slim little lover had hit hard. I wondered for a moment if Greg had intended to go for a kill-spot, but I was not going to ask. The butt of the revolver was visible, half smothered by Logan's hip, still in his back pocket. Had he got a hand to it, we would both have been dead men.

Greg was sitting on his calves, eyes on the carpet. Blood spattered his shoulders. Logan's blood. I rolled the quilt over the body, with the obscenity of his cock jutting from open flies. I did not even touch the gun. The police could have the joy of sorting out this mess. Greg still had not moved, and I went to run a cool bath. I manhandled him to his feet and put him in it.

"Honey? Relax, will you! And stop fretting. It was self-defence." I leaned over and kissed his mouth, tried to forget Logan's cock had ever been in it. It was not Greg's fault.

He leaned back against the side of the ivory tub and closed his eyes. I touched his face, hoping for some positive reaction, but he was immobile. I left him to soak and dressed quickly.

In the passageway outside, I saw the body of our guard. It sat in the chair against the wall, carefully arranged so that the man looked merely asleep. The R/T in his pocket emitted a stream of white noise. I lifted it out and depressed the transmit switch. "Sergeant Calder?"

A pause, and then Calder's well spoken Jamaican voice said, "Who is this?"

"It's Alex Connor. You'd better get over here. You've got a dead bodyguard . . . and Logan is dead too. He got into the room."

I listened to silence for several seconds before Calder said sharply, "Touch nothing. I'll be there as soon as I can."

Back in the room, I plugged in the phone cable and punched up Patterson's private line in Kingston. He took the call at once, and sounded harrassed. He would have been hearing garbled messages for the last two hours – a circus on the river, an officer on his squad shot dead. "Logan won't be bothering you," I said quietly. "You'd better come over as soon as you can get away. He's dead. And no, we did not contravene your fucking gun laws. He was armed. Greg broke his neck in a fight, self-defence." I paused, heard the man's breathing over the line. "I don't want trouble, Patterson. Greg was raped anally and it was a David and Goliath match. Logan was going to do the pair of us and then kill us. There was no choice."

Patterson heard me out in silence. "I'm sorry," he said as I finished, and he meant it. "Look, do nothing, touch nothing. Sergeant Calder's squad will take care of the paperwork. I'll be over myself this evening to collect the *refuse*." The word was said vehemently. "I'll take a formal statement from you then." He hesitated and began again. "There will be a doctor with the squad. He will need to examine your friend. Is this acceptable?"

"I'd be grateful if he would," I said quietly. "It was not pleasant, Patterson."

"No. I'll have to ask you not to leave the island for the moment, of course. With the matter of Logan settled we can close the file on this."

"All right. There won't be trouble, will there?" I asked. "The body speaks for itself, and one look at Greg will speak volumes to your doctor."

"Leave the details to me, Mr. Connor," Patterson offered. "I'll send someone at once."

I hung up and called room service again, sent down for coffee, brandy and chocolate. We both needed picking up. I turned my back on the quilt-wrapped body, gazed blindly out of the window as I waited. Greg probably needed a few minutes' privacy. He's tough, but he's still human.

The tray arrived, and I tipped the boy at the door. The bathroom was steamy and Greg was pink. He had brimmed the tub with scalding water, as if to wash away some terrible taint. I poured his coffee, half and half with brandy, and handed him the cup. He was alive again, his face bleak but mobile as I sat on the side of the tub and looked down at him.

"So?" I finger-combed his hair. "Okay now? Tell me about it?"

"I'll live." He took a sip of coffee. "Did I black out on you? I'm sorry."

"Idiot. You probably saved both our bloody lives. You've checked yourself over, haven't you?" He nodded mutely. "You don't look too bad. Greg, there's a squad coming for the body. Will you let the police doctor have a look at you?" If he refused I was about to insist.

"I have a choice?" he demanded.

"Legally," I said mildly. "But I want to be sure."

He looked up at me with the faintest of smiles. "For you, then. It's over, isn't it? Over."

"All barring the shouting," I said softly. "Lansing'll have the whole lot by now, and we're on bonuses. So long as you're not hurt –"

"I'll live, like I told you," he whispered.

"Hey. Honey." He looked up and I covered his mouth with my own, plundered it, made it mine again after what Logan had done to it. When I was satisfied he sat back with a sigh and closed his eyes.

We were quiet for a long time before a knock at the door heralded the squad Patterson had promised. Heading it was Sergeant Calder, a tall but flabby man a few years my elder. He brandished his identification as the doctor and orderlies followed him into the room. The elderly medic unwrapped the body, crossed himself, kissed his thumb and began to scribble in his notebook.

Calder wanted a report and I gave it in crisp, cold phrases. Logan could have got into the hotel so easily, when the police simply walked out with us. He was probably already in the building when we returned, and with a pass key in his hand the rest was easy. If he came up in the servants' lift, a white steward's jacket and a tray in his hand would be all the cover he needed to jump the man guarding us.

"Look around," I suggested as Calder closed his notebook. "You'll probably find his props somewhere near here. Your man didn't stand a chance." Calder looked sick. He was watching the orderlies load Logan's body onto the stretcher. It looked obscene.

As the doctor stepped back from the bed, I pointed him at the bathroom, where Greg had just pulled the plug for the last time. He had brimmed the bath again and again, as if he could not get clean. I was worried and grateful for the doctor's presence. The exam took ten minutes. By the time Greg emerged, wrapped in the bathrobe that had hung on the back of the door, the body was gone.

Calder wanted a provisional statement from Greg also. His mouth compressed in distaste as Greg gave it in a flat, unaccented monotone. With a few notes in his book, the policeman left us. We stood at the window and I held Greg against me.

"What did the doctor tell you?"

"That I was lucky. One little nick and some bruises. Could have been worse. I don't feel too bad, all things considered." He looked up at me. Those grey eyes were like the sea in a storm. "Are they going to make trouble?"

"Patterson said not." I drew my lips across his forehead. "You want to lie down?"

"Prefer to swim," he said. "Blow the cobwebs away. I'm okay, Alex, really. Just bloody sore. Come with me?"

The afternoon was warm, growing overcast as a weather front marched in. The sea was still a little murky after the hurricane. We only swam in the shallows. Greg turned over, floated on his back as if he was half asleep. I stroked him under the water, making him smile at last.

Patterson flew in on the seven o'clock shuttle. He met us as we were going down for dinner and joined us. I picked at fish in lemon sauce, not hungry, eating out of politeness, as we told the story yet again. Patterson listened in silence and took notes. His expression conveyed disgust and regret. When the story was done he spoke not to me but to Greg.

"The medical report was waiting for me, Mr. Farris. There is no doubt of Logan's – shall we say, condition. Nor of his, um, assault on you. Or that a single blow broke his neck, unintentionally delivered during an unequal struggle. There won't be questions to be answered. As I told Mr. Connor, leave the details to me."

"Thanks." Greg glared down at his plate. In the lamplight I saw a slight flush about his cheekbones.

"I'll have the full, official statement made up, you can sign it in the morning," Patterson added. "And then you're free to go. Oh, here. This was on my desk just before I left Kingston." He handed an envelope to Greg.

Two papers unfolded. Greg scanned them and whistled as he passed them to me. One was from the insurance underwriter in America, the other from the Jamaican government. "The reward money is waiting for you, if you would care to look in to Kingston and collect it. I haven't looked at the papers, but they tell me it's quite a sizeable sum."

"It is," I affirmed. I looked at Greg over the tops of the sheets. "It's enough. There's something we want to buy while we're here." Greg smiled and nodded.

"Well, I'll say good evening." Patterson stood and offered his hand. "Now that all this is finished, I hope you'll stay and enjoy your holiday."

"We will," Greg said as he shook the offered hand. "What about loose ends? We're not at risk now?"

Patterson shook his head emphatically. "We have the whole nest of vipers, I promise you. And I had word before I flew over here, American Federal Agents have taken several members of Rolland's family and a small army of affiliates and employees into custody. It is over, Mr. Farris. You and Mr. Connor are not in jeopardy."

The policeman withdrew, and I leaned back, looking at Greg in the dining room's soft lighting. I wanted to hold him, to revel in the illusion that he belongs to me. As if one human can own another. He was silent, his face drawn taut as Patterson threaded out through the clustered tables. I waited for him to speak.

At last he said quietly and very soberly, "He's wrong."

"Wrong?" I had a glass of wine half way to my lips. "What about?"

"About the unintentional blow." Greg looked away. "I meant to kill him. I knew what I was doing, God help me. What does that make me?"

I put the wine down untouched. "Human. Scared. Hurt. So angry you couldn't see straight. If you hadn't, Greg, I would have."

"Would you?" His voice had the rough texture of coarse silk.

Our corner of the dining room was dim and we were almost alone. Trusting to luck, I set my hand over his beside the candlesticks. "You think I don't fight to protect what's mine?"

A reluctant smile lifted one corner of his mouth. "I think you might."

"Damned right. Same as you do. You kept him off me. I owe you."

"Maybe." He looked at our hands, which lay together on the white table cloth. "Put it on the slate. There's always next time."

"Not if I can help it." I winked at him and withdrew my hand before we overstretched our luck. The band played soft calypso tunes. The floor was cleared for dancing. This hotel was not as lavish as The Grand, but it was comfortable and much more private since it was only half the size. A terrace opened out on the side of the dining room with steps onto the beach. A warm breeze gusted off the sea, wafting in through the open doors. "I'll call Lansing in the morning," I said as the pastry cart came along to us. "We're on bonuses and two weeks' extra time. We haven't even started the holiday yet."

He dropped into that mock-Australian accent to tease. "Fair dinkum. Or do I mean dinki di?" I laughed quietly. "I faxed a month's work home, so make sure Lansing appreciates it. We want a whole fortnight, loverboy. For us."

I laughed at Greg's cheek. "You that eager to join the dole queue?"

The remark won me a smile. My quip was for Greg's amusement. He touched the rim of his glass to mine, smug, sure both of his position at *Perspective* and of me. Although

214

Lansing would crack down on his people when they took real liberties, after the piece of work we had turned in the appreciation would be forthcoming. He had some very fine journalists and photographers on staff contracts. Greg and I were simply the best. If we were complacent, we had good reason to be.

We lingered over drinks, planning how we would return up the river to the *Spirit of Jamaica*, sail around to Kingston for the rewards waiting for us, woo a boy called Jake into signing a bill of sale. I weighed our run-in with Rolland's enterprise against our misadventures in Laos, Beirut, the Falklands, and put it into the past tense. With Logan as dead as Rolland, even Hurricane Rita gone west to rage along the coasts of Honduras and Nicaragua, we had dispensed with reality. We were there to indulge in fantasies. It was time they began.

More adventure stories from Mel Keegan:

Mel Keegan
DEATH'S HEAD

A thrilling sci-fi adventure of interplanetary drug wars, mind-bonding, and gay passion

On the high-tech worlds of the 23rd century, the lethal designer drug Angel has become an epidemic disease. Kevin Jarrat and Jerry Stone are joint captains in the paramilitary NARC force sent in to combat the Death's Head drug syndicate that controls the vast spaceport of Chell. Under the NARC code of non-involvement, each of the two friends hides his deeper desire for the other. When Stone is kidnapped and forced onto Angel, Jarrat's love for him is his only chance of survival, but the price is that their minds remain permanently linked.

"Unputdownable" — *Him magazine*
"Rip-roaring and colorful" — *Time Out* on *Ice, Wind and Fire*

ISBN 0 85449 290 9
UK £8.95 US $12.95 AUS $22.50

Mel Keegan
AN EAST WIND BLOWING

Mel Keegan's latest historical romance is set in the very depths of the Dark Ages, in the north-east of a country not yet known as England. The Romans have recently departed, though fragments of their world still linger on. The native Britons are being pressed back by the barbarian Angles from over the water, as they sail in on the east wind seeking new land to settle. Ronan and Bryn are two young men eager to defend their land against the invaders, but Ronan is a common freeman, and Bryn the son of an overweening lord. As with his *Fortunes of War* and *White Rose of Night*, Mel Keegan conjures up an atmospheric tale in which love between men is forged in the battles they must fight.

"A fine example of this genre" — *Gay Times* on *Fortunes of War*

ISBN 0 85449 286 0
UK £9.95 US $14.95 AUS $24.95

Mel Keegan
WHITE ROSE OF NIGHT

In 12th-century England, fifteen-year-old Paul becomes the squire and lover of a Saxon knight, Edward of Athelstone. Struggling to survive in the Norman world, Edward embarks with Paul on Crusade to the Holy Land, where Paul is captured as a slave by a Saracen captain. The love of the two young men is all that sustains them in their further adventures, where they eventually join with the Arab leader Saladin in seeking an honorable end to this horrible war. Mel Keegan's previous books have offered action-packed gay adventure from future, present and past. This second historical novel from his pen continues his exploration of male love amid the clash of arms.

ISBN 0 85449 256 9
UK £9.95 US $14.95 AUS $17.95

Mel Keegan
STORM TIDE

Sean Brodie, an American engineer on contract in Adelaide, and his partner of eight months, local boy Rob Markham, are struggling to save their relationship by hiring a boat for a week's fishing off the wild south Australian coast. As a storm approaches, they go to the aid of a luxury cabin-cruiser apparently in trouble, only to find that they've stumbled into a drug smuggling gang's offshore headquarters. A lucky escape is only the start of their troubles, as they find their pursuers have unexpected friends on land as well as sea.

Keegan returns to the present with an action-packed and gripping adventure set for the first time in his native Australia.

ISBN 0 85449 227 5
UK £7.95 US $12.95 AUS $14.95

Two true-life adventures from World War II

Noel Currer-Briggs
YOUNG MEN AT WAR

Anthony Arthur Kildwick, born in 1919 to a well-to-do English family, finds the love of his life in a German exchange student at his private school. When Manfred returns to Germany he is seduced by Hitler's nationalist rhetoric, while Tony meets the outbreak of war as a conscientious objector. Yet as the Nazi regime shows itself ever more demonic, Tony decides he must fight, and is parachuted into southern France to work with the Resistance. He discovers Manfred is now an officer with the occupying forces, and their paths cross again in dramatic circumstances.

Based largely on the author's own experience, this fascinating story conveys a vivid sense of the conflicts of the 1930s, and the interplay betwen friendship and internationalism, homosexuality and pacifism, patriotism and democracy, that was characteristic of those years.

"An absorbing account of the conflict between personal integrity and the tyranny of blinkered patriotism" — *Gay Times*

ISBN 0 85449 236 4
UK £9.95 US $14.95 AUS $19.95

Rudi van Dantzig
FOR A LOST SOLDIER

During the winter of 1944 in occupied Amsterdam, eleven-year-old Jeroen is evacuated to a tiny fishing village community on the desolate coast of Friesland, where he meets Walt, a young Canadian soldier with the liberating forces. Their relationship immerses the young boy in a tumultuous world of emotional and sexual experience, suddenly curtailed when the Allies move on and Walt goes away. Back home in Amsterdam, a city in the throes of liberation fever, Jeroen searches for the soldier he has lost. A child's fears and confused emotions have rarely been described with such depth of understanding, and seen as it is from the boy's viewpoint it invites total empathy.

This novel by the artistic director of the Dutch National Ballet appeared successfully in hardback in 1991, and was made into a prize-winning film.

"A beautifully chronicled document of wartime life"
— *Gay Times*

"I was filled with admiration for the way in which Rudi van Dantzig has transformed a difficult and unusual autobiographical theme into a compelling literary work" — *Times Literary Supplement*

ISBN 0 85449 237 2
UK £9.95 US $14.95 AUS $19.95